Excellent

"Did you want something, Bram?"

It had been a long time since she had been in a man's arms, but even then, she hadn't behaved like this... as though anything she did or said or thought was perfectly all right, because she was doing it, saying it, thinking it with Bram.

"Do I want something?" he answered softly, and reaching the end of his limits, he put his hand under Cassie's chin and pulled her lips up to meet his. "I want to make love to you."

Bram continued to hold her gaze while his hands traveled beneath the hem of her sweater and found her warm back. He smiled when his touch made her close her eyes and lean into his body as though she were suddenly boneless. He knew then, that despite her doubts, despite the brief time they had known each other, he could have her if he persisted....

ABOUT THE AUTHOR

Jacqueline Ashley is a veteran romance writer, who began her career many years ago when the union at her work place went on strike. To preserve her sanity Jacqueline started her first book, and by the time she was finished was addicted to "creating imaginary characters in imaginary situations undergoing the very real process of falling in love." Jacqueline has lived in seven different states, but now makes her home in her native Oklahoma with her husband.

Books by Jacqueline Ashley

These books may be available at your local bookseller.

Don't miss any of our special offers. Write to us at the following address for information on our newest releases.

Harlequin Reader Service
901 Fuhrmann Blvd., P.O. Box 1397, Buffalo, NY 14240
Canadian address: P.O. Box 603,
Fort Erie, Ont. L2A 5X3

The Long Journey Home

Jacqueline Ashley

Harlequin Books

TORONTO • NEW YORK • LONDON
AMSTERDAM • PARIS • SYDNEY • HAMBURG
STOCKHOLM • ATHENS • TOKYO • MILAN

Published January 1987

First printing November 1986

ISBN 0-373-16182-4

Printed in Canada

Prologue

THE STEWARTS

Justin

In the richly appointed study of his family's large, sprawling home located on a multiacre estate just outside Barton's Corner, Missouri, Justin Stewart, Jr., stood beside his father looking out the wide windows of the room at the family swimming pool, where his sister and a friend were enjoying the last days of summer.

"Who is that with your sister, Jussie?"

Justin, Sr., who was quite nearsighted but much too vain to wear glasses, finally gave up squinting in the direction of the pool and relied on his son to provide the information he sought.

Justin knew his father wouldn't be pleased by the answer, but with a shrug of his wide shoulders, he gave it, anyway.

"I don't know her name," he drawled dismissively, "but there's no mistaking the red hair. She's got to be one of Harry Palmer's brood. She'd be his youngest if she's Cassy's age and not already working for us like the rest of them—except for Bram, of course."

Though he would have preferred to be, as well as to sound, indifferent, Justin couldn't help the jealousy that hardened his voice as he mentioned his old nemesis, Bramwell Palmer. It was annoying to have to think about Bram when Justin was just home from a successful sojourn at college and was about to come into his inheritance. He would have been content to forget forever that during his high school years he had been bested, more than once, by someone with no social credentials at all.

On learning whom his daughter had with her, Justin, Sr., scowled. "Why the deuce do you suppose Cassandra flouts my authority this way?"

Justin smiled secretly at his father's use of Cassy's full name. When Justin, Sr., was displeased with one of his children, he always used his or her full name rather than their more affectionate diminutives.

"I imagine she was just bored with her own company." Justin wasn't interested in fueling his parent's ire over such a minor matter. They had more important things to discuss.

"If she'd gone to private school the way I wanted, she wouldn't have to be bored enough to seek companionship with young people beneath her social position," Justin, Sr., snapped. "It was all right for you to stay here. You'll be taking my place one day and need to know the townspeople who will be working for you as intimately as possible. But Cassandra's different. I want her to make a good match, and the only way to do that is to go where the suitable men are. Besides," he complained, sounding to Justin almost comically bewildered by his young daughter's lack of discrimination, "haven't I told her often enough that it diminishes respect for all of us when she mingles so familiarly with one of the locals?"

Justin shrugged. "She's young, Father," he pointed out as he turned away and walked across a priceless Oriental rug spread over the highly polished hardwood floor of the study, to sit down in the leather chair fronting his rosewood desk—

an exact duplicate of his father's across the room. "Don't worry," he added absently as he began to peruse the latest income statement of the family company. "It's just a stage she's going through. My advice is not to make too much of a fuss about her democratic tendencies. She'll get over them eventually."

Justin momentarily was amused by his own words as he realized how outraged some of the liberals he had met at college would be if they could overhear this conversation with his father.

"Humph!" Justin, Sr., snorted as, taking one last annoyed look at his daughter's swimming companion, he swung around to sit down at his own desk. "That may be good advice, Jussie, but I can't take the chance you may be wrong. I'll speak to Cassandra after dinner tonight and point out to her, once again," he added with long-suffering pique, "that she has a position in this town and in this family to uphold. I fear she has a great deal too much of your Grandfather Barton in her."

Justin looked up at that, and forgetting for a moment how his father's vanity would be pricked by his words, spoke his thoughts carelessly. "With profits down," he grunted, "we could use some of Grandfather's genius right now. I wish I'd known him."

The immediate expression of displeasure that came into his father's eyes alerted Justin to his error. Justin, Sr., always disliked hearing such flattering references to his wife's now-deceased father, the founder of the family business.

"Not that we don't have our own talents," Justin continued, choosing not to acknowledge his father's ruffled feathers openly, but rather to soothe his ego in an indirect way. "Between the two of us, we'll get those profits back up again in no time. It's the economy that's getting in our way for the present, but with a few adjustments, we can ride things out."

The older man relaxed then and nodded. "Delaying our employees' next pay raise is one adjustment that will help," he said with satisfaction.

Justin leaned back in his chair, his excitement rising as he prepared to make a more radical suggestion than merely delaying a pay raise.

"I was thinking more along the lines of asking them, in a spirit of cooperation, so to speak, to go a little further than that."

Justin saw his parent's patrician eyebrows lift in the expression of surprise that he had expected. "You mean asking them actually to take a pay *cut*?" Justin, Sr., inquired, sounding as surprised as he looked.

"Why not?" his son asked, keeping his tone reasonable, though his excitement was growing. "Without the company, they can't survive in this town. Why shouldn't they take a few of the setbacks, the way we have to?"

"Yes, son," Justin, Sr., answered in a slightly self-righteous tone, "but we do have an obligation to look after these people."

But his father's objection lacked a certain conviction, Justin was glad to note and quickly followed up on. "Father, you know it's dog-eat-dog in the business world," he said lightly. "Everyone has to take his lumps from time to time, including the common laborers."

"Yes, yes, that's true," Justin, Sr., agreed, and Justin concealed a smile when he heard his father trying to sound discouraged, since Justin was convinced now that his parent was actually delighted by his idea. Justin knew his parents well, and he was aware that his father had always felt hampered by his wife's liberal stance toward the family's employees, an attitude inherited from her brilliant yet dismayingly common father. But since Mary Louise Barton Stewart owned the company that Justin, Sr., ran for her, he had always walked carefully where her sensibilities were concerned. Justin, Jr., was counting on the fact that his mother adored him excessively, to get around the restrictions she'd put on his father.

"Why not let me draft a memo explaining to our people why we feel it necessary to institute a ten-percent pay decrease temporarily," he said in a casual fashion, so it wouldn't seem as though he were encroaching on his father's prerogatives.

"Temporarily?" Justin, Sr., inquired, alerting his son that the question was really settled. There were only details to be sorted out.

"Say, six months," Justin suggested, feeling elated by his success at influencing events so soon after taking his place at his father's side. An instant later he had another thought, however, and grimaced. "If Harry Palmer would keep his big mouth shut, we might get away with stretching it another six months, but I doubt if he will."

The older man snorted at the mention of Harry Palmer. "No, Harry won't keep his mouth shut, you can depend on it," he predicted. "If the man wasn't such a genius with machinery, I'd have fired him long ago. But he saves us too much money. If Harry can't fix an engine, it's irreparable."

"I know, I know," Justin agreed irritably. He didn't want his hands tied by anyone, but especially not by a *Palmer*. "But he's a pain in the neck, just the same," he went on. "The man doesn't know his place, and he's taught his kids not to know theirs, either. Otherwise, his daughter wouldn't be splashing in our pool as if she had a right to be there."

Justin paused, thinking, *And Bram Palmer wouldn't have been quarterback on the football team our senior year, much less valedictorian of the class.*

His temper rising, Justin asked his father, "Have you heard Harry brag about how Bram graduated from college cum laude?"

"The boy's smart, I'll give him that," Justin, Sr., nodded. "But he hasn't got a loyal bone in his body. Imagine his turning down my offer to pay his way through college in return for a commitment to come back and work as plant manager under you."

"He got scholarships, remember?" Justin grated.

"I know," Justin, Sr., replied, "but after all the years we've given that family employment, you'd think he would have shown a little appreciation."

Justin didn't reply. He was savoring the fact that despite the many offers of employment Bram Palmer had received from top computer companies after graduating from college, he had foolishly chosen, instead, to go into partnership with a friend to try to start their own business. Justin fervently hoped the two of them were courting disaster.

"But don't worry too much about Harry Palmer, son," Justin, Sr., now said with complacent confidence. "I've always handled Harry, and I always will. Stroke the man's ego, and he's putty in your hands. Remember that, Jussie, for the time when you're totally in charge. Given enough flattery, a man will give on other things, like salary and benefits."

Justin said nothing, though when the time came to take over the reins of the company from his father in the future, he had no intention of wasting his breath soothing his employees' egos. Business was business. And there was no place in business for the sort of sentimental paternalism his father was used to dispensing.

Cassandra

Cassandra Stewart sat on the edge of the family pool, delighted to exchange lighthearted teenage confidences with Maxie—short for Maxine—Palmer. The only thing Cassy regretted about the friendship was that it had taken so long to develop. Though Cassy had admired Maxie all the years they'd gone to school together, it was only after earning parts in the junior-class play the preceding fall that she had rebelled against her father's ideas—ideas that had set her apart from her age group all of her life—and actively sought Maxie's friendship.

"Maxie," she said now, smiling her affection at her friend, "I'm so glad we're friends. I can't believe how much time we wasted."

"I'm still surprised we ever did get together," Maxie responded with a wry quirk of her lips. "Everybody knows your dad and brother consider everyone in town inferior to them."

Cassandra started to make an automatic protest, but the words died on her lips as she realized that Maxie's honesty was one of the things she most appreciated about her. In a town like Barton's Corner, where practically everyone depended on the Stewart family's company for a living, only the Palmers seemed to be unafraid to speak their minds openly.

Cassy knew her thinking was more and more diverging from that of her father and brother, and she was beginning to suspect from stories her mother told her about Grandfather Barton that she had inherited a strong dose of genes from that side of the family. Not that she was a genius. At least, if she was, it hadn't become apparent yet. But she was certainly not an absolute snob, as were the male members of her family. And though her mother wasn't, she was too fond of her husband and son to curb that particular defect in them, though Cassy wished she would at least try.

Glancing behind her shoulder at her home, Cassy thought she saw someone at the study window, and she quickly turned away, a grimace on her well-shaped lips. She knew she was probably in for a lecture from her dad for bringing Maxie to the house for a swim, but she didn't care anymore how much her father lectured her. Maxie was worth it.

"That's true," she bluntly admitted Maxie's assertion. "If daddy had his way, I'd be off to a private school where I could find rich and probably boring friends, and eventually a rich and probably boring husband." She grinned at Maxie then. "I'd rather be here with you, Maxie. You may not be rich, but you're certainly not boring."

Maxie grinned back, her freckled nose crinkling up in a mischievous expression. "I know," she said with exaggerated immodesty, making Cassandra laugh. Then Maxie sobered and ran a hand through the wet strands of her short, fiery red hair. "But just the same, your dad will probably have a fit about your having me over here today."

Cassandra sat straighter, as though preparing for a battle. "You're my friend, Maxie," she said quietly. "If I can't have my friends visit me at home, what good is all this?" She lifted a hand and indicated the swimming pool and the extensive grounds of her family's impressive home. "Except for Mom, it's just a lonely prison."

Maxie shrugged. "Yeah," she agreed, "your mom's nice. But I doubt if your dad or Jussie would describe this place as a prison. This is their pride and joy, their proof that they're better than the rest of us in Barton's Corner."

Cassandra frowned indignantly. "That's not how my granddad felt," she said, "and he was the 'Barton' in Barton's Corner. My dad might have some fancy ancestors, but he wouldn't have anything else if it weren't for granddad."

Maxie shook her head and put a finger to her lips in a teasing manner. "I wouldn't mention that around him if I were you," she whispered with dry humor. "My dad says yours doesn't like to be reminded he didn't start the company and had to marry into it."

Cassandra sighed, feeling slightly disloyal for speaking of her father the way she had. She loved him, but she wished he and Jussie weren't such fanatics about their position in life. She also wished she and Maxie had never gotten on this subject. It was spoiling the good time they'd been having.

"Hey," Maxie said consolingly, and when Cassandra looked up, she saw that her friend's green eyes had softened with good-natured affection. "Don't take it all so seriously. If your dad says I can't come here anymore, you can always come to my house. You might have to sneak around to do it, but you'll be welcome, you know that."

Cassandra shook her head. As much as the idea appealed to her, she didn't dare do what Maxie suggested. "I couldn't sneak around to visit you," she said, hoping Maxie would understand. "If my dad found out, it might get your dad into trouble."

Maxie grinned. "That wouldn't bother Daddy," she retorted. "He thrives on trouble."

Cassandra relaxed, chuckling. "Yes," she agreed thoughtlessly. "Daddy says Harry Palmer is a pain in the—" Stopping short, she looked at Maxie with dismay at having forgotten herself to the extent that she might have hurt Maxie's feelings.

But Maxie's feelings didn't seem to be hurt at all. Her green eyes gleamed with satisfaction. "That he is," she said cheerfully. "In fact, he makes a point of being a pain in the—" She paused, looked around to make sure there was no one other than Cassy within earshot, then whispered daringly, "In the ass." Her eyes twinkled as Cassy at first looked shocked, then dissolved into giggles of appreciation.

"You can't believe how proud Daddy was when Bram beat out your brother for the position of quarterback of the football team and then valedictorian," Maxie continued, her tone expressing as much pride as she was crediting to her father.

At that, Cassandra stopped giggling, and she was unaware that her eyes had taken on a dreamy expression. She was remembering Bramwell Palmer as the smartest, strongest, best-looking boy she'd ever seen. Of course, she and Maxie were far enough behind Bram in age so that he had never noticed her, and she had simply admired him from afar. Now she was wondering what he was like as a man. It had been a long time since she'd seen him.

Maxie slapped Cassy's knee lightly to get her attention, and when Cassy looked blankly at her, her friend grimaced with disgust.

"Stop daydreaming about old Bram," Maxie complained. "I don't know what all the girls see in him, anyway. He's not that good-looking."

Cassy thought Maxie was out of her mind describing her brother as "not that good-looking." But then she realized it would be hard for her to understand any female becoming interested in Justin, knowing him as she did, so she supposed it was a natural sisterly reaction.

"Come on," Maxie said, as she slipped off the side of the pool into the water again. "If I'm going to get banished from this great pool soon, I want to take advantage of it while I have the chance. I love to swim."

Cassandra quickly followed Maxie into the water, determined to give her a good time while she could, because it was entirely probable that her father would forbid her to ask Maxie back again.

I could have been born poor, Cassy thought as she matched her stroke to Maxie's and the two of them glided through the water, *and Maxie could have been rich. If that had happened, would I have thought myself inferior to Maxie?*

Glancing affectionately at her friend's red hair as Maxie turned her face away to breathe, Cassandra admired Maxie anew. She wasn't awed by the Stewart family. She liked herself, and it was evident she didn't feel she needed to prove anything to anybody.

But I do, Cassandra realized with a sense of discovery. *I'm the one who needs to prove myself, to prove that I deserve all this on my own merits and not just through a fortunate accident of birth.*

Feeling a little shaken by the seriousness of her thoughts, Cassandra deliberately turned them off temporarily in favor of simply enjoying the day and the pleasure of shared friendship.

But later that evening, when Maxie had gone home and Cassandra sat listening to her father lecture her on the reasons why Maxie wasn't a fit companion for her and shouldn't be invited back, Cassandra found her rejection of her father's viewpoint hardening into concrete. She was determined to make her own decisions now and in the future.

When the lecture was over, she stood up and looked into her father's eyes, feeling almost as though she were looking at a stranger, though his handsome, aristocratic face was as familiar to her as her own.

"All right, Daddy. I won't invite Maxie back here," she accepted his decree and was angered by the satisfaction in his eyes. "I like her too much to let her be insulted by your attitude. But I intend to continue to be her friend as long as she wants to be mine, and if you're thinking about threatening me that you'll take things out on her father, don't bother. You may think I don't know anything about what goes on at the plant, but I know enough to realize how valuable Harry Palmer is to the company and that you won't fire him over something like this."

Cassandra then turned her back on her father's displeased look and walked out of the study with her head held high to go to her room. On that summer day, at the age of seventeen, she made a firm decision to think for herself and act accordingly. Strangely, however, she felt no need to protest vigorously her right to her own views. She was content merely to voice a quiet statement of her intentions, then demonstrate them.

THE PALMERS

Maxine

Two days before the first day of classes of her senior year, Maxie Palmer sat at the scarred kitchen table in her family's dilapidated but warm and comfortable kitchen while her father told her that he had received a cut in pay and she would therefore have to work even harder at good grades for a scholarship if she wanted to go to college.

"Don't feel so bad about it, Maxie, honey," Harry Palmer said as he reached across the table to enclose one of his daughter's tightly clenched hands in his own large, callused palm. "You'll get your scholarship, just like your brother did."

"I shouldn't have to." Maxie spoke through gritted teeth. She was filled with rage against the Stewart family—even Cassy. Her friend might seem to be different from her father and brother, but Maxie suddenly doubted it. Hadn't Cassy caved in when her father had forbidden her to have Maxie over to swim again?

I wouldn't have given in, Maxie thought, stifling the wisp of doubt that told her she was being unreasonable. She had thought she wouldn't mind being forbidden to visit Cassy's home. She had been wrong. It had hurt her pride enormously, as well as her faith in Cassy's friendship.

What good are friends, Maxie wondered bitterly, *if they won't stand up for you?*

"What do you mean, honey girl?" Harry Palmer said, troubled by the anger he saw in his daughter's flashing green eyes.

"I mean that as much as you've given that company," Maxie said, her heart filled with outrage, "you shouldn't ever have to take a cut in pay. They should be paying you far more than they are, as much as you're worth to them, rather than cheating you out of what's rightfully yours."

Harry shook his head, feeling sad that his daughter had to learn the way of the world through personal experience at such a young age.

"Girl, it doesn't work that way. If they had to, they'd find somebody to take my place." And at Maxie's look of disbelief, Harry smiled. "He wouldn't be as good as me, of course," he boasted playfully, before his smile faded. "But nobody's indispensable, honey."

"The Stewarts seem to be!" Maxie responded furiously.

Harry shrugged. "They own the town," he said simply, "so they call the shots."

"But you're as good as—no, better than—they are," Maxie cried out from the heart. "So why does it have to be this way?"

Harry dropped his eyes, feeling ashamed of his limitations. "Because I don't know anything but engines, honey," he said with quiet acceptance. "Old man Barton was as good with furniture as I am with engines, but he had something I don't—he had business sense. That's why his family is sitting out there in their mansion, and we're here in this run-down kitchen."

Maxie was appalled at herself for causing her father the self-blame she heard in his voice, and she leaned toward him, trying not to cry.

"I love this kitchen!" she said fiercely, meaning it.

Harry smiled. "So do I—" he nodded "—but I would have liked to give you kids, and especially your mama, more than I've been able to. Maybe then, your mama wouldn't be so sick."

The sudden guilt in her father's eyes sobered Maxie. "Money wouldn't cure Mama," she reminded him. "You know that as well as I do, Daddy. You have nothing to be guilty about. And if it's business sense that gets people like the Stewarts ahead," she added bitterly, getting to her feet to pace off the restless, helpless feeling inside her, "then I don't want it."

Alarmed, Harry got up and took hold of his daughter's arms. "Now don't talk foolishness, girl," he said in a stern voice to make her realize he was serious. "You've always wanted to go to college, and if you're going to cave in just because I can't pay for it—"

"Cave in?" Maxie sputtered indignantly. "I have no intention of caving in, Daddy. I'm going to go to college, all right, just like Bram did. I'm going to be a lawyer," she added slowly as an idea took birth inside her and began to grow. "The best lawyer in the country."

"A lawyer?" Harry was puzzled. Maxine had never expressed any interest in the law before.

"A union lawyer." Maxie nodded her head, the idea gaining strength. "Then just let Mr. Justin Stewart or his puffed-up son try to pull something like this again!"

"A lawyer." Harry shook his head dubiously. "What if you're not suited for it, hon?"

"Because I'm a girl?" Maxie was outraged by her father's chauvinism.

"No, no," Harry was quick to reassure her. "I just mean that people have different talents. What if you find out you're not suited to be a lawyer?"

"I'm suited," Maxie assured her father grimly. "You just wait and see how suited I am." Then she looked at her father, loving him passionately and aching for the injustice he was suffering. "Daddy, you've always told us kids we were as good as anybody," she reminded him gently. "And we're going to prove you're right," she added, hugging her father tightly around his waist. "At least Bram and I are, and when we have, we'll help the others."

Harry smiled and stroked his daughter's fiery red hair, loving her spirit, proud to the core of everything she was.

"You bet you will, honey," he said, hugging her and then stepping away to hold her in front of him. "But right now, you're goin' downtown to Hoffman's Store and buy yourself some new clothes for school."

"But, Daddy," Maxie protested, certain they couldn't afford a shopping expedition when her dad had just received a cut in pay.

"No buts," Harry said, turning her around and swatting her bottom to get her started. "I've got a little saved. You just tell John to charge whatever you need. And stop your worrying!" he added when Maxie still hesitated. "Trust me. I've got the money. Now go spend it!"

Maxie smiled at her dad, loving him for his generosity. And rather than hurt his pride, she did as he asked. But the garments she chose were not from the best racks and were fewer than Harry had had in mind. Maxie knew she could do a lot with them, however. She was not unduly modest about her sense of style.

Two days later, when she met Cassy on the school steps, Maxie did something she knew her father would not approve of if he ever heard about it. Her father was a fair-minded man who didn't believe in taking out on the innocent the sins of their fathers.

"What's wrong, Maxie?" Cassy asked instantly upon seeing the look on Maxie's face. "Is your mother sick again?"

Maxie shook her head. "Mom's okay right now," she said, not troubling to conceal her anger. And then, without pause, she asked, "Why didn't you tell me your dad and Jussie were going to cut my father's wages?"

Shocked by the question, Cassandra drew back slightly. "What are you talking about?" she asked. "My dad and Jussie don't tell me anything about the business."

Maxie thought it was probably true that Cassy hadn't known, but she was too angry to absolve her friend from blame.

"Your dad sent a memo around saying it's because of the economy, but I say it's because he and your brother are cheapskates!"

Maxie saw Cassy flinch, but she wasn't about to apologize for speaking what she felt was the truth.

"I'm sorry, Maxie," Cassy said miserably, the look in her large blue eyes asking Maxie not to blame her for her family's actions. And though Maxie knew on one level that she was wrong to take things out on Cassy, she could only pay lip service to denying that she was doing just that.

"I guess you can't help it, Cassy," she said grudgingly. "But I don't feel right about our being friends now," she added, her voice rising as anger clouded her common sense. "I'm so mad at your folks, I can't keep it from spilling over onto you."

Maxie could see that Cassy was stricken by her announcement, and a niggling sense of guilt about what she was doing gnawed at her. But something else inside her argued that this was the way things had to be.

Abruptly, Maxie turned away, intending to put her decision into practice immediately, but then she found she couldn't move. Her conscience wouldn't let her, not like this. She turned her head toward Cassy and inwardly winced at the look of betrayal in her friend's eyes.

Feeling miserable, Maxie tried to explain. "I know I'm not being fair to you, Cassy," she admitted, "but I can't help it. Daddy deserved a raise, not a cut in pay!"

Though Cassy's eyes brimmed with tears, she somehow found the strength to behave with a dignity beyond her years.

"I understand," she said in a quiet, final way.

Given Cassy's background, Maxie doubted she could understand, not really. She found herself saying, "Maybe later—" But then she stopped. She was fairly certain later was never going to come, and there was no use hoping it would.

Maxie had to whirl away before she started to cry over what her principles were costing her. It hurt terribly knowing that Cassy, the best friend she'd ever had, was lost to her. But Maxie was determined not to weaken. There was no way things could be the way they had been, now that she knew what she had to do with her future.

Bram

In an old, crumbling warehouse in Silicon Valley, California, Bram Palmer sat hunched over a computer trying to ignore the ache in his muscles from sitting in the same position for so long.

"You're gonna kill yourself workin' eighteen hours a day like this," Mannie Hillyer, his partner, said as he brought Bram a cup of coffee.

Bram rubbed his red-rimmed eyes with one hand as he took the proffered coffee with the other and sat back from the computer that had occupied his attention for the last twelve hours.

"Look who's talking," he said in a dry tone. Mannie was as hard-working as Bram and never seemed to sleep.

"Ah, but I'm an insomniac," Mannie said, a complacent smile on his thin lips. "You're not."

"No," Bram agreed wearily, rubbing a hand over the ache at the back of his neck. "I get tired."

"So what drives you?" Mannie asked curiously as he hitched a jeans-clad leg over a nearby table.

Bram smiled, thinking Mannie would never understand. Mannie had grown up in New York City where a man could be completely anonymous if he wanted to be. That wasn't so in Barton's Corner, Missouri, population four thousand, where everyone in town knew everyone else's business.

"You'd have to grow up where I did to know what drives me, Mannie," he said with a shrug and took a sip of his coffee. It was foul, the way Mannie's coffee always was, and he grimaced at the taste.

"You think growing up in New York saved me from having to prove myself?" Mannie asked with a slight smile and a faraway look in his dark eyes. "You're wrong, buddy. If you'd had a perfectionist father like I did, you'd understand what I'm talking about."

Bram thought about that. His father had been a perfectionist as well, but only when it came to machinery. With people, he was the soul of tolerance, and Bram loved him fiercely, fiercely enough to do whatever it took to succeed and make Harry proud of him. But he was aware there were other reasons for his determination to come out on top—the same reasons that had made him compete with Jussie Stewart in high school with a fervor that went beyond normal ambition.

"Well," he said dryly, setting his coffee down and turning back to his computer, "whatever it is that drives the two of us, I hope it keeps on doing it. I've promised myself we'll be millionaires before we're thirty, and I don't intend to break that promise."

Mannie stood up, a pleased smile on his lips, but a look of thoughtful calculation in his eyes. "Make that thirty-five, buddy," he said in a perfectly serious tone. "I like to bet on sure things."

"This is a sure thing," Bram said absently. He was about to find the glitch he'd been seeking with deadly patience for hours. "As sure as the sun's coming up."

Mannie shrugged and walked away to go back to his own work. Half an hour later, Bram sat back with a pleased smile on his firm lips and a look of satisfaction in his eyes.

"Look out, world," he murmured as he got to his feet and stretched his muscular arms over his head. "I'm going to prove that I can be a big fish in a big pond, rather than a big fish in a small one, like old Jussie Stewart."

Lowering his arms, he placed his hands on his hips and stared at his computer screen thoughtfully. *You've already beaten him more than once, Bram,* he reminded himself dryly, half impatient with his desire to do it again. *What have you got to do to be satisfied—grind him into the ground?*

But the letter he'd gotten from his sister, Maxie, the week before, saying the Stewarts had cut his dad's pay, answered his question for him and fired a renewal of the grim determination he'd had from the time he'd been a small boy and realized how things stood in Barton's Corner.

"Yeah," he said softly to no one but himself. "I won't be satisfied until I grind him into the ground, until I can buy and sell him and his whole family, until my folks are able to live in a mansion right next door to the almighty Stewarts if they so choose, or anywhere else they happen to want to be."

His energy returning along with his determination, Bram forgot about going to the living quarters of the warehouse he and Mannie rented for a pittance as both workshop and home.

Sleep, proper nourishment and a normal social life could wait. He still had a few bugs to find in the program he was working on before they could market it to the small companies they'd targeted that could benefit from its unique capabilities. He would finish the job before he snatched a sandwich and then collapse on his cot for a few hours of rest. There would be time to live like other people when he got where he wanted to be. For the present, working toward the success that would make a normal life possible was all that mattered.

Chapter One

At a swank restaurant in New York City, Cassandra Stewart sat across from her present employer, Curtis Milburn, thoroughly enjoying her cold shrimp dipped in an exquisite cocktail sauce while she listened to Curtis try to dissuade her from leaving her job with him.

Even though she had no intention of changing her mind about going home to Barton's Corner at her mother's request to live and work, Cassandra listened patiently to Curtis because she felt she owed him a great deal. When she had graduated from college seven years earlier with a double major in marketing and personnel management, she had intended to work at the family furniture business and somehow influence her father and brother to adopt a more liberal stance toward their employees, as well as broaden the market for their product.

She had known it wouldn't be easy, but she hadn't realized it would actually prove to be impossible. The male members of her family had presented a united front of resistance to her ideas, however, and out of despair and a determination to prove herself, Cassandra had stormed off to New York and obtained a junior position at Curtis Milburn's advertising agency.

Luckily, shortly after Cassy started work there, one of the agency's clients, an elderly woman who owned a cosmetics company and was dedicated to helping young women get ahead, had met and taken a liking to her and requested that she be allowed to work on the cosmetic company's new ad campaign.

Cassandra had thrown herself into the job, and her promotion ideas were so fresh and effective that she had been able to prove herself much faster than was generally the case for people so new at the game. She had won Curtis's respect and confidence, in fact, and after that, he had pretty much given her her head without ever having cause to regret it. Now he was trying to protect his investment in her.

"It's medieval, this running off to bury yourself in some backwater town and sacrifice your talent on the altar of family loyalty!" Curtis exclaimed before popping another oyster into his somewhat prim mouth.

Cassandra glanced up from her shrimp, her expression tolerant, even though she thought Curtis's petulant tone and fussy gestures did nothing for his image. She was not surprised at the depth of his pique, since besides being denied her services as one of his best employees, he was also going to miss having her as an undemanding, platonic female companion. She only hoped he wasn't going to really go round the bend and ask her to marry him in order to keep her nearby, since she was positive he would make a terrible husband, even if she felt strongly enough about him to accept a proposal from him in the first place, which she didn't.

"Come now, Curtis," she said in a mild, absent tone, since her mind was made up and nothing was going to change her plans. "Are you saying that if your family asked you—"

"I don't have a family, thank God!" Curtis broke in, sounding both irritable and satisfied.

Patiently, Cassandra continued with her question. "But if you *did* have a family and they needed your help, are you saying you wouldn't give it?"

She knew it was naughty of her to force him to voice the answer she was certain he was going to give, but her gratitude that she had had the good sense not to fall in love with him was growing by the moment.

"I would not!" Curtis said with stern firmness, which was echoed in his cool gray eyes. "It's an outdated, barbaric concept, this family-loyalty thing. And if I *did* have a family," he added rather self-righteously, Cassandra thought, "I have no doubt that no one in it would have the bad taste to request such a thing of me or any other relation. They would no doubt respect my rights, just as I would theirs."

The mild expression in Cassandra's wide blue eyes concealed her thought that Curtis had just insulted her family, which was rather tactless of him. He'd also insulted her, which was *quite* tactless of him, especially if he wanted to persuade her to stay in New York.

Leaning forward, she patted his hand in an innocent fashion, just as if she didn't know that he hated public demonstrations of affection. "Well, Curtis," she said soothingly, "I guess I have to plead guilty to being medieval and slightly barbaric, because I am going to answer the distress call my mother sent for me to come home and help Jussie run the company."

Curtis's prim mouth tightened even more disapprovingly. "That small-time furniture mill?" he said in a disdainful tone. "How can that compare with what you've been doing for me?"

Cassandra abruptly felt her normal tolerance beginning to slip drastically where Curtis was concerned. She might not be proud of the anachronistic policies her father and brother had always practiced, and which Jussie was implementing even more drastically since Justin, Sr., had died two years ago, but she was definitely proud of the quality of product that had kept Barton Furniture in business for so many years.

"I'll try to adjust to the downturn in my personal fortunes," she answered, and there was a definite edge to her tone now.

Curtis sat back in his chair and dabbed at his mouth with a fine linen napkin, all the while staring at Cassandra with grim frustration. Then the grimness departed in favor of one of firm decision.

"Very well, Cassandra," he said, leaning forward to hold her eyes with his own. "If you have definitely made up your mind to take this disastrous step, then I have no choice but to offer you an even better alternative than working for me and being my, ah, companion."

Amused by Curtis's awkwardness, Cassandra reflected that a stranger listening in would no doubt come to the conclusion that she was Curtis's mistress, when in fact they had never been to bed together, an arrangement that had suited both of them. For her part, when she had come to work for Curtis, she had been totally focused on achieving success in her career and had had no desire to be side-tracked by getting seriously involved with anyone. And as for Curtis, Cassandra had immediately recognized that the man was simply too emotionally self-involved, and too physically fastidious, to want to share a full-blown relationship with a woman, which was why she had felt safe dating him.

"I had thought that you were as content as I to let things between us go on as they had been," Curtis continued, sounding half resentful, half propitiatory, "but obviously I was mistaken. Presumably, you, like most women, need something more definite from a man. Therefore—" and here Curtis inhaled a deep breath "—I am prepared to offer you marriage if you will agree to stay on here with me and with my company."

Cassandra blinked at him, striving mightily to keep her unfortunate sense of humor under control. She wanted to ask him which he would miss more—her professional services or her personal companionship. But she knew the answer already. She had brought the company quite a few new clients, and consequently millions of dollars of new business, while all she had brought Curtis was an amiable, fairly attractive, completely undemanding companion to wear on his arm to the theater, to the ballet and to fashionable restaurants, so that he wouldn't have to suffer the perils of more demanding women.

When the silence became awkward, Cassandra forced control upon herself and tried to answer Curtis's proposal tactfully.

"Why, Curtis, how, ah, sweet." She stumbled somewhat over that last word, since Curtis was much too prim and proper to be considered sweet. In fact, she had sometimes pictured in her mind what he might be like on his honeymoon, and she had to hide a grin now as she remembered her conclusion. Curtis would no doubt prepare for bed on his wedding night with a bath, followed by a shower, followed by a vigorous toothbrushing, followed by a good gargle with at least a gallon of mouthwash in order to dispose of any stray germs that might have escaped his determined assault on them.

"However," Cassandra continued in a suitably grave tone that cost her much to produce, "I'm afraid even that, ah, fantastic inducement can't change my mind. I really have no choice, Curtis," she said simply. "I can't let my mother down, not even for your sake."

Cassandra had to snatch up a napkin to cover her mouth when she saw that Curtis was struggling between relief and outrage. While Curtis struggled to resolve his conflicting emotions, she struggled to strangle her laughter into submission. Both accomplished their separate tasks at approximately the same moment.

"I can't believe this!" Curtis spoke first. "Have you no loyalty to me at all!"

Cassandra thought that one over. The answer was not in doubt, of course; she was simply puzzling over Curtis's hypocrisy. If he thought her family had no claim over her loyalty, why did he presume he should?

Her thoughts veered when the waiter approached, bringing with him a dinner she intended to enjoy to the last morsel. Before long she would have to be content with either her mother's cooking or that of the one restaurant in Barton's Corner other than fast-food drive-ins.

Fortunately, by the time she and Curtis were served, he seemed to have forgotten his last question. He was much too caught up in contemplating the glorious perfection of his steak au poivre.

Later, as the two of them sat enjoying coffee and brandy, Curtis started to resume his attack, but by now, Cassandra was replete with food and in no mood to delay getting started on the thousand things she had to accomplish before she could head for Missouri. She cut into his description of her as the single greatest marketing genius in recent history by holding up her hand for silence.

"Curtis," she said matter-of-factly as she gathered up her purse, "I thank you for your high opinion of me, and I realize you must be confused about my behavior, since I've worked so hard to justify that opinion. But I don't intend to change my mind, and since I'm almost late for an appointment with a realtor who is arranging to sublet my apartment, I really must go."

Curtis looked so betrayed by her defection, however, that Cassandra paused a moment to smile with gentle understanding at him.

As she started to push her chair back, Curtis came to life and lunged across the table to grab one of her hands. Startled by his uncustomary vehemence, Cassandra stared at him.

"But you can't just go off and leave me right when we're about to launch Creamy Wheat's new advertising campaign," he said with a touch of desperation in his voice. "You conceived it, and you have to run it. We have a big investment in that campaign, and I don't trust anyone else to..." Curtis's voice faltered and he quickly let go of Cassandra's hand when he saw a look of impatience replace the calm kindness that normally resided in her eyes.

"I've told you three times now, Curtis," she said with quiet firmness, "that Karl Moses is every bit as capable of running that campaign as I am. He's been in on the planning from the beginning, he contributed greatly to the concept, and he has what it takes to fill my shoes. Now I really must go!"

But still Cassandra hesitated, almost allowing her better nature to cloud her quite concrete knowledge that Curtis wasn't really worth her sympathy. But he looked so stunned and helpless by her defection, she thought perhaps even he hadn't realized until now how much he'd come to depend on her, both emotionally and practically.

"You must accept it, Curtis," she said gently. "I'm not staying, and barring some unforeseen circumstances, I'm not coming back."

Curtis flushed and stiffened at Cassandra's rather maternal tone, and he threw down his napkin and sat back.

"Of course, I'll accept it," he snapped. "I never had any intention of doing otherwise. It's just that I don't care for change all that much, at least not from a personal standpoint. I think you'll have to admit that I'm progressive in a business sense."

"Yes, Curtis, you are," Cassandra responded easily as she got to her feet, came around the table and bent to kiss

Curtis's cheek. The action flustered him, both from a hygienic viewpoint and an emotional one.

"Goodbye, dear." Cassandra straightened, smiling at Curtis with good-natured affection. "Thanks for giving me so much autonomy and allowing me to try my wings. I've learned a lot working for you."

"I should hope so," Curtis responded gruffly. He was angry and yet desperate not to seem at a disadvantage.

Cassandra viewed his quandary with tolerance and considered the best thing she could do for him was to get out of his way and give him time to find his equilibrium again.

"Look me up if you ever get to Missouri," she said lightly as she backed away from the table. "I'll give you a tour of my family's small-time furniture mill." And grinning mischievously, she turned and strode away in her graceful, long-legged fashion that Curtis had to admire, even as he fumed inwardly with frustration.

"Not likely," he huffed as he fished in his pocket for his credit card. "No one in his right mind would deliberately go to some hick town with the improbable name of Barton's Corner. No one other than someone like you, Cassandra Stewart, who had the ultimate misfortune of being born there, and whom I heartily wish had stayed there instead of coming to New York to stab me in the back!"

THREE THOUSAND MILES away in California, Bram Palmer sat in his unpretentious office, which in no way reflected his status as half owner of one of the most successful computer companies in the country, with his feet propped on the corner of his desk as he reread a letter from his sister Maxie.

Bram,
I'm worried about Dad. He won't retire, especially now that I'm knee-deep in trying to unionize the plant. He thinks I need him to bring the other employees around

to our way of thinking, and I have to admit he is a big help. Oh, sure, he's always been outspoken about the Stewarts, but people have begun to listen to him a lot more closely now that Jussie is making such an ass of himself. The man's a complete capitalistic pig, worse than his father ever was. At least Justin, Sr., had the sense to sugarcoat the pills he doled out to his employees, where Jussie just grabs people by the throat and forces his potions of injustice on them. The creep! Well, never mind. Forgive me for burdening you with my worries. But if you could see your way clear to come home for a visit soon, it would be a blessing. As much as I want to force a union on the Stewarts, I don't want to do it at Dad's expense, and he just won't see reason. Nor, now that I've started things rolling, will he let me back out, which I've been tempted to do many times, temporarily at least, long enough to get Daddy to retire, anyway. By the way, he's still on my case about getting married and settling down to have grandbabies for him, and if you do come for a visit, you'll get the same sort of harassment. He's literally chomping at the bit to see the next generation of Palmers, and it's no use to try to deflect him onto Patty and Jimbo, because they were smart enough to get away from here, once you paid for their educations, and they're not about to come back. Sometimes I wish I hadn't, but what good is a law degree if you can't use it to pursue justice, right?

Pausing in his reading, Bram lifted his eyes from the letter to stare unseeingly at the far wall. He felt guilty that in his single-minded pursuit of success, he hadn't been home to see his parents very often before his mother had finally succumbed to a stroke as a result of the acute hypertension that had plagued her for years. In fact, he hadn't seen his dad since he had returned to Barton's Corner for his mother's funeral over two years before.

It didn't matter that, since then, he had invited Harry out to see him time and again, offering to pay his way and take as much time off from business as he could to show him around. Harry wouldn't leave Barton's Corner, and for a long time Bram had considered things too precarious to leave California. But now that the partnership was making money hand over fist, and there were any number of good managers under him to take over his duties for a while, he knew it was time to go home again.

His decision made, he returned his eyes to the letter and scanned the P.S. Maxie had tacked on.

One of my other worries right now is that it's rumored Mary Louise Stewart has sent for Cassy to help get Jussie out of the mess he's made. And no matter how much I despise Jussie, I can't hate Mary Louise or Cassy. I've felt guilty for years about withholding my friendship from Cassy during our senior year of high school because of what her dad and Jussie did. So things could get pretty awkward around here if she's as nice as she used to be. I think I'd almost prefer that she come back as hard-nosed as Jussie so I could hate her, too. But that's not likely to happen.

Shrugging away Maxie's last worry, since Bram had never known Cassandra Stewart as other than a younger member of the Stewart family and had no desire to know her now, he set the letter aside and stared at the phone on his desk, aware that for some reason he was reluctant to begin arrangements for his first vacation in years.

Why the cold feet, buddy? he asked himself, frowning slightly. *Does it have something to do with a prophet being unrecognized in his own town?*

Bram smiled at the foolishness of designating himself a prophet, although in some ways that was what he had been. No one except he and Mannie had expected the partnership to become as successful as it now was, but with Mannie's genius for hardware design and Bram's genius for software programming and marketing, the two of them had hit the big time. Bram hadn't missed his goal of becoming a millionaire by the age of thirty by too much. And yet, apart from the satisfaction of having succeeded at what they started out to do, their lives hadn't changed all that much. They lived well, but not with excessive ostentation. They both still put in long hours of work, and neither had as yet found much time to concentrate on his personal life, though Bram was becoming increasingly aware that he was ready, even impatient, to do so.

He smiled again, thinking there weren't too many millionaires who had a first-rate, still-practicing mechanic for a father and a militant union attorney for a sister. Patty and Jimbo were more the sort of family millionaires were expected to have. He had financed their education, allowing them to get out of their jobs at Barton Furniture and go on to bigger and better places and occupations. Patty was a practicing psychologist in San Francisco, and Jimbo, who took after Harry in his fascination with mechanics, owned a Mercedes dealership in Los Angeles.

The smile departed as Bram focused on why he was so reluctant to go back to Barton's Corner. He supposed it had to do with the nature of small-town life. He suspected he could go back to Barton's Corner as the president of the United States, and the town, in particular the owners of the town—the Stewarts—would still think of him as a boy from the wrong side of the tracks.

Since his determination to erase that perception had acted as a spur to him to succeed in business, Bram felt a reluctant, ironic gratitude for the unknowing, backhanded boost the Stewarts had provided in helping him make something of himself. But now, with the maturity he'd gained over the years, he finally realized that his success probably didn't mean much to anyone other than himself and his family.

Objectively, Bram knew it shouldn't make any difference to him what anyone thought of him, yet on some level, he didn't relish returning to a place where his image was stuck in the granite of the past.

His feet came down to the floor with a crash, to accompany the impatient curse that left his mouth at the same instant. "Hell, man, grow up!" he grated as he got up to pace his small office.

The office was small because Bram and Mannie didn't go in for the perks most business owners did. Their common attitude was that it was the job that mattered. They brooked no skimping on quality from their employees, yet they had the devoted loyalty of every one of them because they took care of their people. They recruited the best and paid them accordingly, and they treated everyone from the cleaning crew to their top computer scientist with sincere respect and appreciation. Of course, such a management style worked to their benefit, but it had come about as a result of their innate fairness and not as a calculated technique.

"Grow up, Bram!" he repeated as he stood at a window and looked out over the California countryside. "The Stewarts don't matter anymore, or at least only insofar as they still affect the lives of Dad and Maxie."

He began to feel better at having recognized the source of his discomfort. And he felt a lot better when he realized that the recognition was helping him to come to terms with old scars. At the age of thirty-four he considered it was time to let the reins that had restricted his early years disappear into oblivion, where they belonged.

A feeling of relief eased the tension in Bram's broad shoulders.

"Jussie," he whispered wryly, "I'm a better man than you, whether you recognize it or not. I don't need to prove it anymore. And before Maxie gets through with you, I have a feeling I'm actually going to feel sorry for you. You won't be able to call your soul your own, if you ever did. Sometimes I think you sold it to the devil a long time ago."

And as Bram swung around to his desk and picked up his phone to call and make an airline reservation, his last thought concerning the Stewart clan was that he hoped, for Maxie's sake, that the female Stewart—what was her name, Cassy?—was as hard-nosed as Jussie. Otherwise, Maxie's work was going to be just that much harder, and it was past time for the owners of Barton Furniture to dig their own graves and climb into them.

Chapter Two

As Cassandra drove the new yellow Chevrolet Corvette she had purchased in Springfield at a leisurely speed southeast toward Barton's Corner, she enjoyed renewing her acquaintance with her home state. It was late September, and some of the trees were already dressed in their fall colors, while others were taking things more slowly. The contrast of greens, yellows, oranges, reds and browns was pleasing to the eye, and Cassandra felt her inner metabolism slowing gradually from the hectic pace she had become accustomed to in New York, where things tended to become blurred, to a rather sleepy enjoyment of separate, distinct increments of time.

Enjoy it while you can, Cassy girl, she thought with a lazy smile, *because when you hit the old homestead, the sparks will begin to fly again.*

She wondered if her mother had told Jussie yet that his sister was coming to help him out. She hoped so, but she doubted it. For while Mary Louise was outwardly a very easygoing, warm, uncomplicated woman, Cassandra had known for several years that there was quite a lot more to her mother's character than what showed on the surface.

After college, when Cassandra had tried to work at her family's firm and had her ideas ignored, she had at last gone to her mother for help before eventually deciding to leave town altogether and go to New York. And it was at that time that Mary Louise Stewart had explained to Cassandra some of the realities of her marriage to Justin Stewart, Sr.

It hadn't taken Mary Louise longer than the honeymoon to size up her husband's strengths and weaknesses, but in her love for him, she had elected to allow him the illusion that he was smarter, stronger and better equipped to run the family company than she was, since pride was both Justin's besetting sin and the prop that maintained his self-confidence. She had also gently, tactfully, prevented him from abusing his position past the limits of her own tolerance. But when Cassandra had come to her for help, she had explained that she could not, at this late date, knock the props from beneath her husband's fragile ego by taking her daughter's side.

Disappointed and bitter at the time, Cassandra had come to terms with her mother's decision after her father's death, and she was actually grateful that her mother hadn't allowed her to hurt him. But she had still seen her brother clearly and had had another frank discussion with her mother after the funeral.

"Jussie will ruin the company if we let him, Mom," she had predicted with quiet surety and had been surprised by her mother's assent.

"I know," Mary Louise had said with simple dignity, her lovely blue eyes darkened with sadness at the loss of her husband. "And it's partly my fault," she had admitted with a weary sigh. "I let him get away with things I shouldn't have because it would have upset his father had I interfered."

"Then why not stop it now," Cassandra had demanded urgently, "before he goes too far and—"

But Mary Louise had been shaking her head before Cassandra had finished. "The only way to stop him now is to let him drive the company to the brink of ruin," she had informed her daughter in a quiet, sure voice. "When he's done that, Cassy," she had said calmly, "I'll call for you to come and save us." She had looked at Cassy then with that firm, level, loving look that had always gone straight to Cassandra's heart as she asked, "Will you do it, darling? Will you come when I call?"

And though Cassandra was of a different generation and unable to relate fully to her mother's view of things—had it been up to her, she would have tactfully, but absolutely without equivocation, removed Jussie from his position as head of the company—Cassandra could no more deny her mother's request than she could have slapped the lovely smooth cheek that had so often rested against her own. Therefore, with a defeated sigh and a shrug of her shoulders, she had agreed to Mary Louise's request.

"Yes, Mom," she had forced herself to say. "When you call, I'll come."

That had been two years ago, and now, as Cassandra drove home in response to the call that had finally come, she was both relieved that the waiting was over and unhappy about part of what she had to do. Entrenched in the rightness of his own views, as well as in the habit of running things, Jussie would fight hard to keep the status quo, though it wasn't working and hadn't been for some time. Perhaps, knowing her son's character so well, that was why Mary Louise had insisted she and Cassandra wait before acting against him. Their main weapon would be the failure of Jussie's methods to increase productivity and profits.

Even with that weapon in hand, however, Cassandra was under no illusion that Jussie's pride—a pride even more stiff-necked than their father's had been—would allow him to share power with her easily, or even to accept suggestions, no matter how tactfully given.

But as Cassandra spotted the sign by the side of the road that announced that Barton's Corner, population four thousand, was just ahead, she rested calmly upon the certainty that she would prevail. It might be too much to expect to win without bringing Jussie to his knees, though she hoped that wouldn't be the case, but if necessary she would go even that far to ensure that the company upon which a whole town depended for its livelihood would not only survive, but would grow and flourish.

Cassandra slowed the Corvette, smiling as she drove down Main Street and spotted the stores that had been there all of her life, and a few faces she recognized, faces that stared after her car, obviously sensing there was something familiar about the driver, but unable to relate the sophisticated, self-confident woman behind the wheel with the young, somewhat naive Cassy Stewart who had grown up there.

Leaving the small business district, Cassandra drove by the old red brick high school, and though a smile still remained on her lips, her large, clear eyes clouded somewhat as she remembered the loneliness of her senior year. There had been other friends, of course, after Maxie's defection, but none so compatible, none so special.

Cassandra knew from her mother that Maxie was an attorney and that she was back now, working hard to unionize the company. And since Cassandra's plan was intended to make a union redundant, she supposed there would be no rapprochement with Maxie even now, indeed, she wasn't sure she wanted such a rapprochement. Though she understood the whys of Maxie's behavior all those years ago, the pain of her former friend's abandonment was still in Cassandra's heart, festering there against her better judgment, even against her wishes. She reflected with a wry grimace that some things were apparently stronger than logic and desire.

Just as she was about to speed up and head for home, Cassandra spotted something that made her slow down, instead. At the wheel of a red Jaguar parked across from the school football field was a man she recognized instantaneously, though it had been more than ten years since she'd last seen him. But he had changed very little, physically at least. His hair was still that fascinating shade of auburn, his eyes still as green as hard emeralds. Only the maturity of his face was different, making it more compellingly handsome than it had ever been.

Bram Palmer, Cassandra identified the man silently, her heart beginning to beat faster with excitement. *And what are you doing back in Barton's Corner, Mr. American Success Story?*

Her mother had sent Cassandra the small, weekly local paper for years, as well as keeping her up to date via phone calls on who from Barton's Corner was doing what. So Cassandra had been aware that Bram had done exceptionally well for himself and that he had remained unmarried. And despite her confused feelings about Bram's sister, Cassandra had always been exceptionally pleased over Bram's success. Her pleasure was no less evident at this moment as she saw that Bram was even more attractive than she'd remembered him to be.

Evidently, Bram was on the same sort of pilgrimage Cassandra was. He had his head turned to inspect the playing field where he had shone as a football star years ago. Since the weather was mild and each of them had lowered the driver's car window, as Cassandra drew level with his car, she found herself staring directly into Bram's eyes. The impact of his gaze affected her so pleasurably that, acting without thought, she abruptly braked to a stop and gave him a smile that expressed her pleasure radiantly.

"Bram Palmer!" she exclaimed with spontaneous delight. "It's wonderful to see you again!"

The blank look in Bram's eyes informed Cassandra of what she should have remembered before stopping to speak to him. He hadn't the slightest idea of who she was! But as the blank look disappeared and Bram began to smile at her in the way many men who had wanted to become acquainted with her had smiled at her over the years, Cassandra suddenly realized that when he found out who she was, his burgeoning interest was likely to cool so fast, she'd probably get frostbite standing within ten feet of him.

Since she had no desire to see his look change from one of male interest to cold rejection, she spoke before he could.

"Enjoy your stay," she called, and her smile didn't waver as she stepped on the gas and roared away.

As she looked in her rearview mirror, Cassandra's smile broadened briefly when she saw that Bram was looking back over one of his broad shoulders at her with a puzzled, and clearly disappointed, expression on his ruggedly handsome face.

He'll ask Maxie who the blond in the yellow Corvette is, she thought, her smile fading quickly. *I wonder if Maxie will guess who he means? If she does, and he did find me attractive, it won't matter. He's not likely to do anything about it once he learns my identity.*

It hurt to think that Bram Palmer, whom she'd admired from afar years ago, and who had made her heart race every bit as fast just now as it ever had when she was a girl, would disapprove of her simply because of who she was. And though Cassandra realized objectively that allowing his reaction to matter to her at all was foolish, since she'd never actually known him and didn't really know him now, she had to give herself a strong talking-to, anyway, to make herself feel better.

So what if it matters to him who I am, she thought impatiently. *It makes no sense to indulge childhood fantasies that don't have a chance of becoming real. Even if the man should be mature enough to discount what has happened, and is happening, between our families, he's probably only home for a visit, while I intend to remain here. It would be folly to play with that sort of fire when I've got enough on my plate as it is.*

With a determined lift of her chin, Cassandra told herself to forget Bram Palmer and continued her drive home, to be greeted by her mother with a welcome so filled with warmth and love that she immediately felt much better. Her mood plunged again somewhat, however, when she learned that Mary Louise hadn't told Jussie why she was coming home. That meant the responsibility would lie completely on her own shoulders, and it was one she didn't look forward to.

Several hours later, replete with a delicious dinner her mother had prepared, Cassandra sat beside Mary Louise on a comfortable, attractive sofa in the family den, her gaze assessing as she watched her brother pace in front of the glowing fireplace. She wondered if his restlessness stemmed from his instincts concerning the reason for her visit. He had to know she was aware of the problems at the furniture mill.

No doubt about it, she thought objectively, *Jussie is a very handsome, very impressive, very determined man. This isn't going to be easy.*

"Stop pacing so, Jussie, darling," Mary Louise scolded her son gently. "You're making me dizzy. Come sit down and have some coffee."

Jussie paused, the look in his strikingly attractive blue eyes unguardedly impatient for an instant, before he forced a thin smile onto his beautifully sculptured lips, shrugged and threw himself into the large comfortable chair that had been their father's for as many years as Cassandra could remember.

Still watching him, her frame of mind still objective, almost detached, Cassandra wondered, as she had many times before, why Jussie hadn't yet married. He was thirty-four, handsome, reasonably wealthy, even with the recent decline in the company's fortunes, and when he set out to be charming, he was impressively successful at it. Perhaps, due to his overweening pride, he had simply never found a woman he considered good enough for him. Cassandra smiled wryly at the thought.

"What are you thinking, to bring on such a mysterious smile, Cassy?" Justin asked with lazy humor.

Cassandra shrugged as she leaned forward to place her empty coffee cup on the beautifully carved walnut table in front of the sofa. The table was a product of the family's furniture mill, and Cassandra absently took instinctive pride in the craftsmanship of the carving and the beauty of the hand-rubbed wood.

"I was thinking how handsome you are, and wondering why you've never married, Jussie," she said in an amiable tone. "Is it because you're so successful with women without marriage, you've never seen the necessity to tie yourself down to just one?"

For the first time since Jussie had come home from the mill and found Cassandra ensconced in her old room, looking as though she had every intention of staying awhile, Jussie relaxed, and a short burst of laughter issued from his mouth, while a teasing light of caution gleamed from his eyes as he glanced warningly at his mother.

Mary Louise smiled blandly. "Lord knows, it's not because I'm a possessive mother," she said with dry humor. "I'm dying for grandchildren, but neither of you seems inclined to give me any."

Jussie seized upon his mother's remarks to turn the discussion away from himself. "Mom has a point, Cassy," he teased his sister. "Why haven't *you* married? You're an old spinster of what—twenty-nine? Getting a little long in the tooth, aren't you?"

Cassandra inclined her head gracefully, an easy smile on her lips. "In case you haven't heard, these are the days of women's liberation, Jussie," she gently teased him, knowing that the opportunity to satisfy Jussie's curiosity, and most likely arouse his temper, had arrived. "Many women prefer to establish their careers before taking on a husband and children." She shrugged, her smile tilting charmingly. "Besides," she added, "I haven't yet found a man who excites me as much as business does."

At that, as Cassandra had known he would, Jussie sat a little straighter, and the look in his eyes became more alert.

"Ah, yes—" he kept his tone light "—how *is* your career going? Still making marketing history in the Big Apple?"

"I was," Cassandra admitted without undue modesty, "but I'm ready for a change now, I think."

"What sort of a change?" Justin asked quickly, his tone cold now.

Cassandra lifted her eyes, as blue as his, as determined as his, but without the underlying hardness of Jussie's, and said, as quietly as though she were discussing the weather, "Why, I'm going to come into the business with you, Jussie. I think it's about time, don't you?"

For an instant Jussie looked as though he'd been kicked in the stomach, but he immediately got control of himself and leaned back in his father's chair. The expression on his handsome face was inscrutable.

"We tried that once before, remember, Cassandra? It didn't work out then, and I don't expect it would be any different now."

Cassandra noted the distancing use of her formal name, but remained calm. "I agree it won't be easy," she said softly, "but it *will* work, Jussie, one way or another."

The look in Jussie's eyes sharpened at her addendum. "And what does that mean, 'one way or another'?" he said with harsh impatience. "If you think I'm going to be any more amenable to your knee-jerk liberal style of management now than I was when you first got out of college, you're in for a disappointment. A few years in New York don't qualify you to come down here and tell me how to run my business."

Cassandra lifted her finely arched brows in an expression of cool surprise. "*Your* business, Jussie?" she said in a gently chiding tone. "I was under the impression the company still belonged to Mom. Has something changed during my absence?"

Jussie automatically looked at his mother for confirmation as he replied, "Mom depends on me to run the business, just as she always depended on Dad to do it. Right, Mom?"

Mary Louise, who had been silent, staring into the flames in the fireplace, now looked at Jussie, and as Cassandra watched her brother smile at their mother in the charming way that had always softened Mary Louise's indulgent heart, she felt a clutching sensation in her chest. Would her mother hold firm against a lifetime habit of indulging her son?

"Cassy has an interest in the company, too, Jussie," Mary Louise said with gentle firmness. "She's qualified to help run it, and she's entitled to a share in the responsibility."

Jussie looked blank at first, as though he couldn't believe he'd heard right. Then his face flushed, and Cassandra watched as he fought down his temper in order to reason with his mother.

"Other than that short period after she came home from college, Cassy has no experience at our company, Mom," he said impatiently. "She never spent her summers working there the way I did, nor did she seem to understand what it required when she worked with Dad and me before."

Cassandra seized the opportunity Jussie had given her. "You're quite right, Jussie," she said quietly. "I don't have the experience in running Barton Furniture that you do. That's why I intend to start by getting thoroughly familiar with all aspects of the business. And then maybe a fresh outlook could be of help in turning things around there."

Jussie ignored the part about turning things around. "What are you talking about?" he snorted. "Do you fancy operating the big saws the way I did? If so, I won't stand for it. It's too dangerous."

Cassandra fought down her anger at Jussie's chauvinism and said, "I don't consider that necessary. But if I did, I would do it, make no mistake about that." She got to her feet and walked to stand in front of her brother, who sat in his chair looking stiffly combative.

"Jussie," Cassandra said quietly, "we can go about this in a spirit of loving cooperation, or we can have the fight of the century. But you might as well know now, I intend to take my place at Barton Furniture, and I don't consider my place to be under your thumb. I will learn the business from *A* to *Z*, and when I know what I need to, you'd better make room in your office for a new desk and some new ideas. Because yours aren't working, and you know it," she added as gently as possible.

Her effort to be gentle proved futile. Jussie came to his feet, forcing Cassandra to step back.

His eyes were as cold as a winter sky as he stared first at Cassandra and then at his mother, asking her a silent question. When he didn't get the answer he wanted or expected from Mary Louise, his jaw tightened into a line of granite stubbornness, and he returned his gaze to his sister. Cassandra stared back, not giving an inch.

"So you want to sit in my chair, little sister?" he asked, his tone softly dangerous.

"Not the way you mean, Jussie," Cassandra said with a deliberate lack of hostility, but without a lessening of determination in her firm voice. "I told you, I'd rather we worked together. But if that isn't possible, I'll do what's necessary to get our company back on its feet and then progressing toward a bigger future than it has ever had."

Jussie's firm mouth twisted into a mocking curve, and he stepped back, making a courtly bow of false obeisance.

"Enter the conquering queen," he drawled. As he straightened, the harsh, cold expression came back into his eyes. He shrugged then, and a caricature of a smile twisted his lips as he turned away and strolled toward the double walnut doors that led from the den into the rest of the house. When he reached the doors, however, he turned back, and now his smile was easier as he adopted a jaunty stance of unconcern, one fist on his hip, his shoulders relaxed.

"All right, kid—" the smile slipped into a cocky grin "—you come get me if you can. But don't expect me to go easy on you just because you're a member of the family. I don't play the game that way."

"I won't, Jussie," Cassandra said lightly, her smile confident. "Contrary to what you seem to think, my years in New York weren't wasted. In fact, I outdid a lot of men there who had more experience than I. I bested them partly because they underestimated me, but mostly because I was better than they."

At seeing something move behind her brother's clear eyes that resembled hurt and then, surprisingly, fear, Cassandra regretted giving in to her petty desire to brag a little. She reminded herself that he was her brother, and despite their many differences, their many conflicting viewpoints, she loved him deeply.

But if she had seen those things in Jussie's eyes, they were quickly gone, and he gave her another mocking bow before he turned and left the room without another word.

Cassandra sighed and slowly turned around to face her mother, expecting her to be distressed by what had happened. To her surprise, however, there was no distress in her mother's expression. Rather, Mary Louise was nodding, as though satisfied.

"You've frightened him, Cassy," she said as she got to her feet and came to face her daughter. "That's an advantage for you. Don't throw it away by remembering too often that Jussie is your brother and that you love him. If you do, he'll take the advantage, I assure you."

Puzzled by her mother's seemingly callous attitude, Cassandra shook her head wonderingly.

Mary Louise's smile was both sad and wry, but the look in her eyes was determined. "Don't make the mistake of thinking I don't love Jussie," she said softly. "I love him more than life itself, just as I love you."

When Cassandra started to say something, her mother put a finger gently across her lips. "It's for him more than anything else, Cassy," Mary Louise said quietly, turning to look at the door through which her son had left the room. "For him and for this town. If Jussie isn't stopped, he'll ruin himself and he'll destroy the livelihood of too many others."

She looked back at Cassandra, her gaze clear and lucid. "Jussie's got a lot of growing to do, darling," she said gently. "I let his father encourage too much of the bad side of our son to flourish. And I've left it until almost too late to try to turn things around. But with your help, we'll make a man to be proud of out of Justin Stewart, Jr. And when we've succeeded, I'll have grandchildren to love, because both he and you will have something else on your minds other than business."

Mary Louise dropped a kiss on Cassandra's cheek, then stepped back, turned, gathered up the knitting she hadn't touched as yet that evening and crossed to the chair her son had occupied until a few moments earlier. When she was comfortably settled, she glanced up at Cassandra, still standing and looking at her with bewildered astonishment.

"While you're up, why don't you turn on the television, darling?" she said with a mild, but somehow mischievous, smile. "I think it's about time for *Dallas* to come on, and I never miss it. There's a lot to be learned from J.R.'s nasty shenanigans if one is of a mind to pay attention."

Her mouth curving into a smile as mischievous as her mother's, Cassandra ran a hand through her shoulder-length, blond-highlighted hair, then crossed to switch on the television as her mother had requested. As she turned back to seat herself on the sofa, however, she gave her parent a grave look of reproach.

"Mom," she said, the chiding note in her voice tempered with love, "just tell me one thing."

"Yes, dear?" Mary Louise glanced up, her expression mild.

"Do you own a pair of trousers you take out of your closet and wear when the rest of us aren't looking?" Cassandra teased.

Mary Louise's response was delivered straight-facedly. "Why, of course not, Cassy," she said, and Cassandra had never heard her sound more innocent. "I don't have the right sort of figure for them."

Chapter Three

Regretting that he hadn't followed the lovely, and mysterious, woman who had stopped to speak to him at the school to find out who she was, Bram pulled the sleek red Jaguar he had bought on impulse in Springfield into the cracked driveway of his father's modest home, the house where Bram himself had lived until leaving Barton's Corner for college.

As he came to a stop and killed the engine, his thoughts turned from hoping the woman he'd seen wasn't married to an awareness of the contrast between the car he was driving and his boyhood home. Suddenly, he wondered at his motives for purchasing such an expensive and exotic automobile for the final stage of his trip.

Showing off? he asked himself with dry self-mockery. *Probably,* he acknowledged with a mental shrug and wondered without really caring if the foolish gesture would backfire on him. Unless Harry had told them, the townspeople weren't likely to know that after he had the money to do so, Bram had offered to buy or have built a much better house than this one, but Harry had refused to move. He wanted to stay in the home where he had known such happiness with his wife and children.

As Bram climbed out of the car, he let his eyes wander, with affection, the yard, which contained a spreading oak tree he had climbed many times, and the simple two-story white frame house. The house needed a coat of paint, but then it probably had since the last time Bram had painted it himself. Harry had always been more interested in tinkering with machinery than in performing household maintenance, and his sons had always taken care of such things as mowing the lawn, cleaning the gutters and painting.

I'll have to call old Charlie over to spruce the place up while I'm here, Bram decided, then realized old Charlie, the town handyman, might be dead. He had been in his sixties when Bram had been in high school.

Shaking his head over how quickly time had seemed to pass during his years away from Barton's Corner, Bram walked up the ancient sidewalk, which was cracked and bowing in places, climbed the four rickety wooden steps leading to the front porch and reached for the leaning screened door to pull it open. As he did so, the door came loose from its hinges, and Bram had to grab it to keep it from falling onto the porch.

A sharp, to-the-point expletive left his lips as he set the door against the wall of the house. He felt angry with his dad for letting things get so run down. But the anger was quickly followed by guilt for having stayed away so long. Though Maxie was living here, Bram knew she didn't have the money to hire such things done, and neither she nor their father would take the money Bram had offered countless times to help out.

That's going to change, Bram thought grimly as he turned the ancient knob on the warped front door and pushed. The door, which the Palmers had never bothered to lock in their entire lives, opened reluctantly—probably, Bram thought, because his father and sister usually used the back entrance. He added a new front door to the mental list of purchases and repairs he intended to accomplish before he returned to California.

The living room was exactly as Bram remembered it, containing an old, lumpy, little-used sofa that his mother had covered in a cheap but cheerful print during his senior year at high school, two equally lumpy armchairs clad in a solid color coordinated with the sofa print, a really beautiful hand-carved oak rocking chair Harry had gotten from the furniture mill's reject pile, placed there because it had a minor defect, and an equally beautiful coffee table obtained from the same source.

I have to hand it to the Stewarts, Bram thought wryly as he tried to divert his emotions from the empty, sad feeling in the room caused by his mother's absence. *They've never sold anything but quality furniture. These so-called rejects are better than a lot of companies' top lines.*

While waiting for his father and sister to get home from the plant, Bram wandered the house—looking, touching, remembering—ending up finally in his old attic room at the top of the house. Despite the fact that the room had been frigidly cold in the winter and swelteringly hot in the summer, Bram leaned in the doorway and smiled while a thousand happy memories chased through his mind. When he finally turned away and headed downstairs for the kitchen, he was aware of feeling a deep gratitude for the sort of family he'd had. They might have been poor, but they were also loving and supportive.

In the kitchen, Bram started a pot of coffee, and when it was ready, he sat at the familiar scarred table, staring out the back screened door at a yard where he had practiced football with neighborhood friends too many hours to count. Most of those friends had left Barton's Corner to find futures with more potential than working in the Stewart's furniture mill, and Bram couldn't blame them.

Bram felt a fleeting regret that Justin Stewart, Sr., hadn't lived long enough to see how right Bram had been to turn down the old man's offer to finance his education in return for coming back here. But there would be satisfaction enough at having Jussie know, he thought, and then again wondered why he should care.

I thought you had put all that away, he mused irritably. *The past is over and done with. Let it stay dead, for Pete's sake!*

Bram purposely turned his mind again to the woman in the yellow Corvette who had such a stunning smile and warm, beautiful blue eyes, and who had seemed so delighted to see him again.

Who the hell was she? he wondered, amused at how quickly and thoroughly she had aroused his interest. *Surely, I would remember someone that attractive if we'd gone to school together.*

But he accepted that they must have known each other at some time in the past, even if he couldn't remember her, or else she wouldn't have spoken to him as familiarly as she had, and it intrigued him that though she obviously had been delighted to see him, she had disappeared too quickly to give them an opportunity to get reacquainted. He hoped that didn't mean she was married, but he was afraid it did. Otherwise, judging by the way single women normally reacted to him, she would have stuck around, hoping he would suggest they go somewhere for a drink.

Since success had recently given Bram some time, if not a lot, to pursue a sporadic personal life, he had become aware again that he apparently was one of those fortunate men women found attractive. They always had, from grade school on. But Bram had almost forgotten the fact while burying himself in his work. He had also become aware that it wasn't just his personal charm they found attractive now. His wealth was an added inducement, a development he viewed with a certain tolerant cynicism, since even Mannie, who wasn't blessed with either good looks or charm, was receiving attention from women who wouldn't have looked twice at him before he'd become wealthy.

Bram suddenly grinned as he thought of a line Mannie had stolen from Woody Allen as a result of his newfound popularity with the opposite sex.

"I'm being turned down by a better class of women these days," Mannie would quip—his way of handling a situation he hadn't been prepared for and couldn't quite accept as yet.

Bram's thoughts veered quickly as he heard car doors slam outside, and he was on his feet and out the back door to greet his father and his sister without an instant's delay. Seconds later, his heart torn with guilt and grief, he held in his arms the father he had always thought of as strong and vigorous and ageless. It had taken only a glance to ascertain that Harry Palmer was no more immune from the ravages of time than any other man, and Bram knew he would never forgive himself for waiting much too long to find that out.

AFTER THE CONFRONTATION with Cassy, Justin had left the house to drive a few miles outside of Barton's Corner to a ledge overlooking a small river, where he parked and killed the engine. This was where he always came when he needed to do some deep thinking, and as he stared out the windshield, his eyes were blind to the splendor of the setting sun turning streaks of cloud to an unbelievable shade of fuchsia.

"Damned women!" Justin muttered to himself as he thought about the rotten day he'd had.

First, he'd had a confrontation with Maxie Palmer over his firing of an incompetent employee whose job it was to plane the rough edges off lumber to be used for furniture. It was a delicate job, but nothing that couldn't be handled by any reasonably intelligent twelve-year-old, in Justin's opinion, yet this idiot managed to end up with three-fourths of the wood at his feet in piles of sawdust—wood that cost as much as four dollars a board foot wholesale.

"Threaten to take me to court, will she?" Justin snorted his disgust as he balled one of his hands into a fist. "What does she want me to do? Run a business with a bunch of morons doing the work?"

There was more to Justin's anger with Maxine Palmer than her attempt to unionize his company, however, and he knew it.

Maxine Palmer had grown from a skinny, redheaded, freckle-faced kid into a stunningly attractive woman. She wasn't beautiful. At least, Justin didn't think so. But she had a flair that was as unusual as it was disturbingly appealing. When he'd first seen her upon her return to Barton's Corner, he hadn't been able to keep from staring...and admiring.

Justin knew Maxine's finances shouldn't have allowed her to dress as well as she did. Once he'd discovered why she'd really come back, hadn't he made it clear to everyone in town who might have been tempted to seek her legal services and make it financially easier for her to stick around that there would be repercussions from the Stewart family? Yet she wore outfits any New York model would have been at home in, and with a style many of those models might envy.

"She probably gets an allowance from that damned brother of hers," Justin muttered softly as he slumped behind the wheel of his pickup.

But her manner of dress wasn't all there was to Maxine's appeal. She wore her red hair in a sophisticated yet casual style that practically every woman in town had tried to copy. Her makeup might have been done by a professional. She walked in a graceful, ground-eating stride that invariably drew Justin's eyes to her hips and legs, and her manner was so cool and self-contained, Justin doubted if there were a man alive who could resist wanting to take up the challenge those green eyes of hers seemed to offer with every sparkling glance.

Certainly, he couldn't. And it grated on him every single time he came in contact with her that not only did she apparently remain impervious to him as a man, a reaction Justin had never experienced from a female before, but she actually seemed to find him detestable.

"I should have fired her old man years ago," Justin muttered resentfully, knowing even as he said the words that the idea was ridiculous. Even now, when Harry Palmer was getting old and frail and even more outrageously disrespectful than he'd ever been, he was still the best damned mechanic in the state. And not only that. He had come to be an institution at the mill. Any move against him would have every employee from the janitors to the finish men up in arms and walking out.

With a weary sigh, Justin rubbed his eyes. *I'm tired, damn it!* he admitted with uncharacteristic honesty. *Tired of the responsibility. Tired of the hassle. Tired of getting blamed for everything from a slow economy to the price of lumber. Maybe I ought to just hand it all over to Cassy and let her sink or swim.*

It was a foolish piece of nonsense he was thinking, Justin admitted to himself a moment later. The mill was his. He'd put years of his life into it. He wasn't about to let anybody, not even his own sister, push him out of it at this late date. Things were bound to turn around soon. It wasn't his management that was at fault, but the economy. When it changed, the fortunes of the mill would change for the better.

But what if they don't?

Unbidden, the chilling thought lodged in Justin's mind, bringing the bitter taste of fear along with it, as well as an uncharacteristic self-doubt.

Justin immediately acted to shore up his unexpectedly flagging self-confidence by blaming Maxine Palmer for his state of mind. She never lost an opportunity to hammer away at his management, calling it feudal. She chipped away at his self-respect, calling him inhuman in the way he treated his employees, when he didn't treat them any differently than he would expect to be treated if he were in their place. He wanted an honest day's work from them and was perfectly willing to pay them for it, but they wanted more and more money, more and more benefits, without increasing their productivity.

Hell, Justin thought with disgust, *they want to run the damned mill themselves, when none of them has a clue what is involved on my end of the deal.*

Justin ran a hand through his thick, blond-streaked hair in a gesture of frustration, then slapped the steering wheel sharply as he remembered that his mother was acting as though she supported Cassy against him. Cassy had never made any bones about the fact that she disapproved of his style of management. She was as bad as Maxine Palmer, only it was less understandable in Cassy, since she was his sister.

"I could have used her help," Justin murmured with bitter honesty, "instead of her threats to take over from me. Why couldn't she just have offered to take some of the load off my shoulders instead of throwing down a challenge like that? God, what's happening to women nowadays? Why can't they be like Mom?"

But in a sad, lonely little corner of his mind, Justin knew he was shouting at the wind. Even his mother was behaving uncharacteristically, and Cassy and Maxine were more typical representatives of the female sex than exceptions to the rule. And in truth, Justin knew that his reaction to Maxine Palmer, as abrasively arrogant and independent as she was, was far stronger than any he had ever experienced toward a woman before, and he had always gone for the more traditional type.

"Fat chance of doing anything about it," Justin grated as he sat up and started the engine. "Even if she were willing, it would be like going to bed with another man instead of a woman. She'd probably insist on being the aggressor."

Thinking about Maxine Palmer had put a fever in Justin's blood, but as he backed out of his parking spot, turned the pickup onto the two-lane road and headed toward a dirt lane leading to the home of a young divorcée who was accustomed to accommodating his needs in exchange for some help with her household bills, Justin was aware of a restless lack of enthusiasm for easing his body's hunger while his mind and emotions went begging for satisfaction.

"Damned women!" he repeated his earlier lament as the pickup bounced along the lane toward a lighted house in the distance.

Yet, as Justin headed home an hour later, his physical needs eased temporarily, his mind was still in turmoil. He had every intention of fighting Cassy's unrealistic ideas, as well as Maxine Palmer's bid to encroach on his privileges as the firm's owner, of course. But he was aware, for the second time in his life, of feeling uncertain of his own ability to triumph over the odds against him. He had felt that way when competing with Bram Palmer, and his fears had proven accurate.

"Cut it out," Justin whispered to himself as he drove along the darkened road toward home. "Why undermine your own confidence when there are enough people to do it for you? Take it one step at a time, Jussie. One step at a time. Save your energy for the fight instead of sapping it, thinking about losing."

MAXIE PALMER kissed her dad good night, and after Harry had shuffled off toward his downstairs bedroom, she started clearing the coffee cups and dessert dishes from the table where she and Bram and their father had sat for hours catching up on one another's news.

Bram was out for a walk to get in the mood to sleep, or so he said. Maxie thought he simply needed some time to deal with the knowledge she'd seen in his eyes that night, that their dad wasn't going to live forever.

"If he had come home a little more often..." Maxie started to mutter irritably, then stopped herself and took a deep breath as she concentrated on the relief she felt that there was at last someone to ease the burden of looking after Harry.

Taking care of Harry wasn't easy—not when she also had to work like a Trojan to try to get a union started at the plant, with no compensation other than personal satisfaction. Sometimes she wondered if she was crazy to have come back to Barton's Corner to live like a nun with a mission. Not only was she taking valuable time off from starting a lucrative career somewhere else, but Harry was getting too much in the habit of having her here to look after him. He might *say* she could leave at any time, but Maxie knew it would be a severe blow to him if she took him at his word.

As she filled a pan with hot, soapy water and started washing the dishes, Maxie's thoughts automatically turned to Justin Stewart, as they so often did these days.

Damn him! she thought with helpless bitterness. *Why can't he be an ugly pig physically, the way he is in business?*

Coming home and seeing Justin Stewart for the first time in years, Maxie had expected to find him repulsive. Didn't she loathe everything he stood for? Hadn't he denied her family their rights for years?

But the physical reality of Justin Stewart as a full-grown, exceptionally attractive male had hit Maxie in the stomach like a heavyweight's punch. She had been fighting her attraction to him ever since. And the battle wasn't made any easier when she knew, with a knowledge that was soul-deep, that Justin wanted her as badly as she would want him if she ever let down her guard.

His desire was in those clear blue, hungrily assessing eyes of his every time he looked at her, no matter how hostile the words they might be exchanging at any given time. It was in the way his voice changed to a rasping burr when he spoke to her. He never sounded like that when speaking to anyone else. And it was in the way he always moved physically closer to her the longer they were around each other, until Maxie had to force her legs to carry her away from him before they ended up within a breath of one another.

Away from Justin, Maxie was appalled at herself for wanting a man who was her exact opposite emotionally, spiritually, ethically. Near him, she performed an act she knew no one had as yet tumbled to, and she hoped fervently it would continue to aid her in keeping her distance from him. With Justin Stewart, she played the role of a coldly hostile, ever-contemptuous adversary, never giving an inch to the underlying emotions he aroused in her. She was positive that if she didn't remain strong, if she ever gave Justin an opening, she wouldn't have an ounce of respect left for herself. And self-respect, Maxie admitted in the long, cold hours of the nights she spent alone in her bed, was all she had going for her for the time being.

The back door opened, and Maxie, startled out of her thoughts, swung around as Bram came into the house.

"Welcome back," she said, making an effort to sound cheerful. "Did you have a nice walk?"

Bram nodded but said nothing, just looked at her in a way Maxie couldn't fathom, before he came across the room, pulled her hands out of the dishwater, and heedless of the fact that she was getting his spotless white shirt wet and wrinkled, pulled her into his arms for a tight hug.

"Hey," she giggled, squeezing him back. "What's this for?"

Bram straightened and set her away from him, looking into her green eyes that were so like his own. "For taking care of Dad," he said, his mouth curving into a mirthless smile, "for following your conscience, and most of all, for not calling me an insensitive clod, which is exactly what I've been all these years."

Maxie understood immediately what Bram meant, and she shook her head as she looked up at him with a fond smile on her lips. "We all have our own personal devils, Bram," she said, ashamed of herself for blaming him earlier because he hadn't been home enough in the past few years. "You wanted to make something of yourself, and you would never have been content until you had. You couldn't do that here, not like you could in California. And after all, you tried to get Daddy to come visit you, just as you tried to get him to accept a new house and money for a few luxuries."

She shrugged and moved out of Bram's grip to go back to her dishwashing. "It's not your fault that he has enough pride for six people and wouldn't take anything from you," she concluded her efforts to make Bram feel better.

Bram studied his sister's profile, thinking she had grown into a beautiful woman, and remained unconvinced by her attempt to get him off the hook of his conscience.

"He wouldn't take anything from me that way, no," he said quietly. "But he would have let me do things for him if I'd been here. And believe me, before I leave again, there are a lot of things I'm going to insist he take, like fixing up this house, for example."

Maxie glanced at him, her eyes filled with love. She shook her head, however. "No, Bram, that's not a good idea."

Bram frowned. "Why?"

Maxie sighed, turned away from the sink and picked up a tea towel to dry her hands. "Because I can't stay here forever," she said levelly as she looked into her brother's eyes. "Once the union is flourishing, I'm going to have to go someplace else to make a living."

Bram's frown deepened. "But you could set up an office here," he started, and then with a look of comprehension in his eyes, he added, "that is, if you want to. I can't blame you if you'd rather practice law someplace else, though. You aren't likely to make much of a living here." His look turned wry then. "I'm assuming you take after our father, who has enough pride for six people, and won't let me support you?"

Maxie grinned and wrinkled her nose at him. "Don't be so sure," she teased. "Maybe I'll take anything I can get."

Bram's look gave her his answer to that—patent disbelief.

Maxie made a face at him, then shrugged. "It isn't so much that I'd mind practicing my profession here, Bram," she explained. "It's just that Justin Stewart would make anyone who used my services pay much too high a price for the privilege. He isn't going to forgive me for unionizing the mill, and he's not the type to let the chance for revenge go by without taking advantage of it."

Seeing the anger rising in Bram as a result of her explanation, Maxie reached over and patted his arm.

"Be realistic, Bram," she chided him gently. "Change comes slowly, if at all, and even then, it's often incomplete. I'll be satisfied if I can make a difference in the lives of the people the Stewarts have taken advantage of all these years. I'm not doing it to gain a material reward for myself. When the union is functioning and I leave here, I'll look for my reward someplace else."

She frowned then, as she remembered why she didn't want Bram spending a lot of money on the house.

"When I go, Bram," she continued, "Daddy will have to move somewhere smaller. This place is too big, even if we get a housekeeper for him. It's old-fashioned and not worth the fortune it would take to modernize the place. I know he'll hate the idea of living anywhere else, but it's the only thing that makes sense."

Maxie saw Bram's jaw tighten, and the stubborn Palmer look she knew so well come into his eyes, and she sighed in defeat.

"All right, all right," she complained in an exasperated tone. "It's your money. If you want to practically rebuild this house—which is what it will take to make it really comfortable—and pay for someone to live in and take care of Daddy, be my guest. It will be a few years before I can afford to match your generosity."

Bram relaxed then, and his grin told Maxie she would be wasting her breath to try to talk him out of doing exactly what she'd just told him would be necessary to let their father spend his last years in the home he'd lived in and loved for most of his adult life.

"You're lovable but dumb," Maxie said bluntly.

"True." Bram's grin widened farther, and Maxie threw her damp tea towel at him. Bram caught it, folded it neatly, and laid it on the scarred counter.

"Say," he changed the subject as Maxie let out the soapy water in the sink, "do you know a good-looking blonde who drives a yellow Corvette?"

Puzzled, Maxie glanced at him and shrugged. "No, why?" she asked.

"I was parked at the high school today, and she pulled up and spoke to me as though she knew me, but I couldn't remember her." Bram shook his head, a baffled expression in his green eyes. "I don't know how I could have forgotten someone like that, though. She was something. Either she's changed a lot since I supposedly knew her in school, or she's new in town and somehow knows who I am without our having officially met before.''

Suddenly, Maxie froze as it occurred to her who Bram might be talking about. ''Did she have blue eyes?'' she asked in a strained voice.

Bram nodded, then frowned. ''And come to think of it,'' he said slowly, ''there was something a little familiar about her, though I can't put my finger on just what.''

''She didn't, by any chance, resemble Jussie Stewart, did she?'' Maxie prodded Bram's memory and felt resigned when an expression of recognition suddenly came over his face. ''That's what I was afraid of.'' Maxie sighed. ''It had to be Cassy. No one else in town has a car like that. No one else in town can *afford* a car like that, except you,'' she added with wry humor as she remembered the expensive foreign car sitting in the driveway.

Bram felt disappointed on learning the woman he had been attracted to instantly and who had spoken to him in such a friendly manner was a Stewart.

''But how did she know who I was?'' he asked Maxie. ''And why was she so friendly to me?''

Maxie gave him a look of sisterly exasperation. ''Looked in the mirror lately, brother dear?'' she drawled. ''Not to mention that car you're driving. Any single woman would perk up with you on the scene, and maybe even a few married ones as well.''

When Bram looked annoyed—and indeed, he didn't like the idea that the lovely Cassandra Stewart had merely responded to an attractive face and a fancy car—Maxie relented.

''But to give Cassy her due,'' she went on as she wiped off the counter, then put the dishcloth over the faucet to dry, ''she's probably not a predatory female on the prowl. She had a crush on you years ago when you were too much the local football hero and scholar to notice girls our age.''

Feeling pleased by Maxie's explanation, for no reason that made any sense, Bram grinned and walked with her as she headed for the kitchen door.

"Ready for bed?" she asked.

"More than ready," Bram confirmed. "It's been a long day."

After turning out all the lights, as Bram and Maxie were climbing the stairs together, she turned her head and gave him a curious look.

"So what did you really think of Cassy Stewart?" she asked lightly, uncertain herself how she felt about her former friend being back in town. There was a longing inside her to have Cassy for a friend again, though that was a very unrealistic desire, Maxie knew. Cassy was here to help Justin keep the union Maxie was determined to form from taking hold. The two of them were more likely to become active enemies than friends with that gulf between them.

Bram glanced at her, and Maxie saw a twinkle in his eyes. "Very fetching woman," he drawled. "It's odd that I don't remember her at all, when she's such a stunner."

Maxie snorted. "It's not so odd," she stated flatly. "We were too far behind you for you to consider us worth your lofty attention."

Bram feigned hurt. "Hey, I remember *you*," he protested. "You're the little twerp who took over the bathroom at the age of twelve and didn't give it up until I'd left home for good."

Maxie sniffed. "A girl has to work at looking her best," she confided loftily, "which reminds me, there's still only one bathroom in this house, and though you're probably used to sybaritic living out in California—hot tubs and all that—I'll thank you to remember that I'm a working girl and have first dibs on that lone bathroom in the mornings."

Bram adopted a long-suffering look. "You mean I'm going to have to stand outside the door and plead for mercy the way I used to?"

"Exactly," Maxie said firmly as she paused outside her bedroom. "Either that or get up by five to beat me to it."

"But I'm on vacation!" Bram complained, scowling now.

"Tough." Maxie shrugged and flung her door open. "This is Middle America, pal. We don't put up with any guff from you California weirdos."

And with that, she sailed into her room and shut the door in Bram's face. He eyed the unyielding panel for a moment before strolling off toward his own room, whistling "Home Sweet Home" in a mournful manner that made Maxie smother her giggles as she prepared for bed.

Chapter Four

To his surprise, Bram slept late the next morning. *I guess my body knows I'm on vacation, even if my mind hasn't quite realized it yet,* he thought as he threw back the sheet and light blanket and got up.

The house was silent, and upon realizing that his dad and Maxie had already left, Bram smiled ruefully, feeling as sybaritic as Maxie had accused him of being. But he couldn't deny he was grateful not to have to wait for the bathroom. Living alone had weaned him from the sort of patience it took to live with other people in a house with only one bath.

Later, as he sat at the kitchen table drinking coffee and eating a cold biscuit with a piece of cold sausage in the middle of it that Maxie had left for him, he thumbed through the Barton's Corner telephone directory, to make sure the same firms he remembered from his earlier years were still in business. He needed a hardware store first, where he could pick up a few things to make some minor repairs he'd seen were needed, and while there, he would inquire about hiring someone to do the major repairs on his father's house.

A short while later, having decided the Jaguar was entirely too ostentatious to drive the short distance to town, Bram ambled down the tree-shaded sidewalk he had walked countless times as a boy and as a teenager, turning his head from side to side as he inspected the familiar houses and yards he had once known like the back of his hand.

Nothing had really changed, except that everything seemed smaller than it had during his youth, and the change in his perception made Bram smile as he wondered why that should be so. Was it because he was now used to skyscrapers and freeways? Or because he was a man now, rather than a boy?

Shrugging, he decided it didn't matter. He was in a strange mood where nothing seemed to matter all that much. There was nothing urgent that had to be done, no place to rush to, no deadlines to meet. It felt good in a way, but strange.

As he reached Main Street, Bram slowed his pace even more, stopping at times to look in the windows of shops he remembered. The town seemed just now to be waking up, and the proprietors he recognized were busy either with customers or getting ready for customers. No one saw him, and Bram began to feel almost invisible until he turned a corner on the way to the hardware store and approached the bus station.

The bus station was nothing more than a tiny coffee shop where the proprietress also sold bus tickets. There was an alley beside it where the buses had room to pull in to pick up or discharge passengers. And in front of the station were two old-fashioned wooden benches that had been there as long as Bram could remember, and looked it. Unprotected from the sun, rain or anything else, carved with indecipherable runes by the penknives of generations of boys, they might have been there since Creation began, judging by their appearance.

Presumably they had originally been put there for the use of passengers waiting for the bus. But since there were never that many people waiting, succeeding generations of elderly men had appropriated the benches for sitting and viewing the world and occasionally commenting upon what they saw to their companions.

As Bram came within sight of the benches, he didn't know whether to be glad or sorry that the benches were occupied by a full complement of the town's eldest male citizens, who were no doubt drawn out by the pleasant Indian-summer weather. Soon it would be too cold for their favorite pastime, and they seemed to be soaking up the sun in preparation for the months of hibernation they would be forced to suffer.

As Bram had anticipated, as he drew nearer the benches, every one of the occupants, to a man, turned his eyes in his direction, and he was relieved when the first one to speak was someone he recognized, old Charlie Miller, formerly the town's most dependable handyman.

"Who's this?" Charlie demanded, poking his head forward and peering intently in Bram's direction. "Looks familiar, don't he, boys?"

Most of Charlie's companions nodded, but all of them, though it was apparent they were pleased by the diversion Bram's presence provided, looked puzzled as to who he could be.

Bram came to a stop in front of Charlie and with a big smile, held out his hand. "It's Bram Palmer, Charlie," he said loudly, in case the old man's hearing was gone. "I'm Harry Palmer's boy."

Charlie's face beamed his delight as he took Bram's proffered hand and shook it vigorously. "Course you are!" he said, as though he'd known it all along. "I'da known you anywheres!"

Doubting that, but careful not to show it, Bram stood smiling and nodding and shaking hands as all the other elderly men greeted him. Some of them he knew, others he wasn't certain about, but he treated each as though he remembered him well.

"Well, son, whatcha' doin' home?" Charlie began the questions all of the men were dying to hear the answers to, once the greetings were over, except that Charlie didn't give Bram a chance to answer.

"Come to see your dad, I expect." Charlie nodded wisely. "And that lawyer sister of yours. What's her name? Maggie? Marcie?"

"Maxie," Bram supplied.

"That's right." Charlie nodded, again sounding as though he'd known it all along. "The one that's put a burr up old Jussie, Jr.'s—"

"Heard you was rich now, Bram," one of the other old men interrupted Charlie. "That true?" And again, before Bram could answer, he continued, "Heard you was. Heard you was one of them millionaires now." The old man, who was one of the ones Bram didn't remember, eyed him skeptically, clearly doubtful that what he'd heard was accurate, perhaps because Bram was dressed in faded jeans, an old gray sweatshirt and running shoes.

Faced with admitting in a bald fashion that he was, indeed, a millionaire, Bram felt embarrassed and, instead, started to say something to the effect that he was half-owner of a computer firm, but Charlie saved him the trouble.

"Course he's rich!" Charlie scowled at his companion. "My girl, Betty, drove by old Harry's place yestiddy aft'-noon and come home sayin' Harry had some fancy red foreign jobbie in his driveway." Charlie looked up at Bram again, nodding. "Reckon that was yours, huh, Bram?"

Bram smiled and nodded. He was getting the hang of talking to this group now. They didn't so much want him to say anything as they wanted an audience who would corroborate their speculations.

"What kind of car you got, Bram?" another old man spoke up, one Bram recognized as a former mechanic at one of the town's gas stations.

"Ah, it's a Jaguar, Mr. Hammer," Bram admitted, and almost laughed as the man's eyes opened wide.

"A Ja-gu-ar," Mr. Hammer mispronounced the name in a reverent tone before turning to his fellows and nodding wisely. "He's rich," he pronounced in a tone of absolute certainty.

"Told you so," Charlie said in a testy manner before taking over the questioning again. "How long you stayin', Bram?"

"I'm not sure yet—" Bram started to answer before being interrupted again.

"Always knew you'd make somethin' of yourself, Bram," an old fellow at the end of the bench spoke up. Bram looked at him and suddenly realized the man had been one of his Boy Scout leaders.

"Thank you, Mr.—"

"Knew it, 'cause you always took everthin' you did serious." The man nodded. "Woulda made Eagle Scout if you hadna got so inersted in football, but I guess that was all right. You did good in that, too."

"And smart," Charlie chimed in again, peering up at Bram with a look of such pride on his face, one would have thought Bram was his boy. "Didn't you beat out old Jussie, Jr., for vad...val..." Charlie stopped, annoyed, and demanded of the man next to him, "What the sam hell do you call that award they give the smartest kid in the school?"

"Valedictorian," the former Boy Scout leader spoke up proudly.

"That's right...val...well, whatever," Charlie said, returning his attention to Bram.

Deciding he might be there all day if he didn't take a hand in things, Bram said quickly, "Well, I might have been valedictorian, but I could use some advice from you right now, Charlie."

Charlie puffed up like a bantam rooster. "Glad to give it, son," he said in a dignified manner. "What's your problem?"

"I want to get some work done on Dad's house," Bram explained. "I was going to get you to do it, of course, but I'd forgotten you'd probably be retired. I was wondering if you could tell me who I can trust to do as good a job as you always did."

Charlie cast a triumphant glance at his companions before turning back to Bram to give his answer. "Well, there ain't nobody as good as I was, of course," he said immodestly. "Fellas nowadays don't take the time to do things right, and ain't got no pride in their work, anyways. Most of 'em's just out for the dollar. But I got a nephew I trained myself who's pert near as good as I was in my day. Name's Jodie Wilson. Want me to bring him along over to your dad's place this evenin' after he gets home? I could ride along with him and make sure he spots everthin' that needs to be done."

"I'd surely appreciate it, Charlie," Bram replied in a respectful tone, "if it's not too much trouble..."

"Ain't no trouble a-tall." Charlie slapped his knee for emphasis. "Me and Jodie'll just amble on over there 'long 'bout six-thirty. Ya'll oughta be done with your supper by then, and there oughta still be enough light to see."

"Well, thank you, Charlie," Bram agreed and reached to shake Charlie's hand again. "Right now," he said as he continued down the line, shaking each man's hand in turn, "I've got to get to the hardware store and pick up a few things. It was nice visiting with all of you."

A chorus of reciprocal phrases echoed from the line of men, and then Bram was free to go on his way, looking back and waving as he walked.

When he was far enough down the street, he let the grin he'd been holding back take over. He supposed there were other old men in other small towns like Barton's Corner who behaved exactly as the ones he'd just left had, but he felt more at home after the exchange with these old-timers than he had since he'd arrived.

The clerk in the hardware store was no one that Bram remembered, but when he presented his credit card to pay for his purchases and the man saw his name, the clerk's manner was suddenly friendlier.

"I think my wife went to school with you, Mr. Palmer," he said, sounding satisfied. "Do you remember Betsy Blake?"

"I certainly do." Bram nodded. "We went from first grade through twelfth together. How is Betsy?"

"Doin' just fine," the clerk responded, eyeing Bram curiously, "but not as good as you're doing, from what I hear. Don't you own some company out in California?"

"A computer company, yes," Bram said as he pocketed his credit card and picked up his brown paper sack full of washers and hinges.

"Well, I'll tell Betsy I saw you," the clerk said with a smile. "She'll be tickled to death to hear it. She's always goin' on about some kind of class reunion, and I'll bet hearin' you're back will really get her started."

Bram wasn't certain he wanted to spark a class reunion, but he smiled and nodded and reached over to shake the man's hand.

"Tell her hello for me," he said as he started for the door.

"I'll do that, for sure," the clerk called after him, and then Bram was on the street again, trying to decide if he wanted to stop at the one decent restaurant in town to get a cup of coffee, and probably meet other long-term Barton's Corner residents, or go home and get started on the minor repairs he planned to do himself.

AFTER SLEEPING LATE for the first time in years, then dawdling through a leisurely breakfast while she chatted with her mother as Mary Louise stirred up a batch of peanut butter cookies, Cassandra decided to go for another drive to further refamiliarize herself with Barton's Corner. It was Friday, and though she was eager, in a way, to get started at the mill, she had decided to give herself a three-day vacation first. She needed it. It had been months since she'd had any time off from work.

It was only after making a leisurely tour through the town, then stopping off at Baker's Café for a cup of coffee and finding no one in the place she knew, that Cassandra realized how much she'd been hoping to come across Bram Palmer again.

Didn't you listen to your own lecture yesterday? she asked herself with wry self-mockery. *Chances are he knows who you are by now and would spit in your eye if you did see him.*

With a resigned mental shrug, Cassandra paid for her coffee and went outside to get into her car again, intending to drive out to the mill. She didn't plan to go in, just look around a bit. But as she approached the local hardware store on her way out of town, her heart skipped a beat. Bram Palmer, looking better in jeans, sweatshirt and running shoes than most men did in tuxedos, was standing outside the store looking in the opposite direction.

Drive on by, Cassandra told herself, even as she lifted a foot to press on the brake. Her body apparently knew what she was going to do before her mind did, and as she brought the car to a stop directly in front of Bram, she justified her action to herself, thinking, *You've lived in New York, remember? Anyone who's faced an irate New York cab driver can certainly stand up to rejection from a more civilized type.*

As Bram stood on the curb trying to make up his mind about going for a cup of coffee, he saw the yellow Corvette suddenly pull up immediately in front of him, and the blonde who had spoken to him the day before leaned across the seat to peer up at him from the passenger window, her blue eyes twinkling with humor.

"Need a ride, Mr. Palmer?" she said in a light voice that Bram found easy on the ear. Her smile, as well as the rest of her, was also as easy on the eyes as he remembered from the day before.

Courteously, Bram leaned down so that Cassandra wouldn't have to look up, and as he studied her, taking in the sophisticated hairstyle, the warm curve of her deliciously shaped mouth and the slender body in the designer jeans and tailored white blouse, he said, "Good morning, Miss Stewart. How are you today?"

Cassy tensed up at hearing that Bram knew who she was, and though she continued to smile as she answered, "Just fine. It's a lovely day, isn't it?" she was wondering how soon his apparent friendliness was going to dissolve into hostility.

Bram wasn't feeling hostile, however. Despite the fact that Cassandra was a Stewart, he was as attracted to her today as he had been the day before. Attracted and curious about this woman Maxie had once considered a friend. Bram thought he could understand why Maxie had liked Cassy Stewart. While she resembled the Justin he had gone to school with, there was considerably more human warmth in her eyes than Justin had ever had.

"Yes, it is a lovely day," he answered smoothly as he continued to let his eyes roam her pretty face. "I was just thinking about going to Baker's for a cup of coffee."

Cassandra wrinkled her nose and shook her head. "I was just there," she informed Bram, "and Baker's is not what it used to be. New management."

"Then I guess I'd be better off fixing my own coffee." He smiled.

"Better yet," Cassandra suggested, against every bit of common sense she possessed, "let me take you home to Mother. I guarantee she makes the best coffee in town, and she was also stirring up a fresh batch of peanut butter cookies when I left home this morning. Sound good?"

Bram inspected the apparently innocent light in Cassandra Stewart's eyes and decided to trust that innocence, though he was still somewhat puzzled by the way she kept going out of her way to be friendly to him.

"It sounds very good," he said lightly and bent to open the passenger door of the Corvette as Cassandra straightened up behind the wheel.

When he was settled beside her, he watched as she shifted gears as smoothly as a racing pro and drove away from the curb.

When they had turned a corner and were on the road leading out to the Stewart estate, he turned in his seat to stare at Cassandra with unabashed concentration.

Cassandra had been aware from the instant Bram settled his large body beside hers in the car that she had probably made the biggest mistake of her life, giving in to the insane impulse to pick him up. Her senses were tingling with an awareness of him as a man that was unnerving, and his stare wasn't making things any easier for her. But there was no sign of her inner agitation in her voice as she said, "Do you always stare at women so intensely, or is there something about me that strikes you as odd?"

Glancing away from the road and looking into Bram's eyes for a second was an even bigger mistake than picking him up in the first place, and Cassandra quickly returned her attention to the road, her pulse pounding like thunder.

"Well, it does strike me as a little odd to be invited to the Stewarts for coffee," Bram admitted in a dry drawl. "I can't remember Justin ever asking me home for a visit in all the years we knew each other."

Cassandra grimaced. "He wouldn't," she said with simple directness. "But I'm not like Jussie. Never have been. Never will be."

"I'm beginning to believe it," Bram said truthfully, "but that leaves me with another puzzle."

"And what's that?" Cassandra asked, and now her smile was wary. Was Bram the type of man who knew instinctively when a woman was interested in him? Or did he think she had an ulterior motive for seeking his company, something to do with the mill? She wasn't certain which alternative she preferred he believe.

Bram's gaze focused on Cassandra's lips, lips he found disturbingly inviting.

"Why the friendly greeting yesterday and the invitation for coffee today? I wouldn't have thought you'd remember me."

Relieved laughter bubbled up from Cassandra's throat as she realized Bram seemed genuinely puzzled and she'd been worrying for nothing.

"Don't you remember how it was at school?" she asked teasingly. "All the younger kids knew who the older ones were, but the older ones couldn't care less about those behind them. Besides," she added lightly, "Maxie must have told you that she and I were friends once. Of course, I knew you were her brother, and you haven't changed all that much." *Except to get even better looking,* she added silently and with a certain grim acceptance of her own foolishness in putting herself into a position to react so much to his appeal.

Before Bram could reply, Cassandra turned into the long driveway leading up to the Stewart home, and Bram was distracted from the discussion by his curiosity about the place. He'd seen it many times, of course, but only from the road skirting the edges of the estate. And despite the intervening years, he still found the house and surrounding lawns impressively attractive. Again, he realized that whatever else there was to say about the Stewarts, one couldn't fault their taste.

He turned back to Cassandra when she braked the car and turned off the motor. Then he was amused when she turned to face him and held out a hand.

"Since we've never been formally introduced," she said, her eyes smiling at him, "and are about to break bread together, let me remedy the lapse. I'm Cassandra Stewart, late of New York City, more recently of Barton's Corner, Missouri."

Bram took the proffered hand and looked down at it encased in his own large palm. Cassandra's hand was slim and soft, yet somehow capable looking, as though she didn't confine herself to applying hand cream and lifting delicate silverware and china.

He raised his eyes to stare into Cassandra's and found that the smile was gone and she was staring back at him with a look that had become seriously disturbed. He couldn't know that she was cursing herself for seven different kinds of a fool for not realizing how his touch would affect her. Hadn't she had enough warnings since the moment she'd spotted him the day before?

"I'm happy to meet you, Miss Stewart," Bram replied softly, not letting go of her hand. "But I'll be even happier when I learn what's on that no doubt intelligent mind of yours right now."

God forbid! Cassandra thought with a touch of panic.

She took a deep breath and pulled her hand from Bram's grip, noting somewhat wistfully that he seemed reluctant to release her.

"At the moment," Cassandra lied through her teeth as she opened her car door, "there's not a thing on my mind but coffee and some of my mother's peanut butter cookies. Come on, Mr. Bram Palmer. I'm about to introduce you to a woman who's going to make you sorry she's not twenty years younger.''

Bram opened his door and climbed out of the car, and though there was a smile on his lips, he was as certain as he'd ever been about anything in his life that he wasn't going to be sorry he was too young for Mrs. Justin Stewart, Sr. From the way he'd reacted to Cassandra's touch, it was much more likely he was going to be sorry he'd ever met her daughter.

As Cassandra led the way into the house, she wished desperately she hadn't acted on impulse upon spotting Bram Palmer standing at the curb. It was bad enough to have stopped and offered him a ride, but to have asked him home for coffee was nothing short of idiotic. What could possibly come of fueling an attraction that was distracting and hopeless? She had known yesterday that her former schoolgirl infatuation with him could escalate with the speed of lightning into a woman's full-blown fascination. And she had known, as well, that since she would shortly be on a collision course with Bram's sister and father, it was stupid to court his attention.

So I made a mistake, she told herself as she led the way to the kitchen, where she expected to find her mother, unaware that Bram was dawdling behind her as he inspected her home with mixed feelings of objective appreciation and a totally subjective resentment sparked by the contrast between this house and his father's.

Mistakes can be corrected, Cassandra continued to talk to herself as she glanced into the kitchen and saw that her mother wasn't there. *The thing to do is feed my guest his coffee and cookies, take him home as fast as possible and stay completely out of his way from here on out.*

As she turned around, expecting to find Bram directly behind her, she saw that he had stopped in the doorway to the living room and was looking at it with a peculiar expression on his face.

Don't ask, Cassandra told herself firmly. *Don't even wonder what he's thinking. You're better off not knowing.*

"Mom's not in the kitchen, Bram," Cassandra said with breezy politeness as she passed behind him to head for the den. "I'll find her."

Bram nodded absently, and Cassandra called out "Mom!" as she walked on. She was becoming alarmed as she began to wonder if her mother had gone somewhere. It wouldn't do to be left here alone with Bram. "We have a visitor, Mom. Where are you?" she called in a louder voice.

Cassandra's relief was intense when Mary Louise came walking down the hall from the direction of her bedroom.

"What is it, darling?" Mary Louise inquired as she joined Cassandra. "Who's here?"

"Bramwell Palmer, Mother," Cassandra said, giving her parent a warning look not to act too surprised. "I saw him downtown and asked him home for coffee and some of your cookies."

Aside from raising her brows slightly before adopting a warm smile, Mary Louise acted exactly as Cassandra wanted her to.

"How nice," she said as she walked to where Bram was just turning away from his inspection of the formal living room. "I remember you so well, Bram," Mary Louise said informally, reaching to take his hand as she looked up into his face with nothing but warm acceptance on her own.

And then Cassandra's heart sank as her mother spoiled her warm greeting by saying, "You were the bane of Jussie's existence in high school."

Puzzled by Mrs. Stewart's open reference to the old rivalry he had shared with her son, Bram shrugged and smiled back at her. "I can't say I'm sorry about that," he said lightly, and to his further puzzlement, Mary Louise Stewart laughed as though she were genuinely amused.

"Of course you can't," she replied, squeezing his hand before letting it go. "Jussie needed to learn that not everything comes easily. It's made him try harder later in life."

Bram's instincts were telling him that Mary Louise Stewart was quite serious, and had meant exactly what she'd said, but Bram wasn't sure he should trust his instincts. It was hard for him, even after all these years, to take a Stewart at face value.

While he was trying to think of something to say, Cassandra, appalled by her mother's bringing up the past so bluntly, certain that Bram Palmer didn't believe a word her mother had said, jumped into the conversation with a nervousness that was so unlike her, her mother looked at her in surprise.

"Let's have that coffee and some of those cookies," she blurted, unconsciously taking Bram's arm to steer him toward the kitchen. She could have kicked herself when she saw Bram looking at her with a perceptive gleam.

"Sounds good to me," he said blandly, uncertain why Cassandra had aroused his protective instincts. "Your daughter tells me you make the best coffee in town, Mrs. Stewart," he continued trying to take the heat off Cassandra, though he couldn't have said why. Surely there was no one in the world as unlikely to need his protection as the daughter of the almighty Stewart family.

"Cassandra exaggerates," Mrs. Stewart replied, smiling warmly as she recognized what Bram was doing, "but maybe you won't be too disappointed."

Fifteen minutes later, when Cassandra was feeling unutterably grateful to her mother for having carried the bulk of the conversation with Bram while they were at the table, and in a way that skirted past history, she was wondering how soon she could suggest taking Bram home. The sooner the better, she decided and she forced herself once again, as she had had to do for the entire fifteen minutes, to stop staring at him.

God, who would have thought I'd find the man of my dreams back home in Barton's Corner, she thought with wry, disgusted humor. *And to have him be the one man in the world who is totally off limits is the height of irony. I just hope I get out of this one unscathed and can look back fondly at Bram Palmer someday as the one who got away.*

"I guess it's about time I got back," Bram suggested, looking at Cassandra and feeling irritated when he saw the relief in her eyes. Why the hell had she asked him home, he wondered, if she was so glad to get rid of him now?

"Thank you for the coffee and cookies, Mrs. Stewart," he said politely as he stood up. "I think you do make the best coffee in town, as well as the best cookies."

To hell with it...I like her, Bram thought as Mary Louise's face lit up with simple pleasure over his compliment.

"I'm delighted Cassy brought you home to try them," she said as she got to her feet as well.

Cassandra quickly stood up and leaned over to kiss her mother on the cheek. "Thanks, Mom," she said. "I'll take Bram home, then be right back to help you in the garden."

Cassandra looked into her mother's eyes and willed her fiercely not to comment upon the fact that Cassandra had never helped in the flower garden in her entire life.

"Hmm...all right," Mary Louise said with only a slight trace of dryness in her voice. Then she turned to Bram again and did exactly what Cassandra had hoped she wouldn't. "You mustn't be a stranger, now that you know the way here, Bram," she said with a warm invitation in her voice.

Bram couldn't resist. "Oh, I've always known the way here, Mrs. Stewart," he said lightly, then was ashamed of himself for indulging in pettiness. He was grateful when

Mary Louise didn't seem to take his statement in the way he'd meant it.

"Of course you have," she said simply. "I forgot for a moment that you lived here all your life before you went away to college." Then she brightened, and started to say, "Why don't you join—"

"I just remembered I have to go by the plant after I drop Bram off," Cassandra hastily interrupted before her mother could invite Bram to dinner. "So I'll be late getting back to help you in the garden," she continued as she headed for the side door. It was too risky to go all the way back through the house, giving her mother the opportunity to finish the invitation she'd been about to extend to Bram. Cassandra was certain he wouldn't want to come, but more to the point, she was positive it would be a mistake, from her standpoint, to see any more of him.

"Thank you again, Mrs. Stewart," Bram said as he followed Cassandra to the door. "I enjoyed meeting you." He kept the irony he was feeling out of his voice, thinking that it was strange indeed that he had lived in the same town with this woman for years, played on the same football team as her son and yet never formally met her before or been in this house.

"And I enjoyed seeing you again, Bram," Mrs. Stewart said, and for a moment, Bram was positive she had picked up on his thought. Did she perhaps regret that he was entirely accurate?

Cassandra hurried around the house to her car, while Bram followed at a more leisurely pace. He was debating whether to challenge her directly about her reasons for bringing him home and then making it obvious she couldn't wait to get rid of him, or let the whole thing drop. From Cassandra Stewart's attitude, he was positive the invitation wouldn't be repeated. And then he hit upon an idea that he freely admitted was an unworthy one, but that he knew he wasn't going to resist implementing.

In the car, he said nothing until they were back on the road that led into town. Then, watching Cassandra out of the corner of his eye, he said, with perfect innocence, "You must allow me to return your hospitality. Are you busy tonight?"

Cassandra just stopped herself from jerking her head around to stare at him with dismay. "Why, ah..." She was stumbling to find a reason to refuse his invitation when Bram interrupted.

"I thought since you and Maxie used to be such good friends, you'd like to come to dinner at our house tonight. I'm sure she'd be delighted to see you."

Cassandra knew better, and she was positive Bram did, too. She was suddenly angry at him for posing such an obvious trap. An instant later, the anger she had long felt toward Maxie erupted inside her as well, and with reckless abandon, Cassandra acted on impulse for the second time in one day.

"Why, that would be lovely," she said with only a trace of grimness in her voice. "What time would you like me to be there?"

Her reaction took Bram completely by surprise. He had been certain she would make some excuse to turn down his invitation. Against his will, he found himself admiring her for turning the tables on him.

Bram thought about rescinding the invitation and letting her off the hook, then realized he wanted to see Cassandra again. The realization aroused a burgeoning sense of caution inside him.

"I imagine around seven would be fine," he said thoughtfully, wondering why he was courting danger this way. Surely he had more sense than to contemplate getting involved with a Stewart?

Neither of them said anything else until Cassandra had pulled her car to a stop in front of Harry Palmer's dilapidated house. She wanted desperately to back out of coming back for dinner, but a certain stubborn pride prevented her from doing so.

"Should I bring anything?" she inquired as Bram reached for the door handle. "A bottle of wine, perhaps?" She was thinking she might need a bottle of something to get her through what would almost certainly be a totally awkward evening.

Part of Bram recognized she was only being polite in making the offer, but in his current mood, he deliberately chose to react negatively.

"No," he drawled with an edge to his voice, "I think we can manage."

Puzzled by his tone, Cassandra swung her head to look at him in surprise.

Feeling disgusted with himself for taking such a cheap shot, and because of the situation he'd gotten himself—and Maxie—into, Bram opened his door.

"See you at seven," he said. "Thanks for the ride."

"You're welcome," Cassandra answered, but doubted Bram heard. He had already shut the car door behind him.

As Cassandra pulled away, her former anger descended into depression. "Great," she muttered to herself as she headed back home. "You're doing swell so far today, Cassandra Stewart, and before the night's over, I expect your score will be even more impressive. Maybe you ought to bring Jussie along with you tonight and really make a mess of things."

But then she wondered why she should worry about what any of the Palmers thought of her, or of her family. Maxie was a fair-weather friend, and Bram was a subtle, complex devil—a *handsome*, subtle, complex devil, which only made him more dangerous.

"Well, at least I like Harry," Cassandra muttered, resigned to getting through the night somehow, "and with any luck at all, this will be the last time I have to have anything to do with the Palmer family outside of business, which will suit me just fine."

Ha-ha, her mind mocked her lie without showing the slightest bit of mercy, and mercy was certainly a quality she could have used right about then, especially from her own mind regarding her own mistakes.

Chapter Five

"You did *what*?"

Bram ostensibly kept his attention on chopping avocados for the guacamole he was making, but out of the corner of his eye he ascertained that while Maxie wasn't yet in the grip of an all-out temper tantrum, she was getting there.

"I invited Cassandra Stewart here for dinner," he repeated, keeping his voice patient and calm. And before Maxie could voice the indignation and anger he saw gathering in her eyes, he assigned himself the blame that he knew she would eventually heap on him.

"I know it was a dumb thing to do." He nodded as he reached for an onion. "I let my baser instincts get the upper hand. I invited her out of sheer perversity, in an attempt to embarrass her. I didn't really think she'd accept."

"Then it's clear you don't know Cassy Stewart!" Maxie snapped as she flung her purse down on the kitchen table and set her hands on her hips.

"I don't pretend to." Bram shrugged. "She put me off balance, inviting me home with her like that. I guess I was really trying to regain the upper hand."

"And here I thought you were above such dumb male games," Maxie snorted, and then she shook her head and gritted her teeth. "Don't you know what an impossible position you've put me in? The past Cassy and I share would make things awkward enough, but add to that what I'm trying to do to their company, and it's positively idiotic to expect the two of us to sit down for a sociable meal together!"

"I know." Bram was feeling guilty and his reply was given softly. He stopped chopping, wiped his hands on a tea towel, then came to stand in front of his sister, placing his large hands on her shoulders.

"Look," he said, "I know it's going to be a hell of an evening, but short of calling up and telling Cassandra Stewart she can't come after all, we're stuck. So while I'm fixing dinner, why don't you go upstairs, relax in a hot bath, fix yourself up and make the best of it." He grinned and eyed Maxie mischievously. "You can call me all the names you're thinking when the evening's over. Chances are you'll have thought up some new and even more appropriate descriptions of my character by then."

"You can count on it," Maxie agreed, but in truth, she couldn't stay mad at Bram, even though she knew she would be entirely justified if she screamed her head off at him.

Bram further increased her mixed feelings toward him by pulling her close for a hug. "You love me, remember?" he teased with gentle humor.

"I *used* to love you," Maxie grumbled, reluctantly hugging him back.

"And you will again, I'm positive of it," Bram assured her with mock gravity. "Now go get ready. I promise you, I'll cover up any awkward moments that develop this evening with my vast store of small talk."

"Ha!" Maxie snapped, pushing him away and grabbing up her purse again. "There won't be any awkward moments, brother dear. The whole evening will be an unequivocal disaster!"

As Maxie stormed upstairs, Bram watched her go, feeling half amused, half chagrined. Then his father came in from the backyard, where he'd been inspecting the pecan tree to see what the harvest would be after the first frost, and stopped short in surprise at seeing Bram standing in the kitchen with an apron around his middle.

"Son?" he asked, as though he wasn't sure it was really his boy standing there grinning at him.

"It's me, Dad," Bram said cheerfully as he went back to the counter to continue his chopping. "I've invited someone over for dinner and decided to cook it myself to save Maxie the trouble."

Harry Palmer's expression lightened. "Who's comin?" he asked as he set down his lunch pail on the kitchen table. "One of your friends you used to hang around with?"

"Ah . . . no," Bram hesitated, then mentally shrugged, thinking he might as well give his father time to get over being upset if he, like Maxie, disapproved of having a Stewart in his house. "She was Maxie's friend, not mine. It's Cassandra Stewart, Dad. I met her in town today, and she took me home with her for coffee and cookies. I felt I had to return the courtesy."

Harry looked surprised, but since he had never had anything against the female members of the Stewart family, he merely shrugged.

"Fine," he said amiably, surprising Bram by his reaction. "Reckon I better spruce myself up a bit if we're gonna have a lady to dinner. You think I need a shave?"

He held his chin up for Bram to inspect and ran his hand over it, checking for stubble.

"No, Dad." Bram smiled, loving his father immensely at that moment. "You look just fine."

Harry looked down at his grease-stained overalls and work shirt and shook his head. "Your mama wouldn't think so if she could see me," he said with conviction. "Reckon I better wash up a little and put on my Sunday suit."

Bram opened his mouth to protest, hating to put his father to the trouble because of his own unfortunate lapse of good sense, but then closed it again, thinking his father was right. Letty Palmer would have insisted her husband clean up for a guest, regardless of who it was.

"I think Maxie's in the bathroom right now," he said, instead. "Why don't you rest and watch the evening news until she's done?"

Harry nodded, but there was a smile on his lips. "You reckon your sister will really let us have our turn?" he said teasingly. "I swear, that girl would spend her life in the bathroom if she had her druthers."

"Maybe so," Bram said lightly, "but I have a feeling she's not in a mood to dawdle tonight."

Bram was right. But even though Maxie cut her usual time in the bathroom by half, she still managed to look strikingly turned out by the time she showed up in the kitchen, silently putting an apron around the waist of the tailored black slacks she wore with an emerald-green dolman-sleeve sweater, and proceeded to help Bram put dinner together.

"You don't have to help, you know," Bram pointed out gently, then fell silent when Maxie merely glared at him and slammed the pan of enchiladas he had prepared into the oven.

In truth, Maxie was beseiged with a welter of various emotions. Though she would never have admitted it to Bram, part of her wanted to see Cassy again. She was under no illusion that the meeting would be an easy one, and if she hadn't been forced to it, she knew she would have avoided dealing with her shame over the past. But now that she couldn't avoid facing Cassy Stewart after all these years, she wondered if she would have guts enough to apologize for abandoning her friend so long ago.

At the same time, Maxie resented the guilt that made her feel an apology was called for. And since she expected that she and Cassy couldn't avoid becoming enemies in the present—never mind the past—she tried to tell herself an apology would be a useless exercise. But she couldn't convince herself of the truth of that, and therefore, her mood was irritable and anxious.

When everything was done except wait for the enchiladas to finish baking, Bram went upstairs to clean up and Maxie settled herself with her father in the living room to watch the last half of the evening news. But she couldn't concentrate on the present. It was the past that paraded through her mind, bringing with it a wistful desire to be a girl again instead of a woman, with all the adult problems a woman faced.

"BUT I WAS GOING TO invite Bram to dinner here tonight if you hadn't interrupted me," Mary Louise said with an irritable frown upon being informed that Cassandra wouldn't be home for dinner and why.

"Mom," Cassandra said, unable to believe that her mother wasn't aware of what problems that might have brought about, while keeping to herself the most important reason why she'd interrupted her mother in the middle of her invitation, "what do you think Jussie's reaction would have been if he'd come home and found Bram Palmer sitting in our living room?"

Mary Louise lifted her chin and said coolly, "The living room belongs to me, and I wasn't aware that I have to ask my son's permission before I invite someone to dinner."

Cassandra swung around from her bureau mirror, where she'd been inspecting her makeup for any flaws, and stared at her mother in surprise.

Mary Louise continued to look and sound stubborn. "It's time Jussie got over his jealousy of Bram Palmer," she declared, and then, eyeing Cassandra speculatively, added, "especially if you're going to be seeing much of him."

Cassandra flushed and hurriedly pivoted toward the mirror again. "I don't intend to be seeing much of Bram Palmer," she said, forcing a calm, disinterested tone into her voice as she picked up a lipstick and set it down again when she realized she had already used it three times. "He's only here on a visit. I intend to stay here. What would be the point of seeing much of him?"

To her consternation, as she glanced at her mother's image in the mirror, Mary Louise's expression told her she hadn't succeeded in fooling her parent with her pretended indifference to Bram Palmer.

"Don't you ever intend to marry, Cassy?" her mother asked in an innocent way as she stepped forward to smooth a stray wisp of blond-streaked hair away from Cassandra's cheek.

"Certainly," Cassandra said, stepping around her mother to search in her closet for a light jacket to wear.

"And just where do you intend to find a man in this town?" Mary Louise said dryly. "The last time I looked, there weren't that many single males available, and those that aren't married are not exactly your type."

"I wasn't aware I had a type," Cassandra said distractedly as she debated between a navy-blue blazer and a plum-colored one.

"Every woman has a type." Mary Louise smiled as she crossed toward the bedroom door. "And if you ask me, Bram Palmer is yours." Before Cassandra could protest that assertion, her mother said, "Wear the blue one, dear. It brings out your eyes," and she disappeared out of the room.

Cassandra did wear the blue blazer, and as she went to kiss her mother goodbye, she dared her with a look to comment upon the fact. But Mary Louise merely smiled and said, "You look lovely, dear. Have a good time."

Not likely, Cassandra replied silently as she headed for an evening she would have given a lot to have over and done with.

By the time Cassandra parked at the curb in front of the Palmer house and climbed out of her car, her dread about the reception Maxie would give her had escalated until she was disgusted with herself.

She bolstered her courage as she strode determinedly up the cracked sidewalk. *I haven't anything to be ashamed of, and if Maxie wants to give me a hard time, that's her problem.*

When Cassandra saw the broken screen door leaning up against the side of the house, she felt inexplicably guilty, as though it were her fault that Harry Palmer's house was in disrepair.

Don't be silly! she inwardly protested the feeling and lifted a hand to knock on the warped front door.

Upon hearing the knock, Harry quickly got up to answer the summons, and after he'd wrestled the front door open, he smiled at his attractive guest, who seemed somewhat uncertain of her welcome.

"Well, Cassy, how nice to see you," he said warmly, instinctively trying to put Cassandra at ease.

"Hello, Mr. Palmer." Cassandra smiled back, warming to his kind manner. "It's very nice to see you, too."

"Come in, come in," Harry invited, holding the door open. "Bram and Maxie are here in the living room."

As Cassandra stepped inside the house and saw Maxie Palmer standing stiffly across the room, eyeing her with an expression Cassandra didn't find especially welcoming, she quickly switched her gaze to Bram, who stood beside his sister, and her heart rate sped up as she noted that he, at least, seemed glad to see her, even if Maxie didn't.

Returning her gaze to Maxie, Cassandra stood for a moment trying to gain control of her chaotic reaction to seeing her old friend for the first time in many years. She thought Maxie had grown beautiful, but she would have given a lot to see the old Maxie—the one who was so impish and kind and fun to be with. But the old Maxie had betrayed their friendship, and so Cassandra resented her desire to have her back.

Finally, Maxie, who was thinking Cassy was more beautiful than ever and hadn't lost the sweet expression in her eyes and the warm, humorous curve to her mouth, both of which Maxie had always admired, inadvertently stepped forward and half lifted a hand to her old friend.

"Cassy?" she said, knowing she was asking an unspoken question and knowing that Cassandra had heard the question when Cassy's expression became filled with uncertainty. "Oh, Cassy!" Maxie exclaimed, suddenly impatient with her own stubbornness. Quickly she closed the distance between them to catch her friend up in her arms. "It's so good to see you again, Cassy," Maxie said in a choked voice, her cheek against Cassandra's.

Cassandra stood unyielding for a bare second, then, unable to resist, her arms came around Maxie as her eyes filled with tears.

"I'm so very sorry," Maxie whispered, tightening her hold at feeling Cassandra's response. "I was rotten to desert you the way I did. Please forgive me. Oh, Cassy, please say you forgive me."

Maxie didn't cry easily, but on feeling a sob shake Cassandra's chest, she was suddenly weeping herself.

When she felt Maxie's tears on her cheek, something tight inside Cassandra's heart began to loosen, and oblivious of Bram and Harry Palmer for the moment, she began to smile through her tears.

"It's all right, Maxie," she choked out. "It's all right, really it is." And to Cassandra's amazement, it was that simple to forgive old wounds. She hadn't believed it could be, but the resentment and hurt she had felt at thinking of Maxie's behavior all these years was suddenly gone as though it had never existed.

For a few moments, Maxie and Cassandra clung to each other, trying to get their tears under control, while Harry Palmer looked at them with puzzlement in his eyes and Bram smiled, relaxing now that it seemed his mistake had turned out all right. It felt good to watch his sister be reunited with a friend who obviously had meant a great deal to her, and as his glance traveled from the back of Maxie's head to Cassandra Stewart's lovely, tear-streaked face, he finally believed that she was different from her father and Justin Stewart, Jr.

However, Bram found the knowledge both comforting and disturbing. For while he was able to accept that a friendship between Maxie and Cassandra was possible and be glad of it, he still couldn't really believe that the attraction he felt toward Cassandra was wise. She might be different, but surely not different enough to consider a romantic relationship with a man who came from the wrong side of the tracks.

When Maxie and Cassandra drew back from each other, smiling in an embarrassed way and wiping the tears from their faces, Harry spoke up.

"What's it all about, Maxie girl?" he asked, for she had never told him about how or why her friendship with Cassandra had ended.

Maxie glanced at her father in an embarrassed fashion. "Never mind right now, Daddy," she said in a muffled voice. "I think we'd better eat, or the food will be ruined."

Cassandra smiled at Maxie, then glanced up at Bram, her eyes warming with gratitude. "Thank you for inviting me, Bram," she said quietly.

"It was my pleasure." Bram smiled back with more warmth than he'd meant to display. But the look in Cassandra's eyes had touched him on a number of levels he couldn't fail to respond to naturally.

"Well," Harry said a little irritably, "if nobody's gonna tell me what's goin' on here, I guess we *had* better eat. It's past my dinnertime."

Everyone relaxed then, smiling at Harry's grumpy manner, and followed as he led the way to the kitchen. The Palmer house had no dining room.

Bram was used to cooking for himself and, living in California, had learned to fix Mexican food, which he especially favored. Cassandra, however, presumed Maxie had cooked the dinner.

Turning to her after they'd all seated themselves, she grinned. "It looks delicious, Maxie, but I thought you said once you only knew how to cook plain foods."

Maxie glanced slyly at Bram, who was dishing up the enchiladas. "I didn't cook this, Cassy," she informed their guest. "Bram did the honors tonight, and I won't guarantee that we won't all end up poisoned."

Bram adopted a mock scowl. "Such ingratitude," he growled. "I'll have an apology from you before the night's over, or you'll find the bathroom occupied when you get up tomorrow morning."

Maxie wasn't worried. "Tomorrow's Saturday," she scoffed. "I'll sleep late and won't need the bathroom early."

Bram shook his head. "Is there no justice?" he mourned playfully.

Cassandra looked from one to the other of them, divining that the Palmer house must have only one bathroom. Again, she felt guilty, as though it were her fault. Furthermore, she felt guilty because she was appalled at the idea of having to share a bathroom with the rest of the members of her household. She had always had a private bathroom off her bedroom, and that was one luxury she knew she couldn't give up willingly.

Harry Palmer eyed the food on the table with wary disfavor. "Is this somethin' you learned to eat in California?" he asked Bram doubtfully.

Bram put a hand over his mouth to hide his smile. "Yes, Dad," he said when he was able to do so calmly. "Just try it. I think you'll like it if you give it a chance."

Harry still looked doubtful, but he picked up his fork and cut a piece of his enchilada, bringing it warily up to his mouth. Everyone watched with smiles as he chewed for a moment, then nodded.

"I guess it'll do in a pinch," he allowed. "Not like meat and potatoes, but edible, I guess."

"Thanks, Dad," Bram said gravely, gazing across the table into Cassandra's laughing eyes with a twinkle in his own.

Throughout dinner, everyone carefully avoided mentioning Barton Furniture, concentrating instead on Cassandra's experiences in New York and Bram's in California. After they'd moved to the living room, however, and were having coffee, Maxie decided to test the atmosphere and determine whether she and Cassandra were going to be able to communicate as honestly as they'd been able to do in the past.

"Why did you come back home, Cassy?" she asked, though she knew the answer. "Considering how well you were doing in New York, I would have thought you'd prefer to stay there."

Cassandra gazed at her friend, her expression open, though she sensed that the pleasant evening might be about to go downhill now.

"I've always intended to come back," she said quietly. "I tried to when I graduated from college, but it didn't work out."

Bram was frowning a warning at his sister, but Maxie persisted.

"But why?" she asked. "Why come back to Barton's Corner after getting used to all that New York has to offer?"

Cassandra glanced down at her coffee cup. "Perhaps for the same reason you did, Maxie," she said calmly, then lifted her eyes to her friend's face again. "I had some unfinished business here."

Maxie was frowning now. "I doubt that you came back for the same reason I did," she said, her tone impatient. "We might as well stop beating around the bush, Cassy. You know I came back to unionize your family's business, and I can't believe you're happy about that."

Cassandra shrugged. "No, I'm not happy about it, Maxie," she said bluntly. "In fact, I don't intend to let it happen."

Maxie felt her temper begin to rise and fought to keep it under control. "Then we're going to be fighting each other from different sides of the fence, Cassy," she said with level firmness, "because I'm not going to give up until I succeed in getting your family's employees what they've deserved all these years—a competitive wage and decent benefits and protection from your family's arbitrary decisions."

Cassandra's voice was quiet as she answered. "We don't have different goals, Maxie," she said simply. "Merely different ways of accomplishing the same thing. I want exactly what you do. I just don't happen to believe that it has to be done through a union."

Maxie frowned and leaned back against the lumpy cushions of the sofa where she sat. "I can believe that you mean that, Cassy," she said dryly, "but you must be aware that Jussie doesn't feel the way you do. How do you propose to change his mind? Have him brainwashed?"

Cassandra let a small smile play across her lips as she glanced at Bram. He looked interested, if somewhat uncomfortable that Maxie had forced this discussion on all of them. Then she looked at Harry Palmer, who was gazing at her without animosity, though the determined look on his face matched Maxie's.

"I doubt that Justin would stand still for forcible brainwashing," Cassy replied lightly, "but I intend to do my best to raise his consciousness." And before Maxie could protest that Cassy had set herself an impossible task, she added, "I don't feel comfortable going into details about what I have in mind," she said with the natural authority she had honed in New York. "Jussie is, after all, my brother, and our differences should remain private. But I'm not your enemy, Maxie," she finished with soft sincerity. "I hope you believe that."

"I don't consider us personal enemies, Cassy," Maxie replied in a serious tone, "but I don't see how we can keep from becoming business enemies. I'm committed to the union."

Cassandra blinked and looked thoughtfully into the distance, saying nothing, which provoked Maxie into further speech.

"Jussie could drop dead tomorrow and you could take control, Cassy," she said earnestly, "and though I'm sure you'd try to be fair, without a contract, the employees wouldn't have any guarantees, don't you see? They would still be at the mercy of your goodwill—or that of your successor. And that's not acceptable."

Cassandra noticed that Bram was looking at Maxie in a thoughtful manner that connoted some degree of disagreement, and instinctively she addressed a question to him.

"How have you handled things at your computer company, Bram?" she asked curiously. "Are your people unionized?"

Bram felt caught between the two women, but he could do no more than answer honestly. "No," he said simply. "It never seems to have occurred to them."

Again acting on instinct, Cassandra smiled and pursued the matter. "Why is that, do you think?" she asked softly, noting that Maxie was frowning at her brother. It was apparent she didn't appreciate his contribution to the discussion.

Bram shrugged and explained the style of management he and Mannie had adopted. "It seems to work well for everyone concerned," he finished, speaking as much to Maxie as to Cassandra, though he was well aware that Justin Stewart's generosity toward his employees didn't match his own and Mannie's.

Maxie felt impatient. "That's all very well," she stated the obvious, "but the management is different here than at your company, Bram. Justin is a lot like the old-style capitalists before unions were established, who didn't care anything about the welfare of their workers."

"That's a little unfair, Maxie," Harry spoke up. "Justin, Sr., and now Jussie haven't skimped on safety procedures—just on salary and benefits."

"That's because they didn't want to get into trouble with the government," Maxie said stubbornly. "But unless he's forced to, Justin won't ever pay a fair wage and upgrade the medical and retirement coverage for his employees. And he's still able to fire anyone at the drop of a hat, whether they deserve it or not!"

Her green eyes snapping with frustration, Maxie faced Cassandra and demanded, "Can you deny that what I say is true?"

"Not for the present," Cassandra answered truthfully, deciding it was time to end this discussion before it got out of hand. She had plans to change things eventually and erase Maxie's and Harry's entirely justified complaints, but it would take time, and she doubted anything she could say now would convince Maxie, at least, to be patient.

She set her coffee cup aside before getting to her feet. "I've enjoyed the evening very much," she said to the three Palmers. "Thank you again for asking me to come, Bram," she directed her attention to him, then switched it to Maxie. "And I think you know how much I've enjoyed being with you again, Maxie," she said with soft sincerity. "I hope nothing will stand in the way of our friendship again. It would be a shame."

Maxie opened her mouth, then didn't know what to say. She was frustrated at having their discussion cut off so soon. She was doubtful of her own ability to set aside her feelings about business enough to be able to take Cassandra's offer of renewed friendship. Yet she wished with all her heart she could. The almost magic compatibility they shared had begun to wrap her in its seductive folds again, and she realized how much she'd missed having Cassandra's friendship, even over the years when she had refused to think about it.

She stood up and crossed to where Cassandra was standing, taking her hands into her own. "I hope we can overcome all the outside interference and be like we used to be," she said wistfully, looking into Cassandra's warm eyes. "I've missed you, Cassy."

"I've missed you, too, Maxie," Cassandra said with quiet sincerity. "If we can be patient with each other, I think we'll be all right."

Cassandra squeezed Maxie's hands, then let go and reached for the purse she'd set beside the chair she had occupied.

"I'd better get home," she started to say, but was interrupted by a knock at the door.

Bram looked puzzled for a moment; then his expression cleared as he realized who it must be. "I think that's Charlie and his nephew, Dad," he said to Harry. "I asked them to come by and give us an estimate of what needs to be done to the house."

As Bram moved to open the door, Harry looked as though he might protest, but he quickly changed his mind. He couldn't imagine living anywhere else, but he knew the house needed repairs he couldn't afford to make. Furthermore, he knew how anxious Bram was to do something for him, and so he remained silent.

"Sorry we're late," Charlie said after greeting everyone. He looked about to burst with curiosity on finding Cassandra Stewart visiting the Palmers, but he managed to mind his manners. "Jodie was finishing up a job over at Custer and didn't get home till a few minutes ago."

"That's all right, Charlie," Bram spoke up. "But I'm afraid it's too dark to see what needs to be done tonight. Can you and Jodie come back tomorrow?"

Jodie, a large, capable-looking man in his thirties, who seemed to suffer from shyness, answered as his Uncle Charlie looked at him.

"We can come back in the mornin'," he assured Bram. "I'm finished with the job at Custer and haven't got anything else goin'."

"Good." Bram smiled, both from gratitude and from amusement at the way Jodie was directing sneaking looks of admiration at Maxie and Cassandra. Before he could add anything else, Harry spoke up.

"Why don't you sit a spell and have some coffee, Charlie?" he invited his old friend. "You, too, Jodie. I think we got enough in the pot, don't we, Maxie?"

Maxie smiled and nodded and started to leave the room, then hesitated as Cassandra made a move toward the front door.

"I'll go on," Cassandra said to Maxie, then smiled at Charlie and Jodie. "It's nice to see you again, Charlie—and nice to meet you, Jodie," she added, smiling at the large man who was nervously crumpling his billed cap in his hands and who nodded shyly at her.

"I'll walk you to your car," Bram said, moving around the other men in the room to come to Cassandra's side.

"Good night," Cassandra said to everyone in general in a light, pleasant way, though she had tensed at Bram's suggestion.

Amid a chorus of good-nights in reply, she stepped out the front door with Bram right behind her.

Seeking to fill the sudden silence between them in an innocuous way, Cassandra smiled slightly up at Bram as they walked down the sidewalk, and said, "You're a good cook, Mr. Palmer. It's too bad you'll be going back home soon. The one thing I do miss about New York is the food. There are so many wonderful restaurants there."

"In California as well," Bram responded, wondering why he suddenly felt slightly depressed by the reminder that he would soon be going back.

But he knew the answer the moment he glanced down at Cassandra Stewart. The moonlight glinted from her blond-streaked hair, he could smell the perfume she wore, and there was something about her walk that made him want to stop, turn her toward him and put his arms around her.

Don't get carried away, he thought with wry self-directed amusement, and an instant later they had reached the yellow Corvette and had turned to face each other.

For a long moment they simply stared at each other's faces, wrapped in their separate private thoughts that, if they had only known it, were running along the same lines.

I want to kiss her, Bram thought with sudden urgency, and unconsciously moved closer to Cassandra.

Oh, Lord, what will I do if he kisses me? Cassandra was thinking, knowing that she was on very dangerous ground. She was certain that a kiss from Bram Palmer would have a devastating impact on her.

She opened her mouth to say something, but the words wouldn't come out. She couldn't seem to move or speak or do anything other than stare up into Bram's attractive, masculine face, while she wished that she weren't Cassandra Stewart and he weren't Bram Palmer. She thought it would have been heavenly to have met Bram with nothing in the past or present between them other than mutual attraction.

Bram's eyes settled on Cassandra's parted lips, and he couldn't seem to look away. He was positive that her mouth would taste delicious, that her body against his would fit with devastating magnetism.

"I . . . don't want you to go," he said, surprising himself as much as Cassandra by speaking his thoughts aloud.

Cassandra at last closed her mouth and swallowed. "I have to," she said without much conviction, and then added, sounding even to her own ears as though she were trying to convince herself, "It wouldn't be wise to stay."

"Do you think not?" Bram spoke so softly, Cassandra could barely hear him. "I'm not so sure . . ."

And I want you, Cassandra Stewart, regardless of the consequences. Bram stopped, reluctant to finish his thought.

"Did you really have a crush on me when we were in school?" he asked, to keep himself from saying anything more revealing. A smile curved his mouth into a shape Cassandra longed to touch with her fingers and then her mouth.

"All the girls did, I think," she answered with halting softness. "But you were too far ahead of me to notice a little junior high fan."

"A fan . . ." Bram repeated, his smile twisting somewhat.

"I admired you," Cassandra said. "You were the stuff heroes are made of—handsome, smart, strong."

Cassandra's eyes dropped to Bram's shoulders. He was wearing a white long-sleeved shirt, but she could imagine the strength of the muscles she was positive he still had. Unconsciously, she half lifted a hand to touch him. She caught herself before she completed the motion, tightened her hand into a fist and dropped it to her side, quickly looking down to hide what she knew must be in her eyes from Bram's discerning gaze.

"Cassandra," Bram said with soft determination, "it's been a long time since I've been able to pay any attention to my private life. And there are a lot of reasons why you're probably the wrong woman to help me make up for what I've been missing, but . . ."

Bram paused as Cassandra jerked her head up to stare at him with amazed consternation.

"But," Bram continued as he raised his hands to place them on Cassandra's waist and pull her gently, inexorably toward him, "I've already played the fool once today. I might as well finish up the way I started."

Bram lowered his head, gratified when Cassandra didn't turn her mouth away, though the look in her eyes said she wished she could. Their lips met, melted at the contact, then fused into a joining that shook both of them into an awareness that they were playing with a fire that was even more potent than they'd both suspected it would be.

It had been a long time since Cassandra had been kissed with such intensity by a man to whom she was drawn with a terrible need. She hadn't been aware of just how physically and emotionally hungry she'd become. And at the moment, she wasn't capable of resisting her own hunger, much less Bram's.

Bram, who had starved his personal needs for years, was as ready as Cassandra for the sort of nourishment he sensed she could provide.

Without thinking, he tightened his arms around Cassandra, aware on a primal level that merely holding her like this, with their clothes between them, wasn't enough. He wanted to join them completely, wanted to feel her warm, naked skin with his hands and with his lips, wanted to sink into her body and find release for more than his physical needs. The loneliness he had borne without fully realizing he carried it inside him now flared into an aching demand for surcease.

Cassandra, caught in the same need that held Bram, circled his neck with her arms and thrust her hands into the thick hair at the base of his neck. She stretched on tiptoe and abetted his attempt to meld their bodies together ever tighter. She opened her mouth under his and accepted the immediate, urgent thrust of his tongue with joyous welcome, then met the thrusts with delicious, parrying darts of her own tongue.

The headlights of an approaching car startled them into releasing each other, and when it had passed, neither made a move to touch the other again.

"This…" Cassandra made an attempt to speak, then had to stop to clear her throat. The tremor in her voice was so evident, she knew Bram had heard it and understood its cause. "This," she continued, making a powerful effort to control her voice, "can take us…" Again, she paused, afraid to voice her thoughts.

"To paradise," Bram finished for her, but there was a wry twist to his lips, and despite the need still raging inside him, he made no move to touch Cassandra again. He was as wary of the sudden conflagration they had provoked in each other as she was.

"Or to hell," she whispered, gazing straight into his eyes, her own showing the fear and longing she was feeling.

Bram nodded, taking her meaning immediately.

"I almost wish we were children again," Cassandra said with soft regret. "Then we could take what we want with the thoughtlessness of youth and worry about paying for it later."

"You sound as though we're ancient now," Bram found himself protesting. He knew what Cassandra meant, but part of him didn't want to face the consequences of what could happen between them. He would have turned off his mind—and Cassandra's—if he could have and simply gone with his senses.

Cassandra felt uncertain. She had so many things to do, there was no time for a love affair now. Yet she craved what this man could offer, craved it, yet feared where it could lead.

Bram finally broke the silence that had fallen between them. "I guess we have a dilemma. Maybe we ought to sleep on it."

Cassandra couldn't restrain the short burst of ironic laughter that filled her at Bram's words. Sleep on it? She doubted she would close her eyes before dawn.

Bram nodded, a slow grin coming to his mouth. "It won't be easy, will it?"

Cassandra shook her head, distressed by the whole situation. She had never in her life become so attracted to a man so quickly. It didn't matter that she'd had a silly crush on him as a schoolgirl. She hadn't known him personally, and yet here they were, behaving as though they were old and intimate associates.

"Go home, Cassandra Stewart," Bram said with wry humor. "Go home before I won't let you go. We'll talk tomorrow. Tonight we think."

Oh, yes, Cassandra knew she would spend the rest of the night thinking. Or at least, remembering how it had felt to be held and kissed by Bram Palmer.

Bram was thinking the same about her as he reached down and opened her car door for her. Cassandra quickly scrambled inside, afraid if she didn't move forcefully, she would stand there at the curb indefinitely just for the pleasure of looking at Bram.

"I'll call you tomorrow," Bram said softly as he bent to look at her and held the car door open. "I have the feeling I can think from now until eternity and still end up demanding to see you again."

Cassandra's heart swelled with spontaneous happiness at Bram's words. And acting with a matching spontaneity, she leaned toward him, reached a hand to his cheek and pressed her mouth against his. Bram responded with gratifying intensity until each sensed they were getting into deep water again and broke apart with reluctance.

"Go home," Bram said before straightening and closing the car door with unnecessary force. He stepped back and watched as Cassandra fumbled for her key, then brought the motor to life with a startling roar. She lifted a hand briefly, drank in one last sight of Bram, then pulled away and headed her car toward home.

You're a fool, Cassandra, she told herself in an effort to still the rapid beating of her heart. *A complete and utter fool... I think.*

As Bram watched the taillights of the yellow Corvette disappear down the street, he was telling himself much the same thing, yet with even less conviction than Cassandra felt. And before the dawn reached the windows of his attic room the next morning, he knew that, foolish or not, he wasn't going to be able to resist his need to see Cassandra Stewart again. She had breached the barriers he had erected against his emotional needs too thoroughly to allow him to ignore those needs the way he had been doing for years. And if there were reasons why he should stay away from her, he deliberately decided to discount them for the time being. He was used to taking risks.

Chapter Six

"Jussie, the mill's closed today, isn't it?" And at Justin's wary nod, Cassandra added casually, "Would you mind taking me for a tour of it?" Cassandra bit into a piece of toast, but she kept her eyes on her brother whose sudden stubborn look wasn't encouraging.

He shook his head. "I have other things to do today. Sorry."

Cassandra kept her annoyance out of her voice. "It wouldn't take long," she persisted. "It's been years since I was inside the place. You must have made a lot of improvements."

Justin looked at his sister and felt a deep anger start up inside him. She didn't fool him with her mention of "improvements." He would have bet money she had so little respect for his abilities, she presumed he hadn't upgraded a thing he hadn't been forced to.

"As a matter of fact," he said, and hearing the tight, harsh note in his voice, he made an effort to tone it down, "the equipment and techniques we use are state-of-the-art. But since you've never known that much about our methods, you probably won't recognize that when you see it."

Justin's accusation made Cassandra feel both uncomfortable, because he was entirely accurate, and angry, because it wasn't her fault that she didn't know more about the operations at the plant than she did.

"You're right—" she kept her tone level "—but I'll learn, Jussie. I'll have to know a lot more about the furniture business than I do now to take full advantage of any marketing opportunities there are, but as far as employee relations are concerned, I happened to major in the subject, and I can help you with the problems you're having there, beginning Monday morning. I don't have to know how to plane a board to understand the people who do it and what they need and want."

Justin leaned back in his chair. He could feel the flush of temper in his face, and he considered taking the time to gain control of his anger, then dismissed the idea. Why should he?

"Has it ever occurred to you to think about why the plant is closed now on weekends?" he demanded of Cassandra. "It wasn't a few years ago, you know."

Cassandra was not intimidated by her brother's anger. "I imagine," she said calmly, "that the present economy won't support that much production."

Justin really lost control then. He threw down his napkin on the table, scraped his chair back, stood up and glared down at Cassandra's calm face, wanting to wipe the smug self-righteousness he thought he saw there into oblivion.

"Think again, Miss Perfect," he grated harshly, "though I don't suppose it would matter if you did. You've got yourself convinced that I'm Simon Legree's descendant!"

Cassandra stirred uncomfortably, for he wasn't far off the mark.

Seeing that conclusion on her face, Jussie gritted his teeth. "Oh, to hell with it!" he ground out, stepping away from the table, but before he left the room, he couldn't resist a parting shot.

He spoke contemptuously. "You not only want to show me the error of my ways, but you want me to help you do it. Well, think again, little sister. You find out how the plant operates on your own. Then you check the books and tell me how I'm supposed to maintain profits at the level you're accustomed to receiving as your share." Justin flung what he considered Cassandra's hypocrisy in her face. "And show me how I can give your precious employees everything they say they want as well."

With that, Justin swung out of the room, positive that when it came to a choice of her own financial well-being versus that of the people she was supposedly so intent on championing, Cassy would back off.

Climbing into his pickup a few minutes later, Justin had no idea of where he was going, and he wished heartily, not for the first time, that Barton's Corner was big enough to support a health gym. He could have used a good workout to ease his temper.

But there were different ways to get exercise, and just before backing up the pickup, Justin remembered that the wood supply for the family's fireplace was low, and the good weather they'd been having couldn't last forever. Normally, he had one of the local men cut their winter supply of wood, but today he decided to cut it himself.

Killing the pickup's motor, Justin climbed out, walked to the garage and picked up a power saw and a can of gasoline, then after throwing them into the back of the pickup, he headed for a place outside of town that the Stewart family owned but didn't use. The few acres were heavily timbered.

As he drove, hell-bent for leather, he had the ironic thought that in his present mood, he hoped he didn't injure himself. But the restless feeling of being alone and misunderstood that rode with him needed to be eased. It was depressing to realize that there was no one, not even his family, who was on his side and to whom he could talk about his feelings and frustrations, and count on a sympathetic hearing. He had never, until recently, regretted being single, but he would have given a lot just then to have a wife who understood and supported him.

DESPITE HER INTENTION to sleep late, Maxie's relentless mind had her wide-eyed and unable to stay abed by 6:00 a.m. Since her father and brother were still asleep, she moved quietly through the house doing her Saturday cleaning chores, and when Bram and Harry came downstairs two hours later, she had the house spotless and breakfast cooking.

Noticing the preoccupied frown on her face, Bram spoke up.

"What's on your mind, Maxie?" he asked sympathetically. "You look like you're in a bad mood."

Maxie didn't know how to answer, how to explain the restlessness inside her. She felt overburdened by responsibilities she couldn't shrug away, and which she could have handled a lot easier if she'd had the counterbalancing support of someone she loved and who loved her—and not just her father and brother.

She sighed, then had a thought she hoped might help negate her mood. There were times when she just needed to get away for a while, take a long walk and let nature soothe her troubled mind. And since Bram was here to keep Harry company, there was no reason why she couldn't do just that.

"I think I just need some exercise," she said, looking pleadingly at Bram, then indicating their father, who had his head in the morning paper. "Would you mind if I disappear for a while after breakfast? I won't be gone long."

Bram shook his head, his gaze sympathetic. "Stay as long as you like, Maxie," he encouraged her. "Charlie and his nephew will be here soon, and Dad and I will be busy with them for quite a while, probably.''

Smiling her relief, her mood considerably lighter, Maxie finished cooking breakfast and put it on the table. And later, as she picked up a light jacket, then ran outside to climb into her secondhand, battered Dodge Colt, she was determined to take advantage of the opportunity Bram's visit was giving her to think of absolutely nothing having to do with Barton Furniture or the Stewart family. She would concentrate solely on the peace of nature while she recharged her batteries.

HALF AN HOUR after leaving her father's house, Maxie was strolling in a leisurely fashion through a wooded area that was one of her favorites, soaking up the Indian-summer sun in the spaces between the trees and enjoying watching the squirrels about their urgent business of burying nuts for the coming winter, when she heard the noise of a power saw and frowned.

Maxie had no desire to have her peaceful sojourn disturbed, and she was about to turn around and walk in a different direction when she began to wonder who else had discovered her favorite place to get away. Perhaps she could find out who it was without being seen.

A few minutes later, Maxie heartily regretted her curiosity. Had she approached from a different direction, her idea might have worked and she would certainly have disappeared from the scene in a hurry. But as it was, she stepped through a gap in the trees and found herself suddenly face-to-face with Justin Stewart.

Oh, God, Maxie thought angrily. *There goes my peace of mind for sure.*

An instant later she was even more furious to find herself admiring Justin's body, which was outlined clearly from the waist up in a tight T-shirt; he had taken off and left in the pickup the expensive light blue cashmere sweater he'd put on before he'd decided to cut wood. He wore tight, sawdust-covered jeans as well, and as Maxie's eyes traveled the length of him, she was disgusted to find that her stomach was tightening with a totally unwanted physical reaction to him.

Justin had finished cutting through a dead limb and glanced up just as Maxie appeared in front of him, and for a moment, he simply stared at her, with the power saw still roaring in his hands. But when, after giving him a look that erased every bit of the calm he had found while engaged in satisfying manual labor, she started to turn away, Justin abruptly switched off the power saw and filled the resulting silence with a taunting challenge.

"Don't run away, lawyer lady," he mocked. "You're trespassing on my land, and I may want to press charges."

Maxie tightened her lips and turned back to face Justin. "I didn't know who owned this property, but I'm not surprised it belongs to you. Doesn't almost everything around here?"

Actually, Maxie was more grateful for Justin's typical greeting than angry about it. It helped her to keep her emotional distance, steeling her against the sensuality in his mocking smile and in his blue eyes, which, as usual, were glinting a challenge at her she was aware had little to do with anything exterior to the fact that they were a man and a woman.

Justin straightened. Though he would have had it otherwise, he was aware of a deep sense of disappointment raging within him over Maxie's hostility toward him. But then, upon reflecting that his greeting to her had hardly been conducive to eliciting other types of emotion from her, he suddenly smiled at her more naturally, unaware that the action breached a wide hole in Maxie's defenses.

"Hey," he said in a much more amiable tone, "it's too nice a day to fight. Let's call a truce for the time being, all right? I was only teasing about pressing charges."

Maxie's constant wariness toward Justin escalated alarmingly at his suggestion. If Justin, hostile and nasty, wasn't enough to kill her desire for him, how was she supposed to resist a friendly, charming Justin?

While she was thinking, she stared at him, unconsciously taking another inventory to store with all the others she'd taken every time they were near each other. And while her eyes focused on his thick, sun-streaked hair, which even a coating of sawdust couldn't dim, Justin put down his saw, withdrew a handkerchief out of his back pocket and wiped his face of the sweat and dust of his labors, walking toward her as he did so. He stopped only a pace in front of her.

Maxie came out of her haze as her screaming senses woke her up too late to the danger his nearness represented. "I have to go," she said quickly and started to turn away.

Justin reached out and caught her arm to stop her, aware only after touching her of the sudden need to share one peaceful, mutually honest interval with Maxie Palmer before they met again in the hostile arena they normally shared.

"Stay, Maxie," he said softly, and when she looked up at him, startled disbelief clear in her translucent green eyes, he smiled and added even more softly, "Please."

Maxie swallowed. "Why?" she asked, hating the hoarseness in her voice that probably revealed to Justin how much his touch, even muffled as it was by the light jacket she wore, disturbed her unbearably.

Justin did detect Maxie's unusual vulnerability, and he was enormously pleased by it. In their so-far-tumultuous acquaintance, he'd never once caught her off balance, and as he speculated about why she should be feeling nervous now, his conclusion elicited a sharp arousal in his loins.

"I don't think you really need to ask that, do you?" He spoke without inflection, but his smile was intimate.

Maxie wondered how she could avoid acknowledging that she understood what Justin meant. She feared honesty between them, at least, she feared honesty regarding their personal feelings toward each other. Such understanding could imperil her public goals.

"I'd better go," she said again, pulling back slightly against Justin's hold on her arm.

Justin tightened his grip. "No," he said simply, and when he saw the distress in Maxie's eyes, he gentled his smile. "I'll make a deal with you," he proposed, keeping his voice light, though he'd never been more serious. "Let's pretend we just met and we don't know a thing about each other. Let's forget our normal relationship entirely and get to know each other as people rather than business adversaries. I promise it won't hurt a bit."

That's what you think! Maxie thought, desperately tempted by Justin's suggestion, and just as desperately afraid to accept it.

"That's impossible, Justin," she said aloud, forcing herself to look into his eyes, though doing so weakened her. "We have too much common history behind us. We can't talk about our childhood because I'll get angry about how rough your family's policies made it on families like mine. We can't talk about our work because...well, you know why not," she interjected impatiently, before adding, in a cool, dismissing tone, "That doesn't leave us a lot to talk about, does it?"

Justin stared at her thoughtfully for a moment, then an idea came to him that had him smiling again.

"You're wrong, Maxie," he said firmly. "We can talk about anything we want to. The trick is to really pretend we're strangers. You can say anything you want to about your childhood or your job or anything else that comes to mind—and so can I—just as though you aren't the Maxie Palmer who's been making my life hell lately, and I'm not the Justin Stewart you loathe and despise.''

Intrigued by the possibilities of the idea, yet reluctant to spend any more time in Justin's dangerous company, Maxie started to shake her head, but Justin ignored her and pulled her with him to a nearby fallen log. Pushing her down onto it, he then straddled it with his long legs and sat down facing her.

Maxie couldn't tolerate being on view without having the same advantage, and though she would have preferred not to look directly at Justin, she swung her leg over the log so that she was facing him.

Amused by Maxie's action, and by their positions, sitting knee-to-knee on a log out in the country, with no one around them for miles, Justin grinned at Maxie, inviting her to share his amusement.

''Maybe we ought to conduct our negotiations out here from now on,'' he teased her. ''The atmosphere is certainly friendlier.''

''What negotiations?'' Maxie replied, straight-faced. ''I've never seen you before in my life.''

Justin threw back his head and laughed straight from the heart. Suddenly, he felt as though his problems had dropped into a deep well from where they might never surface again.

Maxie groaned inwardly, terrified by her own fascination with Justin's charm. The sound of his laughter was beautiful . . . and contagious. Before she could stop herself, she was smiling at him.

Finally, they were smiling into each other's eyes, and Justin became so caught up in his fascination with how much more beautiful Maxie was when she was smiling approvingly at him than when she was behaving with cold contempt, that he forgot about playing their game.

Maxie didn't. It was the only lifeline she had to keep from leaning forward and pressing her mouth against the sculptured curve of Justin's. "Where are you from?" she asked, attempting the polite tone she would really have used with a stranger.

Justin came out of his bedazzled inspection of Maxie's face and, smiling, answered, "Timbuktu. How about you?"

"Nowheresville, Missouri," she answered pleasantly.

"Never heard of it." Justin shook his head.

"Not many people have," Maxie admitted. "It's hard to find, that is, if anyone actually wanted to find it, which not many people do."

"Ah, I see." Justin nodded wisely. "Small town?"

"Very," Maxie agreed.

"Kind of old-fashioned? Stuck in the past?"

"You might say that," Maxie drawled, "but I have a feeling it's going to enter the twentieth century before too much longer."

"And why is that?" Justin inquired, though he knew the answer.

"Well—" Maxie took a deep breath, certain their game was going to come to a fast end when she finished the little speech she was composing in her head "—you see, I'm an attorney who specializes in union law. And I'm working very hard to unionize the company that more or less owns my little hometown." Eyeing Justin warily, she added, "Of course, the family that owns the company is fighting tooth and nail to stop me."

"But you intend to win," Justin said gravely, surprising Maxie by his refusal to get angry. "Tell me," he invited, gazing at Maxie interestedly, "what made you decide to become a union attorney?"

Maxie gave him a faint smile, puzzled by his manner. "Ah, now we have to delve into my childhood. Are you sure you want to hear this?"

"Positive." Justin nodded, keeping his gaze directly on Maxie's face in a way he saw disturbed her. She kept looking away, which was highly unusual for the Maxie Palmer he knew and had come to desire.

Maxie lifted her shoulders in a slight shrug. "Well," she said, her smile deepening for an instant, then departing in favor of a mock gravity, "once upon a time . . ."

Justin held up his hand. "Is this going to be a fairy tale?"

"No, only told as one." Maxie frowned at him sternly.

Justin's mouth twitched as he nodded.

"Well, as I said," Maxie continued, "once upon a time, there was a little girl who grew up as the daughter of a man who was truly a genius."

With her sparkling eyes, Maxie challenged Justin to deny her evaluation of her father's talents, but he merely sat quietly watching her in that unnerving way of his, so she glanced away, pretending an interest in the surrounding area she distinctly didn't feel, and continued.

"However, the little girl's father wasn't the type of man to take advantage of his own talents. He was born and had grown up in Bar—Nowheresville." She stumbled a little, flashed Justin a quick glance, then looked away again. "His wife had, also. Neither of them wanted to live anywhere else." Frowning as she thought about it, oblivious of Justin's intent gaze for a moment, Maxie added, "But things might not have been different if they had moved, because Daddy was too contented to tinker with his machinery to pay attention to much of anything else—other than his family, of course."

Maxie glanced at Justin, but his calm, interested gaze didn't waver, and with a mental shrug, thinking, "*In for a penny, in for a pound,*" she continued. "The elder brother and sister in the family went to work for the family that owned the town. There was no money for college, you see, and though the parents had tried to create a feeling of self-confidence and ambition in their children, these two, at that time, merely went along with tradition, which said the children of the town, upon graduating from high school, went to work at the town company." Maxie flashed Justin a look filled with pride then, and added, "But the third child—a son—was determined from a very early age to be different."

Justin, knowing Maxie was referring to Bram, felt an inner tension begin inside him, but he was careful to keep anything he felt from showing in his face. He didn't want to spoil Maxie's recitation. Sitting here and talking with her, without either of them displaying animosity, was weaving a seductive spell around him.

"This son," Maxie continued, "proved he was a match for the son of the town's leading family whenever they came up against each other."

Maxie paused, waiting for a negative reaction from Justin, but when he displayed nothing other than interest, she felt almost ashamed at indulging her desire to prick his ego, then alarmed at finding herself actually sympathizing with Justin over his defeats at her brother's hands.

"He worked hard and got a scholarship to college," she quickly went on, "and he did brilliantly at his studies there. After graduating, he took a chance that paid off. He went into a partnership with another man, and after a lot of hard work and struggle, they made a huge success of their company."

Maxie was unaware that she was smiling proudly. Justin was very much aware of it, as well as a feeling of jealousy toward Bram. But somehow the jealousy had less power to sting than it had had in the past, now that he was associating Bram with Maxie.

"This son helped the elder brother and sister to get an education, and they were able to pursue a better life away from Nowheresville as a result of his help,'' Maxie said, her pride in what Bram had done evident.

"What about the youngest daughter?" Justin asked softly, watching Maxie's face very closely. "Didn't she get any help?"

Maxie shrugged. "She didn't need it," she said simply. "She always felt self-confident. She even became friends with the leading family's daughter. In fact, she loved her dearly."

Justin knew she was talking about Cassy, but his sister had never confided in him concerning her relationship with Maxie. He decided there had been a lot more to the friendship than he had suspected, and became aware that he was feeling slightly guilty that his family's snobbery had probably ended the friendship.

"But something happened when the youngest daughter was seventeen," Maxie said, watching Justin's face with a grave expression in her eyes that made him uneasy. "The town's leading family cut the father's pay, when he actually deserved a substantial raise, considering the contribution he was making to the family's business. That outraged the youngest daughter, enough so that she broke off her friendship with the leading family's daughter and determined what her career would be—one that would allow her to redress the wrongs her father had suffered, and those of others in Nowheresville as well. She studied very, very hard, and as her older brother had done, she got a scholarship to college. It wasn't easy, but she finally got her law degree, spent a few years getting some experience, then came home and is active now in fulfilling her purpose."

For several very long moments, Maxie stared at Justin and he stared back at her with a succession of feelings flickering through his clear eyes. He was remembering that it had been his idea to cut the pay of the family's employees, and that at the time he had felt very smug about it. Now he realized what it had meant to those employees, and his regret was sharp that his action had resulted in present problems, especially the animosity Maxie felt toward him.

Unaware of his thoughts, Maxie was nevertheless cognizant of some sort of bond forming between her and Justin. She couldn't decide why this should be happening, and she was having a hard time dealing with the pleasure—and the danger—of that bond.

Then it was Justin's turn to talk about himself, and Maxie unconsciously leaned toward him, her curiosity about him sharp.

"That was a very interesting story," he said quietly, holding Maxie's gaze. He meant what he said. He had very seldom made an effort to understand the feelings of other people, and he was disturbed by the empathy Maxie's story elicited inside him. "Would you like to hear a story I have to tell?" he then inquired, and something in his heart lightened when Maxie nodded.

"Very much," she said softly and felt she was betraying herself when she realized she meant it.

"Once upon a time," Justin started, speaking in a low, firm voice, "there was a young man who grew up in a wealthy family. The young man's grandfather was a genius at designing furniture, as well as having a smart business mind. He created a place where his designs could be built, and in doing so, he made it possible for people who didn't want to move away from their childhood homes to find employment there."

Maxie's glance slid away from Justin's for a moment as she took his message. She was alarmed, telling herself she mustn't let herself become too understanding about Justin's side of things and thereby weaken the purpose that had brought her back to Barton's Corner.

"While the grandfather was alive, everything went smoothly," Justin continued, aware on some level that telling Maxie these things was making him think about them in depth himself for the first time in his life. Justin looked away from Maxie and stared into the distance without seeing anything other than the story that was unfolding in his mind.

"But his daughter married a young man whose family was a member of the aristocratic poor. Her husband had very definite ideas about class position."

Maxie tightened her jaw, but she said nothing.

"He taught his son his way of thinking," Justin went on thoughtfully, "and his son accepted his ideas." Justin took a breath and turned back toward Maxie. He knew from looking at her that his story so far hadn't overcome her prejudice toward his father, or probably toward him.

Speaking with deeper sincerity and more insight into himself than he'd ever had occasion to elicit before, Justin said slowly, "The son bought the idea that he and his family were better than other people. But he didn't know how to reconcile that view with the fact that another boy—one of a lower class—was more talented than he."

Justin stared into Maxie's eyes as he continued. "Aside from that conflict, however, he has a great deal of trouble believing that he doesn't deserve to reap the benefits of the genius of his grandfather and the hard work he himself puts into the family business, while those who work for him, while they deserve what they earn with their labor, have no right to call the shots concerning the business."

Justin's last words created an overwhelming sense of disappointment inside Maxie. She wondered sadly how she had allowed herself to become caught up in Justin's story to the point where she had begun to actively expect a change of heart in him.

"Tell me, stranger," Justin asked with a slight mocking lilt to his tone as he wondered how objective Maxie could really be, "this youngest daughter you were telling me about, does she believe that her brother—the one who had the brains to conceive a company and took the risks that could have resulted in failure instead of paying off— shouldn't reap the benefits of his own hard work, ideas and risk taking? Or does she think he should turn the bulk of his reward over to his employees?"

Maxie frowned. "My...the young man who became successful realizes that he can't stay a success without the people who work for him, and he pays his people generously, sees that they have adequate health and retirement benefits, and treats them with respect and appreciation for their efforts on behalf of his company," she said coldly. "It might be worthwhile," she added with grim emphasis, "for the young man you were talking about to consult with the young man I was talking about to learn something about how to develop a loyal work force."

"That might be a little hard," Justin said, his anger beginning to rise, "even if the young man I was talking about felt he had anything to learn from your young man."

Maxie straightened, her eyes flashing with temper. "I can assure you your young man has some things to learn," she said flatly. "And why would it be hard? My young man is here in Nowheresville right now!"

Justin was startled by the news. No one had told him Bram Palmer was back, and he wasn't particularly happy about the possibility of running into him again.

His mind veered off Bram when Maxie stood up and swung her leg over the log, preparing to leave. Justin stood up as well, regretting heartily that the game they'd been playing had somehow gotten off track.

"I need to get home," Maxie said coolly, eyeing Justin with the same hostile look she normally gave him.

Justin's frustration swung out of control, and without thinking, he reached out and took hold of Maxie's waist to stop her from leaving.

Startled, immediately apprehensive, Maxie reached down and covered Justin's wrists with her hands, trying to get him to release her. Instead, he stepped closer and pulled her up against him.

"So we're back to normal?" he said, his voice tight and soft. He slid his arms around Maxie and held her hard against him. Something primitive and determined rode him as he looked into her eyes and saw that, though she seemed alarmed, there was a part of her that savored their contact as much as he did.

"Well, I'm not ready for it," he said, and lowered his head to seize the mouth that had haunted his dreams for months.

Maxie struggled against the senses he was bringing into flaming life inside her. But as though Justin knew her double mind intimately, his sensuous attack on her mouth increased. Every tiny hesitation in Maxie's fight seemed to inflame Justin further until, finally, Maxie's struggles stopped. She was weakened as much by her own desire as by his.

The instant Maxie gave in, Justin automatically changed his assault to a determined seduction, which Maxie reacted to as predictably as she'd always feared she would. There seemed to be no distinct transition between her efforts to push him away and her subsequent efforts to blend her own body into his. Her response to his fevered, enveloping kiss was eager, and she felt desperate to have more and more of his lovemaking.

Seconds slid into moments as their mutual hunger raged, and each attempted to satisfy needs too long banked, to touch and taste the other, while every other consideration disappeared from their minds.

"You wanted me, too," Justin whispered between kisses. "God, I wish I'd known!"

"But I didn't want this to happen—I wish it would stop," Maxie gasped her half lie before Justin seized her mouth again.

Driven by the heat of his desire for Maxie, Justin at last lifted his mouth from hers and took her head in his hands while he looked deeply into the emerald fire of her eyes.

"Let me love you, Maxie," he grated with husky desperation. "God, I want you. Let me show you how much..."

He began punctuating his plea with searing kisses that drove sense from Maxie's mind and left her only her own hunger to guide her, and when Justin lowered one of his hands to her breast to touch it with skilled tenderness, then traced his lips over her throat and down to the breast he held to mouth its tip through her blouse, Maxie's breath sobbed in her throat, ragged with need and thoughtless hunger. She held her hands to his head, abetting his efforts, and when he pushed her blouse aside and touched her bare skin with his warm lips, she groaned audibly.

Justin straightened and lifted Maxie in his arms, intending to lay her down on the cushion of leaves covering the ground and assuage their need for each other completely, and it was only then that Maxie surfaced from her senses enough to face the consequences of her weakness.

Laying her head in the hollow of his neck and clinging tightly to his shoulders, she gasped out, "No, Justin, don't!"

Justin frowned and paused in the motion of lowering her to the ground.

"You want me as much as I want you," he argued fiercely for what he needed from her. "I won't hurt you, Maxie. I promise I won't."

"Yes, you will!" Maxie lifted her head to gaze at him with the agony of her choice in her eyes. Cupping his cheek with her hand, she softened her voice. "You won't mean to, Justin, but you will."

Justin gazed back at her, his frustration and puzzlement evident.

"I do want you, Justin," Maxie murmured, "God help me, I do! I have since the first moment I came back here and faced you. But if I give in to my desire for you before I've finished what I came here to do, I'll hate myself. I couldn't stand the conflict of loving you during the night and hating what you stand for during the day. And when I've finished what I came here to do," she concluded with sad awareness, "I doubt very much that you'll want me any longer."

Angry, Justin set Maxie on her feet, but he didn't let go of her. Holding her shoulders, his jaw set and stubborn, he grated, "I've wanted you during every minute of every one of our battles! What makes you think that's going to stop if you win? Hell, I don't have any control over what you make me feel, and I don't think you can control what you feel, either!"

Her eyes wide, Maxie shook her head. "But I have control over what I do," she said with quiet finality. "I can't split myself in two, Justin," she added with soft regret. "And that's exactly what I'd be doing if we became lovers."

Justin lifted his head in a proud gesture that Maxie both admired and hated. Then his expression softened, surprising Maxie, and she was even more surprised when he pulled her closely into his arms again.

"All right," he grated against her cheek. "I'm not sure that you're right, but I can't force you against your convictions. I don't want you that way. I want you to come to me without a single reservation."

Maxie despaired that she ever could be free of her reservations about Justin, but when he set her away from him slightly and looked down into her eyes, she realized that she could never go back to the way she'd felt about him before she'd been in his arms.

"This thing between us is too strong to be denied, Maxie," he said with rough sincerity. "It can be delayed, but it won't go away. I don't even want it to, despite our differences. Someday I'll have you . . . and if you think I'm unaware that when I do, you'll most likely have me, too, think again. Despite that risk, I won't back off. I can't."

Slowly, convinced by the light of honest conviction in Justin's beautiful blue eyes, Maxie nodded.

"Then, I won't, either," she said softly. "When the time is right, I'll come to you, Justin. I'll come to you just the way you want me to. And whatever happens afterward, I won't regret taking the risk."

Justin forced himself to relax on receiving Maxie's promise. "Do I get a kiss to tide me over?" he asked with a wry, humorous twist of his mouth that diverted Maxie's attention to his firmly shaped lips.

Without answering, she came up on tiptoe and wrapped her arms around his neck. Pressing her mouth to his, she allowed herself to kiss him with all the hungry, honest feeling inside her, and Justin's response almost shattered her determination to walk away from him for the time being.

At last, she had to tear her mouth from his and step out of his arms quickly in order to be able to do it at all. "I'll see you Monday, Justin," she said shakily as she backed away from him, her mouth trembling, her eyes huge in her face. "We still have a battle to wage about Larry Manion's dismissal."

Justin devoured her with his eyes, storing her image in his memory until he saw her again. "I'll look forward to it," he answered, telling her with his look how many ways he meant what he'd said.

Maxie nodded, quickly turned on her heel and walked away on legs weakened by the desire raging through her, knowing that the search for a measure of peace that had brought her to this place had, instead, resulted in utterly destroying her peace of mind for some time to come, if not forever.

Chapter Seven

By the time Bram had accompanied Charlie and his nephew on their slow circuit of the house and listened while they discussed at great length what needed to be done, his patience was wearing thin. During his years in California, he'd gotten unused to the amount of time and talk it took in his hometown to get anything accomplished.

Now Jodie was calculating the cost of the repairs they'd decided upon, laboriously adding up the figures on a crumpled piece of paper, and Bram sat across from him trying not to show how impatient he felt. He didn't really care how much it cost to fix up his dad's place, but he was aware that Harry, Charlie and Jodie would never understand such an attitude, so he sat quietly waiting, since there was nothing else he could do.

When Jodie at last gave him the figure he'd arrived at, Bram heaved a silent sigh of relief. "Thanks, Jodie," he said as he got to his feet. He was grateful his father had gone out of the room and hadn't heard the total Jodie had given him. Harry would have probably argued it was too much. "This is fine. How soon can you start?"

"Well," Jodie said with a slowness that tore at Bram's nerves. "If I get all the material bought today, I can start Monday. Would that suit you?"

"That's great," Bram answered, then turned as Harry came into the living room from the kitchen carrying a tray of beer and glasses.

"Thought we could use a picker-upper," he said with satisfaction as he set the tray on the coffee table.

Charlie beamed in anticipation. Obviously, it would be a while before he took his leave, which suited Bram, since Charlie would be company for Harry when Bram himself left to see Cassandra—if she was willing to see him again.

Jodie, however, got up and put on his cap. "I better get to the lumberyard and the hardware store before they close," he said, glancing regretfully at the beer.

"Sure you haven't got time for a little refreshment?" Harry coaxed.

"No, thank you." Jodie shook his head. "Another time, okay?"

"All right, then," Harry said with a shrug. "I'll run Charlie home later."

When Jodie was gone and it was apparent to Bram that his father and Charlie were quite content to chat with each other, he headed for the kitchen.

"I've got something to do," he said to Harry, who looked up as he passed by. "I'll be back after a while, Dad."

"Fine, son," Harry answered and turned back to his friend.

In the kitchen, Bram looked up the Stewart number and dialed it, grateful when Cassandra, rather than her mother or Jussie, answered.

"Hi," he said, unable to keep a soft, intimate note out of his voice. "Can you get away for a while?"

Cassandra had decided it would be best not to see Bram again. After a night of tossing and turning, she had elected to use her common sense rather than give in to her emotions. She needed a clear mind and a steady heart for the job she faced turning things around at the mill, and Bram was a distraction she didn't need, especially when there was nowhere for a relationship between them to go. Her future was tied up in Barton's Corner; his was in California. And she had a suspicion, anyway, that Bram harbored the type of resentment toward her family that would eventually eat away at any relationship they did manage to establish.

She was therefore both surprised and considerably annoyed when her mouth opened and said yes, instead of voicing the no she had intended to give him.

"Fine. It's a beautiful day. We'll go for a ride, all right?"

"All right," Cassandra agreed with only a trace of the ambiguity she was feeling in her voice.

After ringing off, and while she was waiting for Bram to arrive, Cassandra occupied herself fixing a picnic lunch. It kept her from chewing her fingernails, even if it didn't keep her from thinking about how foolish it was of her to see Bram again. Where had all her willpower gone so suddenly? she wondered irritably.

When she opened the door to Bram, however, she realized why she hadn't been able to refuse him when he'd called. His appeal was every bit as potent as it had been when she was a young girl, but now that she was a woman and had been in his arms, he was well-nigh irresistible.

Bram inspected Cassandra with eyes that couldn't seem to see enough. His gaze traveled from her blond-streaked hair to the wariness in her blue eyes, to her delectable mouth and down her body, which in jeans and a navy blue sweater, looked better to him than the bikini-clad figures he was accustomed to viewing in California.

"I still don't understand how I failed to take notice of you when we were in school," he said with soft humor, showing her with his eyes how attractive he found her.

"You were too busy passing a football to make passes at girls, if I recall." Cassandra couldn't help being pleased by his admiration. "Not that you had to try very hard with the girls," she added dryly. "Tell me, did you ever actually ask anyone out yourself, or did they ask you out?"

"I don't remember," Bram said diplomatically, though his eyes twinkled with humor.

"Uh-huh," Cassandra responded with blatant disbelief and handed him the picnic basket. "Well, I suppose I should be honored that you called me, instead of the other way around," she went on with mild mockery. "I'll bet the women are still doing the calling where you're concerned."

As she shut the door behind her, Bram elected not to respond to her last statement. Instead, he said, "You didn't have to feed us."

Cassandra was about to respond when he rested his hand on her shoulder as they walked to the car, and the resulting flood of warmth that immediately shot through her made her pause to swallow before she could find her natural voice.

"Didn't I?" she said as casually as she could manage. "Well, I happen to be hungry, but if you're not, I'll eat it all myself."

"Whoa," Bram teased as he opened the door of the red Jaguar for her. "I didn't say I wasn't hungry. I merely said *you* didn't have to feed us. I could have bought us a meal."

"Where?" Cassandra drawled, looking up at him chidingly as she sat down in the passenger seat. "At Baker's, where everyone in town would have seen us sooner or later and started gossiping about what we were doing together?"

Her words plunged Bram out of the pleasant mood of anticipation he'd been in as effectively as though Cassandra had thrown a glass of cold water in his face. He didn't answer as he shut the door and walked around the car. When he was seated beside Cassandra, he looked directly into her eyes and said, with a tinge of sarcasm, "I'd forgotten it might embarrass you to be seen with a Palmer. Would you prefer that I drive the back roads so no one will have the opportunity to gossip about us?"

Cassandra was appalled that he could have put such an interpretation on her words, and her eyes contained a surprised reproach as she looked back at him.

"That's unfair, Bram," she said quietly, concealing her growing suspicion that Bram harbored a lot of resentment against her and her family. "I only meant that I dislike being the subject of gossip at all, and there's no sense in arousing any, anyway, is there? You'll be returning to California soon, while I intend to stay here. We won't have all that much time together, will we?"

At her words, Bram again felt reluctant to return to California, a reaction that didn't soothe his temper, considering that he didn't believe Cassandra's explanation. Why should it matter how much gossip they caused? he thought angrily. Would she care so much if he were an acceptable escort for a Stewart female?

Seeing the anger flashing in his eyes, Cassandra said quietly, "Bram, would you like to call this off?" She was thinking her earlier decision not to see him again had been right. It was obvious he didn't believe her, which both insulted and frustrated her. How did one get through to someone so steeped in past prejudices? she wondered sadly.

Without answering, Bram immediately turned away and started the car. He wasn't sure whether he wanted to force Cassandra to be seen with him or if he just didn't want to part from her. He was simply acting from instinct.

Surprised by his action, Cassandra speculated about the reason for his refusal to take her offer to end their date before it had really gotten started. When she came to no clear-cut conclusion, she turned to wondering why she hadn't ended the date herself. There would have been time to get out of the car before he started backing up. As she glanced at Bram's profile, however, she had her answer. He was like a flame to a moth where she was concerned, apparently, drawing her on, though she was positive she would end up burned.

"Where are we going?" she asked when, instead of turning toward town, Bram turned the car in the opposite direction.

"I thought we'd try Butler's Meadow," he said without inflection. He was now ashamed of his desire to force Cassandra to be seen with him, but it grated on him that the past was apparently alive and well in Barton's Corner. He was still just a boy from the other side of the tracks where the Stewarts were concerned. So why hadn't he taken her up on her offer to end this farcical date when he'd had the chance? he wondered irritably.

"Do the Butlers still let people use their meadow?" Cassandra asked, her mood lightening a little at the thought of revisiting a place that had many happy memories for her.

"I don't know," Bram answered levelly. "I suppose they can run us off if they don't want us there."

Half an hour later, after an almost silent ride, Bram parked by the side of the road and they got out. But before they started walking a footpath to the meadow, Cassandra stopped him.

"Bram, if you're going to remain upset with me, it might be best if we forget about having a picnic together," she said, her eyes clouded with unhappiness.

Annoyed by her second attempt to call off their date, Bram glanced down at her, reluctantly admiring the way the sun glinted on her hair. "What makes you think I'm upset with you?" he responded in order to gain time to think. He had no desire to get into a discussion with Cassandra that had no resolution as far as he could see.

She gave him an exasperated look. "You haven't said two words in the last half hour, and you have to ask why I think you're upset?"

Bram raised an eyebrow at her tone, and the sudden distancing, disapproving look in his eyes when he met Cassandra's gaze hurt her far more than made any sense. She could hardly credit the strength of her reaction to his attitude, but the tears stinging the backs of her eyes were proof that he had somehow gained a great deal of power over her emotions in the brief time they'd known each other.

When Bram saw the moisture gathering in Cassandra's eyes, he frowned, thinking at first he was mistaken, but when she blinked rapidly and looked away, trying to gain enough control to ask to be taken home, he had to believe that she was about to cry, and he was astonished.

"Hey," he said softly. He set down the picnic basket he was carrying and took a step toward Cassandra, lifting his hands to place them on her shoulders.

Cassandra started to shake him off, but he wouldn't budge. Indeed, before she could stop him, he had enfolded her in his arms and was holding her with his cheek against her hair.

"I'm sorry," he said quietly. "I've been a heel."

Far from disputing his confession, Cassandra nodded her head, gulping down her tears.

Her reaction made Bram smile and his arms tightened around her. "Forgive me?" he asked, trying to put a teasing note in his voice.

Cassandra again shook her head, this time in the negative, and Bram's smile grew into a chuckle, which made Cassandra lean back to look up at his face, her expression resentful. "I don't like what you were thinking, Bram," she said, her voice quavering with emotion.

Bram's smile disappeared as he studied the look in her eyes and digested her words.

"I've told you I'm not like Jussie and Daddy, Bram," Cassandra added more quietly, holding his gaze. "Can't you believe that?"

Bram found himself wanting to believe her far more strongly than was justified by their brief acquaintance. "I want to believe you're not," he replied honestly. "But it's difficult to separate you from them."

Cassandra was disappointed by his reply, and she automatically said the words that seemed called for. "Then, aside from the fact that we wouldn't have much time together, anyway, there really isn't any point in our seeing each other anymore, is there?" she answered, unable to keep the regret she was feeling out of her voice or her eyes.

"I suppose not," Bram said slowly, making Cassandra's heart plummet with disappointment. Against all reason, she had hoped he would answer differently. "Except that I don't think I can stay away from you," he added.

Cassandra's heart was suddenly soaring again, and for a long moment, they stared into each other's eyes, each acknowledging the dilemma they faced, until Bram made the decision to put all else aside, other than the pleasure of being together for a while. He began to smile.

"I could stand here all day holding you and enjoying every moment of it," he teased softly, "but I believe you said something about being hungry."

Cassandra suddenly felt an urgent desire to follow his lead—to take the moment for what it was worth and face the future later.

"Yes, I'm hungry," she answered, a smile tilting her lips.

Bram held her tighter for an instant, then kissed her forehead and let her go. "Come on, then," he said lightly as he bent to pick up the picnic basket again. "Let's have our picnic."

He took her hand as they walked to the meadow, and it felt natural to Cassandra to walk with him that way.

"Here's the old rock," he said as they came off the footpath and approached a huge tree, beneath which was a flat rock that made a perfect picnic table. "Do you want to sit on the ground, or should I search for a proper rock for the lady to use?'' he asked with a formal bow, determinedly keeping the atmosphere between them light and playful.

"I think I'll have a rock, kind sir," Cassandra said airily. "A soft rock, if you please."

Bram nodded as he set the picnic basket down on the large, flat rock, then set off to find another one suitable to serve as a chair for Cassandra.

Cassandra kept an eye on his wanderings as she spread a cloth and began to set out the food she'd brought.

When Bram came back, he held a fairly smooth, good-sized rock in his hands, which he set down on one side of the picnic rock.

"Is it a soft one?" Cassandra asked doubtfully as she eyed it.

"It soon will be," Bram said and reached down to pull his sweatshirt over his head.

Cassandra managed to find her voice as he was making his sweatshirt into a cushion for her. "You'll get cold," she croaked, stunned by her own reaction to Bram's tanned, smoothly muscled, chest, shoulders and arms.

Bram executed another courtly bow. "Never," he said, placing a hand over his heart. "And even if I die of pneumonia," he added, peering up at her with a teasing look in his eyes, "nothing is too much to sacrifice for a lovely damsel such as yourself."

Cassandra, her lips twitching, gingerly sat down on the rock, wriggled for a moment, then smiled her satisfaction at him.

"Comfy?" Bram inquired in a caressing voice. He was in love with that smile of hers.

"Very." Cassandra nodded, then indicated the food with a sweep of her arm. "Help yourself," she invited.

Bram eyed the food consideringly, bent to lift one corner of a piece of bread and asked in a level tone, "Peanut butter and jelly?"

"I was a little strapped for time," Cassandra said, smiling mischievously.

"I see," Bram nodded. Then, sighing in a exaggeratedly long-suffering fashion, he sat down across from her.

Cassandra made a face at him. "Don't quibble," she instructed him in a prim tone. "I assure you I have other virtues besides cooking."

"Such as?" Bram inquired, reaching for a sandwich.

"Such as brains and determination," Cassandra responded airily before biting into a sandwich of her own. "Do you want something to drink?" she asked belatedly, speaking with her mouth full.

"What did you bring, Kool Aid?" Bram teased straight-facedly.

Cassandra wrinkled her nose at him. "You should be so lucky," she said, slipping her tongue out of her mouth to catch a stray dab of grape jelly. "There's only water."

"Water," Bram said in a solemn tone, "in my estimation, does not constitute something to drink."

"So don't drink it." Cassandra smiled blandly at him. "I don't mind."

Bram gave her a speaking look before reaching for the water jug. "Are there any glasses?" he then inquired.

Cassandra stopped chewing for a moment. "I knew I forgot something," she admitted. "Do you have any germs?"

"Many and varied," Bram confirmed with satisfaction.

"Me, too." Cassandra smiled. "Let's hope they get along all right."

As they ate, they chatted amiably about times they'd picnicked in Butler's Meadow before.

"Did they still have the senior picnic here when you and Maxie were about to graduate, as they did when I was in school?" Bram asked.

Cassandra nodded, remembering a little sadly how much more fun that picnic would have been if she and Maxie hadn't been estranged.

"I don't suppose they do anymore, though, since they've put in the new park," she added, failing to mention that her mother had donated the land for the new park. She didn't like the feeling that she had to weigh her words around Bram or risk arousing his resentment toward her family, but she kept telling herself it wouldn't last long, anyway. He would soon be going back to California.

When they were done eating and had put the remnants back into the picnic basket, Bram stood up and held out a hand to help Cassandra to her feet.

"Are we going to eat and run?" she teased, trying not to think about how much she enjoyed having him hold her hand.

"'Tis time to stroll the meadow, dear lady," he said formally as he tucked her hand under his arm and immediately felt a jolt clear down to his toes when her slender fingers brushed the bare skin of his side.

"Would you like to wear your sweatshirt again?" Cassandra asked absently, her mind dwelling on how astonishing it was to be so shaken by the glancing touch of skin against skin.

"I don't think so," Bram said gravely. He much preferred the chance that she might accidentally touch him again.

"Aren't you cold?" Cassandra persisted, curling her fingers to keep them steady. She glanced up at Bram's face. He was looking straight ahead with a secret smile on his lips.

"Not in the least," he said solemnly, though he was laughing inside at the very idea that he might be cold.

"Oh," Cassandra said in a small voice, hoping she could continue to control the urge to stroke his chest with her fingers.

They meandered for a while, pausing to pick up an oddly shaped pebble or a stick to throw. They were headed back when Bram suddenly had the sensation that time was running out. He had been avoiding thinking about what had happened between them earlier, because if he thought about it, it would spoil the sheer pleasure of being in Cassandra's company. But he had the feeling that if they parted that day without discussing their differences, Cassy might refuse to see him again.

He stopped walking and turned her to face him. When she looked up at him, he said in a low voice, holding her gaze intently, "Tell me again how different you are from your father and Jussie."

Cassandra went still inside and gazed at him helplessly, wishing he hadn't spoiled the illusion she'd been weaving that they had no problems to face, no limit on their time together.

"Bram, I can't make you believe anything simply by telling you it's so," she answered with level simplicity. "You'll have to make up your own mind about me, only..."

"Only what?"

"Only we don't have that much time, do we?" she reminded him, a touch of sadness in her voice.

Cassandra looked down, away from the intensity in Bram's eyes, but now her gaze rested on his waistband and the bare tanned skin above it, and she felt a sudden sinking sensation in her stomach.

Bram put a hand on her cheek and raised her face to his again, and when he saw the look in her eyes, he immediately understood and felt a tightening in his groin.

"No, we don't have much time," he said softly, bending to her mouth as though pulled by a magnetic force. "And it would be a shame to waste what time we do have."

A light, shuddering sensation ran through Cassandra's body as Bram's lips brushed hers, and she raised her hands to rest them on his waist as he continued to tease her lips in a gentle, tormenting way. As her longing to have a real kiss from him escalated, she unconsciously tightened her grip on the bare skin of his waist, and her touch made Bram suck in his breath.

"Cassy," he breathed, then smothered her mouth with his own and tightened his arms around her as Cassandra met his embrace by slipping her arms around him and leaning into his body.

The night before, their hunger for each other had escalated so quickly, it had taken them both by surprise. Today, as though they were on the same wavelength, they took their time, savoring each kiss, touching each other in gentle exploration, letting desire grow between them with steadily increasing urgency.

When Bram knew he was reaching the point where the urgency was going to have to be satisfied, he tempered his kisses, then looked deeply into Cassandra's eyes.

"I want to make love to you," he whispered softly, "but not here. We don't even have a blanket."

Cassandra stared into the enveloping, exciting green depths of Bram's eyes for a long moment, then let her lids close and gave a soft little sigh of disappointment as she leaned her head on his shoulder.

Bram's smile was tender as he cradled her against him. "I suppose this is what is known as a romantic delay," he murmured with gentle humor. "But I've put my personal life on hold for so long, I don't appreciate a delay of any kind right now."

Her eyes still closed, Cassandra nodded languidly. "Me, neither," she sighed, making Bram's smile broaden.

But as her heart began to quiet from its frantic race and her mind cleared somewhat, Cassandra remembered that there was a very real danger in letting herself want Bram so much. Reluctantly, she lifted her head and straightened in his arms.

Bram let her put a little distance between them, but when he saw the troubled look in her eyes, his smile faded. "What are you thinking?" he asked, though he was afraid he knew.

Cassandra hesitated, then decided to be honest with him. "I'm afraid, Bram," she admitted softly, then bit her lip and looked away.

Bram was puzzled. "Afraid?"

Cassandra nodded, returning her solemn gaze to his. "I'm afraid if we make love, I won't ever want to stop."

Bram relaxed, his expression lightening. "What makes you think you'll ever have to stop?" he asked, his voice deep.

Cassandra shook her head, and leaned against him again, resting her head on his chest and closing her eyes. "We hardly know each other," she reminded him, though that wasn't her real worry.

"Do you really believe that matters?" Bram's hold tightened until Cassandra was snuggled tightly against him.

"No," she confessed with a sigh.

At that, Bram smiled again, thinking he could never remember feeling so tender toward a woman who could arouse him past thought. Then he stopped smiling as he focused on why Cassandra was really worried about their getting too intimately involved.

He took her shoulders in his hands and made her stand straight while he continued to hold her and look into her eyes, his own gaze serious. "Do you really intend to stay here in Barton's Corner?" he asked.

Cassandra hesitated. Her desire for Bram had weakened her intentions. It took a moment to get her thinking straightened out again. Then she nodded, though there was a reluctant look in her eyes.

Bram was disappointed. If Cassandra was adamant about her decision, it didn't necessarily mean they couldn't work something out, but the logistics would be formidable. But more important than that, if her protestations that his being a Palmer didn't matter to her were either consciously or unconsciously false, she wasn't likely to get over that feeling living in Barton's Corner where the prejudice had been born.

His hands dropped from Cassandra's shoulders, and she saw again that distancing look in his eyes that hurt her and that she hated. But she saw absolutely no use in continuing to try to convince him he was wrong, though it was hard for her to understand how he could believe what he obviously did about her, in light of her friendship with Maxie and her actions since she and Bram had met. Prejudice didn't yield to words, however, or to logic, it seemed.

She gave Bram a helpless look of frustration, then turned away and started walking back toward the picnic rock.

Bram frowned, then slowly began to follow her, again filled with that sense that time was running out. At the rock, when she straightened after picking up the picnic basket, he put a hand on her arm to stop her from walking away.

"If I'm wrong about you, I'm sorry," he said quietly as Cassandra looked steadily into his eyes. "Maybe I'm the one with the problem. I thought I'd gotten over the need to prove myself to this town and especially to your family, but—"

"There's no need for you to prove anything to anybody," Cassandra quickly interrupted. "And if there was, you've already done it."

Bram shrugged. ''Maybe,'' he said, but there was a tinge of doubt in his tone.

Cassandra sighed. ''I suppose I understand.'' She lifted her shoulders in a shrugging gesture. ''I'm trying to prove something myself.''

Bram's brows lifted in surprise. ''You?''

He sounded so incredulous that Cassandra frowned at him. ''Yes, me,'' she said somewhat indignantly. ''Ever since I was seventeen, I've wanted to prove I deserve all the benefits that come to me just for being a Stewart on my own merits, not have them given to me on a platter.''

Bram still looked incredulous. He couldn't relate to what Cassandra was saying. It simply had never occurred to him that someone in her position might feel the way she said she did.

''Oh, stop it!'' Cassandra was suddenly furious with Bram. ''I'm tired of your doubting everything I say! I've never been a liar, Bram Palmer, and if you don't believe that, ask Maxie.'' With that, she spun on her heel and started walking rapidly toward the footpath leading back to the car.

Bram was torn between amusement and chagrin. Then, upon realizing how insulted he himself would be if Cassandra had acted to him as he'd been acting toward her, he snatched up his sweatshirt and started after her, pulling the shirt on as he strode along.

He caught up with her about halfway back to the car. She glared at him and continued walking. He tried to take the picnic basket from her and carry it himself, but she snatched it out of his reach. He prudently decided to wait until they reached the car to apologize. She might not accept his apology, but she would be forced to listen to it, since he had the keys and it was too far back to her house to walk.

When they reached the road, Bram opened the car door for Cassandra; she slid inside and propped the picnic basket on her lap like a barrier, staring straight ahead with a stubborn look on her face. Bram hid a smile and went around the car to slide in behind the steering wheel. When he made no effort to start the car, however, and merely leaned back in the corner facing her, Cassandra at last glanced at him with a frown.

"I'm sorry," Bram said quickly before she could turn away, but he was smiling in such a way that she remained unconvinced.

"I really am sorry," Bram repeated in a more sincere tone, without the smile. Now, she looked half convinced, but still uncertain.

Bram leaned forward slightly and caught a lock of Cassandra's hair between his thumb and forefinger, playing with it as he said, "And I still can't stay away from you," in a low, sensual voice that feathered Cassandra's spine.

"Have dinner with me tonight," Bram suggested. "We'll go to Springfield. Why not, Cassandra?" he persisted, now brushing the strand of her hair he held in petal-soft caresses against her cheek. "As you point out so often, I'll be leaving soon, and I'd rather spend what time we have together than apart."

Bram's voice and actions were imparting a languid sensuality into Cassandra's blood. Her hands had loosened on the picnic basket, the expression in her eyes was softening, and she was unconsciously beginning to lean toward Bram.

He accepted the signals she was giving him and leaned closer until their mouths were a breath apart.

"Say yes," he whispered in a gentle, coaxing tone.

"Yes," Cassandra obeyed, so caught up in her fascination with Bram's eyes and the temptation of his lips that she hardly knew what she was saying.

The light in his eyes deepened, and he smiled very slightly as he touched his mouth to Cassandra's in a kiss as soft as the brush of the wind, at first. On feeling her response, however, he slipped his hand around the back of her neck and held her with warm strokes of his fingers as he deepened the kiss, then teased her mouth gently, then deepened the kiss again.

Overwhelmed with need for him, Cassandra started to put her arms around his neck, but the picnic basket was in the way. Frustrated, she had to content herself merely with cupping his cheek with one hand.

At last, Bram drew back slightly, and as Cassandra looked into his heavy-lidded eyes, a light shudder went through her.

"I'll look forward to tonight," Bram murmured in a husky tone. "If we have differences, they aren't worth spoiling what happens when we touch."

Cassandra nodded. They kissed briefly again, then pulled reluctantly away from each other. Bram started the car and headed back toward town.

At the Stewart house, after Bram had stopped the car, they looked at each other, smiled and clasped hands for a moment before Cassandra opened the door.

"I'll pick you up at six," Bram said, his voice caressing her.

"I'll be ready," Cassandra replied and got out of the car.

It was only as she watched him driving away that she realized she had once again acted against her common sense, and that every moment she spent with Bram was one she might have to pay for when he was gone.

She took a deep breath and shrugged her shoulders in a gesture of fatalism. "So be it." She shaped the words with her lips but no sound escaped, and she quickly turned to enter the house. She intended to sort through her clothes for something to wear that night that might make Bram Palmer remember her when he returned to California and was faced with all the temptations a man of his attractiveness and wealth must inevitably meet.

Chapter Eight

Maxie was so preoccupied thinking about what had happened with Justin that day, she barely heard Bram tell her he wouldn't be home for dinner. It wasn't until he came downstairs dressed in a lightweight, tailored blue suit, white shirt and expensive tie that she came to attention.

Blinking with surprise as she looked him up and down, she asked, "What's the occasion for the splendor? Have you got a date with the governor?"

Bram smiled as he paused in front of a mirror on the wall to straighten his tie. "Hardly," he said lightly. "Someone a little closer to home. Cassy Stewart. I'm taking her to Springfield for dinner."

Maxie immediately felt ambivalent about the idea, and as Bram saw her expression in the mirror, he frowned a little and turned to face her.

"What's the matter?" he asked. "I thought you liked her."

Maxie looked away. "I do," she said hesitantly as she twisted her hands together. "I just don't understand why... well, Bram, you'll be going back to California soon and Cassy plans to stay here. Do you think it's wise to—" Maxie paused, thinking she was making more out of a simple date than was probably called for. Shrugging, she said,

"Oh, it doesn't matter. It's just a date, right? Nothing serious?"

Bram's frown deepened as he came closer to his sister and took her arm. Maxie looked up at him, and he didn't like the troubled look on her face.

"And if it developed into something serious?" he asked quietly. "Would there be something wrong with that, Maxie?"

Bram's question made Maxie uncomfortable. She wasn't certain herself why she should have any objections to a relationship between Bram and Cassy.

"No," she said slowly. "I suppose not."

She sounded anything but definite, and Bram pressed her.

"Come on, Maxie," he said dryly. "Something about it obviously upsets you. What is it? Why don't you like the idea of Cassy and me getting together? Is it because she's a Stewart?"

Maxie spread her hands in a helpless manner and moved away from Bram, turning her back to him as she walked to a wall and started straightening pictures while she tried to think.

Why should the idea of a member of her family getting involved with a Stewart bother her, she thought with self-directed irony, when she herself was so desperately attracted to Justin?

Finally, as Bram watched patiently, waiting for her to speak, though Maxie didn't want to accept her own shortcomings, she thought she understood what was behind her uneasiness at the thought of Bram and Cassy becoming seriously involved with each other. It was sheer selfishness. Given the sort of person Cassy was, there wouldn't be any hesitation on her part about marrying Bram because he was a Palmer. Any hesitation on her part would concern her commitment to the mill and the conflict of giving up that commitment in order to marry a man who lived halfway across the country.

But Justin was different—damnably, heartbreakingly different. He might become involved with a Palmer, all right. But his insufferable pride would most likely prevent him from marrying one. And she had promised to have an affair with him one day. If she followed through on that promise, Maxie had little doubt that the affair would escalate into an emotional commitment—on her part, at least. And since she would have little choice when that happened, other than to leave Barton's Corner and try to put Justin out of her heart and mind, it would make things just that more complicated if their families were tied together by a marriage between Bram and Cassy.

Despite the deep well of sadness Maxie's conclusion brought with it, she knew that she would never do anything to interfere, should things work out happily for Bram and Cassy.

Having identified what was going on inside her, Maxie immediately set about to erase the puzzled concern her reaction to Bram's announcement had caused him. Not for anything would she tell Bram, or anyone else, about the attraction she and Justin shared. For one thing, the people she was trying to help would certainly doubt her commitment if they knew. For another, she couldn't bear the thought of her family feeling sorry for her because she was foolish enough to desire a man unworthy of her love.

Turning around, she smiled at Bram naturally and said lightly, "You just took me by surprise, that's all. But now that I'm over the shock, I think it's wonderful that you and Cassy are attracted to each other. It couldn't have happened to two nicer people."

Bram felt doubtful about Maxie's sudden about-face. He didn't press her about it, though.

"I don't know how wonderful it is," he said with a wry smile. "There are a lot of problems connected with being attracted to a Stewart."

Maxie thought dryly, *You're telling me?* Aloud, however, she said, "If it's meant to be, you'll work things out. Now," she added as she started walking toward the kitchen, "I need to fix Dad's supper, and you need to get started on your date. Have a wonderful time, Bram." She smiled at him and patted his arm as she passed him.

Bram looked after her, still troubled by something he sensed was bothering Maxie beneath her surface cheerfulness. Then he cursed his thoughtlessness as he realized she might simply be lonely and in need of a good time herself. She had been stuck in this town too long, taking care of their father as well as working hard on her goals, and he doubted if she'd had much, if any, social life in all that time.

Bram wrestled with his selfish desire to be alone with Cassandra that evening, then realized he would worry about Maxie all night if he acted on his selfishness. Besides, after dinner, he and Cassy could bring Maxie home and then have some time alone together.

Quickly, he followed Maxie into the kitchen. She was tying an apron around her waist, and though she looked up at him with a smile, he wondered if the glimmer in her eyes might be tears.

"Maxie, come with us," he said firmly. "You can leave something for Dad to eat, but you need to get out and have some fun."

Maxie was extremely touched by the offer, but she merely scoffed at it aloud.

"Don't be silly!" She gave her brother an exasperated look. "What couple wants a third party hanging around their necks on a date? And besides," she added firmly when Bram started to argue, "I don't relish being a gooseberry. It doesn't fit my image."

She grinned at the last statement, encouraging Bram to lighten up, but she was dismayed when he got that stubborn, unbudging look she knew so well on his face. She watched as he crossed to the phone, looked up a number and started to dial.

"Now, Bram, what do you think you're doing?" she asked warily. "I assure you, I don't want to—"

Bram cut her off by holding up a hand as he said into the phone, "Mrs. Rutledge?" He had called the widow who lived a few houses down the street and had helped Harry Palmer out in the past before Maxie had come home. "Yes, this is Bram Palmer. Well, it's nice to hear your voice as well, Mrs. Rutledge. How are you?"

Bram listened for a moment as Maxie crossed to him and started tugging on his arm, making faces at him to tell him to stop what he was doing.

"That's wonderful, Mrs. Rutledge," Bram said, ignoring Maxie's actions. "I'm glad your grandchildren are doing so well. Now, Mrs. Rutledge, I wonder if you would do me a favor."

Maxie was now grabbing at the phone, but with his superior height, Bram evaded her efforts easily.

"Thank you, Mrs. Rutledge, I appreciate that," he said, holding Maxie off with one arm. "Would it be too much trouble for you to come over and fix Dad's dinner and keep him company for a while? Maxie and I have something to do, but we didn't want to leave him." Bram paused again, then with a wide smile on his face, said, "Thank you very much, Mrs. Rutledge. Maxie and I appreciate your help."

After saying goodbye, Bram hung up and turned to face his sister, who was fuming.

"Not a word!" he warned. He held up a hand then grabbed the ties of the apron around Maxie's waist and flipped it off her. She folded her arms and gave him a stubborn look while he inspected her appearance. "You look great." He nodded. "No need to change." And then he grabbed her arm and literally dragged her, sputtering all the way, outside to where Harry was sitting on a wooden bench enjoying the evening.

"Dad," Bram said as he dragged Maxie to a spot in front of their father, and Harry looked up at them with an affectionate smile on his face, "Maxie and I and Cassy Stewart are going over to Springfield for dinner. I've called Mrs. Rutledge to come and—"

"I'm not going!" Maxie interrupted, glaring at Bram.

"She's going," Bram calmly went on. "I'd be willing to bet she hasn't been anywhere to relax in months—right, Dad?"

"That's right, son." Harry nodded, and a fleeting look of guilt flickered in his eyes before he addressed his daughter firmly. "Now you hush up your hollerin', girl, and do what your brother says. If he wants to take you out, you go along politely, you hear?"

Maxie seethed, but since it was clear she wasn't going to get any help from her father, and Bram's grip on her arm was unrelenting, she had no choice.

"All right, I'll go," she said ungraciously, glaring at Bram again. "But I don't like it!"

"You will." He smiled complacently. "Thanks for the help, Dad." He grinned at his father, who was smiling fondly at the two of them, obviously enjoying a situation that reminded him of old times. "Mrs. Rutledge will be here in a few minutes," Bram added as he pulled Maxie with him toward his car. "We won't be late."

"Take as long as you like," Harry called after them. "The two of you are too big for me to issue curfews anymore." And his chuckles reached them both as Bram shoved Maxie into the passenger seat of the Jaguar and went around to the driver's side.

Maxie sat in stony silence on the way to the Stewart home. She was furious, not only that Bram had forced her to come along against her will but that he hadn't given her time to freshen her makeup and change clothes.

"Don't pout," Bram instructed as he pulled the Jaguar to a stop in the driveway outside the Stewart house. "The idea is to have fun. If you're going to be a gooseberry, at least be a cheerful one."

Maxie jerked her head around, a look of furious indignation on her face, but Bram was grinning broadly and that took the wind out of her sails. She settled for sticking her tongue out at him.

"'Atta girl," he said with a satisfied nod. "I knew you couldn't stay mad."

Before Maxie could sputter an indignant reply to that, Bram was out of the car and striding up to the Stewart front door, which Mary Louise opened to him a few seconds later.

"Good evening, Mrs. Stewart," Bram said with a warm smile. "It's nice to see you again."

"And it's very nice to see you again, Bram." Mary Louise smiled just as warmly back at him. "Come in. Cassy will be ready in a few minutes."

Bram followed Mary Louise as she led him into the family den, which Bram found as attractive as any room he'd ever seen, with its thick walnut paneling and the cheerful light of a fire in the grate, but he forgot about his admiration for the room when a tall man he recognized stood up and turned around.

Mary Louise wisely stayed silent as her son and Bram Palmer faced each other for the first time in years and stood inspecting each other with carefully unrevealing expressions on their faces.

For his part, Bram felt curious, as well as slightly uncomfortable. He'd forgotten about the possibility of running into Jussie, and now that he had, he looked carefully for any signs of hostility on his old enemy's face.

Had Bram showed up at his home before the afternoon he'd spent with Maxie, Justin very well might have been hard put to mind his manners and display at least a minimum of courtesy to this man who had caused him a great deal of frustration and embarrassment in the past, and whom he wasn't at all sure he wanted dating his sister, though there wasn't anything he could do about it, given Cassandra's independent nature and Mary Louise's enthusiastic encouragement of the match.

But he was more curious than anything, for the moment. After taking in Bram's expensive suit, good looks and natural air of confidence, his old jealousy niggled at him a little, but not as strongly as it had in the past.

"Bram," he finally said, his voice uninflected, as he stepped around his chair and came to hold out a hand.

"Hello, Jussie." Bram unconsciously used Justin's old nickname as he took the proffered hand and shook it. "How are you? It's been a long time."

"I'm fine," Justin answered, wondering if Bram had meant anything other than a polite inquiry in asking how he was. He must have heard from Maxie, if not from Cassy, that things could be better.

"I'm glad to hear it," Bram said quietly, and Justin was surprised to find that he believed in Bram's sincerity.

An uncomfortable pause resulted, which Mary Louise filled by inviting Bram to sit down. After they were settled, she naturally inquired after Bram's family.

"How are your father and sister, Bram?" Mary Louise said. "I understand Maxie is taking care of Harry."

"They're fine." Bram smiled at Mary Louise's refusal to mention the rest of what Maxie was doing in Barton's Corner. He wondered how Justin was taking the mention of

Maxie. So far he had surprised Bram by minding his manners.

"Yes, Maxie's taking care of Dad," Bram said smoothly, following his hostess's lead in refusing to comment on Maxie's union activities. "She's out in the car right now. I persuaded her to come with Cassy and me to dinner. She doesn't get the opportunity to have much of a social life."

Bram had his head turned toward Mary Louise and missed the sudden attentiveness in Justin's manner.

"But why didn't she come in?" Mary Louise asked with surprise and a certain amount of indignation as she made a move to get to her feet. "We can't leave her out there."

Justin was up before his mother could gain her feet. "I'll see to it, Mother," he said, and was out the door so quickly, Mary Louise didn't have time to thank him.

Bram was surprised by the alacrity with which Justin had made his offer and acted upon it, and he wondered uneasily how Maxie would take having Justin come to the car for her. But surely Justin wouldn't do or say anything impolite in a social situation. It was more likely that Maxie would.

It was hard for Bram to concentrate as Mary Louise chatted companionably with him, and it would have been harder if he could have witnessed the scene going on outside the house right then.

When Justin unceremoniously pulled the passenger door of the Jaguar open, Maxie reacted by turning her head toward him in a startled manner. And when Justin leaned inside, bringing his mouth within an inch of hers, her breath literally stopped in her throat.

"I can't believe my good fortune," Justin murmured, a teasing light in his blue eyes. "I didn't think I'd see you again until Monday, and then we'd have to act as though we still hated each other."

Maxie swallowed and drew her head back, though the temptation of Justin's mouth was hard to resist.

"I'm not sure I've stopped hating you," she said shakily as she remembered the conclusions she'd reached about Justin a mere half hour ago.

Justin frowned and lifted a hand to stroke her cheek. "Don't, Maxie," he said softly. "I thought we were past that." As though to jog her memory, he touched her mouth with his, lightly, with tender honesty, which was exactly the tactic to undermine Maxie's logic and throw her back on her emotions.

He had her trapped, and she couldn't have moved away if her willpower had been up to it, and Justin continued stroking her mouth with his, tracing it delicately with his tongue from time to time before resuming his gentle kiss.

At last, breathing heavily, he withdrew a little and inspected the dazed, softened look in Maxie's eyes.

"You don't hate me, Maxie," he whispered. "You can't pretend you do."

Maxie shut her eyes against the desire and warm longing in Justin's, and he smiled, wanting her so much, he could barely restrain himself.

"Come inside, Maxie," he said on a deep breath. "My mother sent me out to get you." He took her arm to help her out of the car.

Maxie's eyes flew open, the expression in them incredulous.

Resisting Justin's tug on her arm, she said, "Oh, no," and lifted her chin in a proud expression. "The last time I was a guest at your home, I was informed I wouldn't be welcome again. I remember, even if you don't."

Justin frowned, at first failing to understand what Maxie was talking about. But then, as he dimly remembered a summer day a long time in the past when he and his father had watched Maxie and Cassy swimming together, a feeling of shame and regret filled him as he realized she had a right to feel as she did.

"Maxie, if you know anything about my mother, you know she wasn't the one who didn't want you here," he said heavily and hesitated before adding, with simple honesty tinged with regret, "but you're right that I agreed with my father's views concerning your and Cassy's friendship. I'm sorry. I was a fool, and I hope you'll forgive me for it."

Immediately distrustful, Maxie stared into Justin's eyes, and what she saw there plunged her into confusion. He seemed sincere. But the sincerity was probably only the result of his present physical desire for her. She couldn't afford to believe he had changed as much as he seemed to want her to believe. The stakes were too high.

"Justin, we can learn to behave differently," she said quietly, "but it's harder to change our basic natures. I'm not able to yet, and I can't believe you have. I'm sorry, but I don't think I could be comfortable in your family's home . . . not yet."

Frustration welled in Justin at Maxie's stubbornness, frustration and a niggling worry over whether she might be right about his basic nature. Things were happening so quickly, his ideas were being assaulted by others, and now he was questioning them himself.

Since Maxie had come back to Barton's Corner to fight him at every turn, he had been forced to develop respect for her abilities as well as her attributes as a woman. And in his deepest soul he had never really been able to believe in his superiority over Bram Palmer, though he had pretended to himself he did. But was Maxie right? Beneath his infatuation for her, his desire to have her in his bed, his respect for her mind and talent as an attorney, did part of him still think of her as inferior?

Justin became aware that Maxie was watching him out of those fascinating green eyes of hers, which now contained a dawning awareness of the conflict within him.

Quickly straightening to get away from that look of hers, Justin leaned his hands on the top of the Jaguar and stared blindly at nothing as he tried to sort out his feelings. It didn't take long, and he ducked back down to face Maxie again.

"Maxie," he began in a voice firmly urgent, "I may not be the way you'd like me to be yet, and maybe I won't ever be. But, Maxie—" his tone became more urgent, almost pleading, which astonished her "—don't throw away the power you have over me. Use it! What happens between us is enough to pry any man's character out of the concrete it's been set in. Can you at least believe that I'm worth an effort?"

Touched by Justin's plea and shaken by his reference to the power she had over him, Maxie stared at him, her inner confusion in her eyes. But then the thought occurred to her that a man in the grip of an infatuation behaved one way. When he surfaced from it, he went back to being his normal self. Suppose Justin went so far in his present infatuation as to propose marriage to her, and suppose she was foolish enough to accept. How could a relationship between them work if he someday reverted to his type?

As Maxie remained silent, Justin sighed. He hadn't really expected to break down all the barriers between them on the basis of one shared, glorious afternoon. He hadn't expected it, but he had made the mistake of hoping for it.

"I know it's hard, Maxie," he said levelly. "I guess we both need time to come to terms with what's happening between us. You don't have to come in if you don't want to."

Maxie was aware of a slight feeling of disappointment, which made no sense, when she'd had no intention of entering the Stewart house, even if Justin had continued to insist upon it.

"You don't have to come in," Justin repeated thoughtfully, "but that doesn't mean I can't come with you."

"What?" Maxie exclaimed, startled by Justin's constantly changing manner. She would have given much, for the moment, if he would stop making things harder for her and remain the same old snobbish, proud, insensitive, ruthless Justin Stewart.

At that moment, the door to the house opened and Cassy and Bram appeared in the doorway with Mary Louise behind them. Justin straightened up as Cassy and Bram came down the steps to the car, while Mary Louise stayed where she was.

Both his sister and Bram were looking at him quizzically, which made Justin smile in a wry fashion.

"We were wondering what had happened to you," Cassy said lightly, "and since it's getting late, we decided to come see."

Justin's smile broadened, and he said with light good humor, "I was trying to talk Maxie into inviting me to come along with you." He heard a soft gasp come from the interior of the car, but it didn't stop him. "How about it?" he said in a calm manner. "I don't have much of a social life myself, and I could use a night out."

Cassy and Bram unconsciously looked at each other with surprised wariness, each wondering what sort of an evening it would turn out to be in the company of two sworn enemies.

Bram recovered first. "Of course you're invited, Justin," he said with easy equanimity. "But you'd better tell your mother."

Aware of the worries and undercurrents all around him, but feeling mischievous and determined, Justin nodded. "Won't take me a minute," he said lightly and strode toward where his mother was waiting at the door.

When he faced Mary Louise, Justin grinned down at her puzzled expression. "I'm going with them, Mother," he said, leaning down to peck her cheek. "Don't wait up for us. We might be late."

"I doubt it," Mary Louise responded with anxious amazement, grabbing Justin's arm when he would have turned away. "Justin, behave yourself, will you?" she said on a pleading note. "Don't spoil everyone's evening by showing your hostility to Bram and Maxie."

Justin raised his brows as though his mother's attitude surprised him. "What hostility?" he quipped, his grin cocky. And when his reply didn't satisfy Mary Louise, he reached for her and hugged her briefly. "Don't worry, Mom," he whispered. "I promise I'll make you proud of me tonight."

Then he was off, leaving Mary Louise staring anxiously after him, clearly disbelieving his promise.

When Justin and Maxie were settled in the back seat of the Jaguar and Bram and Cassy in the front, and Bram had started the engine and was pulling out of the driveway, Justin surreptitiously reached over and took Maxie's hand in his own. When she jerked and tried to pull her hand away, he smiled at her and leaned close, squeezing her hand to reassure her.

"Don't worry," he murmured with laughter in his voice. "I promised Mother I'd be nice to you. I didn't tell her how much of a pleasure it would be to treat you the way you deserve."

And as he straightened up and looked out the window with a secret smile on his handsome face, Maxie was left to wonder what sort of treatment Justin thought she deserved—that of a desirable woman, or the sort he would display toward any ordinary enemy.

Chapter Nine

The drive to Springfield took forty-five minutes, and Cassandra, alarmed by the silence in the back seat, carried the bulk of the conversation, concentrating on uncontroversial topics. She was disappointed not to be spending the evening alone with Bram, but considering the danger to her equilibrium he represented, she wondered if perhaps it was better that they had chaperons—even if the chaperons might end up at each other's throats before the evening was over.

The restaurant in Springfield was very nice, almost on a par with ones Cassy had patronized in New York. When they were seated and had ordered, however, the four of them looked at one another somewhat awkwardly. Then Justin grinned at his sister.

"Don't worry," he teased. "You aren't going to have to rattle on throughout dinner the way you did in the car to keep Maxie and me from getting into a fight." He directed a mischievous glance at Maxie, who was keeping a blank look on her face, and added, "We've called a truce for this evening, and I promise not to break it if she won't."

Maxie's eyes flashed a disgruntled message at him, but when she looked over at Cassy and saw the strain on her face, she shrugged. "Far be it from me to tear down a white flag," she said lightly. "I'm game." She looked at the other three with a slight smile on her lips. "So what shall we talk about that won't make for a miserable evening?"

Again, Justin surprised everybody, including himself. Looking at Bram, he said, "Well, I, for one, would like to hear about Bram's computer company. I don't know much about computers. There doesn't seem to be much use for them in my business." Leaning back in his chair, Justin sipped at his wine while waiting for Bram to reply.

"But there are applications for one in your business, Jussie," Bram said. "For instance, your office procedures could be automated. A program could be designed to fit your specific bookkeeping, personnel and inventory-record needs. I think you'd be surprised at how much time and money could be saved if you had a computer system tailored for you."

Always interested in anything having to do with making his company more efficient, Justin momentarily forgot about resenting Bram and discussed the matter with him as though he were any other knowledgeable person who might be of help.

Maxie and Cassandra, who had tensed up when Justin had introduced the subject, each thinking that Justin probably meant to make some disparaging remarks about Bram's expertise, relaxed as the conversation went on without unpleasant overtones. Occasionally, they exchanged amused, understanding glances with each other.

Finally, Bram caught them at it and grimaced before looking at Justin with amusement in his eyes. "I think we've been dominating the conversation a little too long, Jussie," he said.

Maxie spoke up, but her tone was agreeable. "You certainly have," she said. "I've been wondering for ten minutes what's keeping our dinner."

As Bram and Justin automatically looked up in search of their waiter, they spotted the man hurrying toward them with a huge tray on his shoulder.

"Ask and ye shall receive," Justin said to Maxie, looking into her eyes so that she would understand his silent message. He was delighted when she looked away in an embarrassed fashion, while the beautiful smooth skin of her face flushed a flattering pink, and he settled back in his chair with a pleased smile on his face as the waiter distributed the food.

When everyone had been served and the waiter had left, the four of them began to eat, and conversation was at a minimum, other than comments on the excellence of the filets mignons. When they reached the dessert stage, however, Justin noticed that Bram and Cassy quite often had eyes only for each other, and it was obvious from the glances they were exchanging that their relationship had progressed far beyond what he had thought would be possible in the short time that Bram had been back in Barton's Corner.

Justin sat frowning, disturbed by the electricity sparking between Bram and Cassy. Surely, considering what Cassy had in mind concerning the family business, there couldn't be anything serious between them. Bram would be going back to California soon...wouldn't he?

"How long are you going to be here, Bram?" he asked casually.

Bram turned away from looking into Cassy's eyes. He was regretting heartily that he had asked Maxie to come along with them, and that Justin had invited himself along. There was nothing he wanted more at the moment than to be alone with Cassy.

"I'm not sure," he replied, aware that he was becoming more and more reluctant to think about returning to California.

"How long can you stay away from your business?" Justin persisted. Bram's manner made it obvious what was on his mind.

Bram shrugged. "Well, not forever," he said wryly. "But I have good people working under me, and my partner can handle things for a while."

Justin wasn't satisfied, but there was no point in badgering Bram, so he fell silent, examining his feelings about a serious relationship developing between his sister and Bramwell Palmer. In a way, he thought, if the two of them should fall in love and Cassy left Barton's Corner, it would be the end of one of his problems. But he was surprised to find that he didn't look forward to that as much as he should have, and upon thinking about it, he realized that no matter how much he and Cassy clashed in their ideas about running the family firm, he was beginning to want her help. Maybe she could do something about quelling the unrest among the employees that was keeping production down.

Glancing at Bram again, Justin studied him objectively, realizing as he did so that it wasn't surprising Cassy found him attractive. Even when he was a teenager, the girls had swarmed around Bram Palmer, and he had more to offer now than he had then.

Which left the question of how he felt about having Bram as a brother-in-law, should things develop that far between his sister and his old nemesis. And his feelings were complex. While he wanted Cassy to have a happy marriage, would he have to spend the rest of his life actively aware of Bram's successes if Bram became a member of the family? Out of sight, out of mind, had been his mode of dealing with the rivalry over the past few years, but a brother-in-law would be hard to ignore.

Justin glanced at Maxie and found her eyes on him, the expression in them perceptive. It surprised him that she seemed to be able to read his mind, and while it pleased him in a way, it was also an uncomfortable feeling when his thoughts were ones he'd prefer she didn't know about.

Suddenly it dawned on Justin that something was happening he wouldn't have believed possible in a million years. Both he and Cassy were seemingly enamored of a couple of Palmers! God, his father would turn over in his grave if he knew!

But he won't know, and Mother won't mind at all, Justin thought with wry amusement. *The question is, do I mind?*

He wasn't certain, and he became too absorbed in looking at Maxie to continue thinking about it. He was unaware, as was Maxie, that Bram and Cassy were neglecting each other for the moment to stare at the two of them with fascinated disbelief.

Cassy turned her eyes to Bram and raised her brows, asking him silently if he was getting the same impression she was.

Bram barely raised his shoulders in reply, but there was a thoughtful look in his eyes. *God help Maxie if she's fallen for a man like Jussie,* he thought with heavy dread. *There's not much chance of a happy ending there.*

The possibility put a damper on Bram's mood. He couldn't believe Maxie would be so foolish, but the evidence was there before his eyes as she gazed at Justin with a curious mixture of longing and rejection.

He'll take everything he can get and leave her with a broken heart, Bram thought, his protectiveness toward his sister raising a deep anger inside him. *Surely she knows that.*

Determining that he would talk to Maxie later, Bram returned his attention to Cassy, who, sensitive to his mood, was looking at him as though she'd like to take him into her arms. Immediately, Bram forgot everything else in his desire to have her do just that, and again he cursed the fact that they were not alone.

"More coffee?" The waiter unobtrusively set a salver containing the check on the table, then hovered with his carafe, capturing the attention of everyone at the table. All of them, as though by mutual consent, shook their heads and the waiter scurried away.

"Are we finished?" Bram asked, reaching for the check just as Justin did the same. The two men paused and looked at each other, while Cassy and Maxie exchanged alarmed looks, expecting the uneasy calm of the evening to erupt with a vengeance with a fight over the check.

As Bram and Justin stared into each other's faces, each was aware of the symbolism of paying this particular check. Then Bram broke the impasse, saying quietly, "We invited you, remember?"

Justin hesitated an instant longer, then sat back with a nod. Cassy and Maxie heaved silent sighs of relief, grateful that the issue had been resolved so simply.

In the car returning home, silence reigned for the most part. Bram was trying to think of a way to have some time alone with Cassy, who wanted the same, and Maxie was trying to think of a way not to have time alone with Justin, who was achingly aware of every delectable scent and gracious movement of the woman at his side, and wanted nothing more than to have her to himself, undisturbed, long enough to tear down the barriers he suspected she had again erected against him.

As Bram turned the car into the Stewart driveway, Justin made up his mind. He'd be damned if he'd spend the night tossing and turning and burning with a fever for a woman who reached him on such a visceral level that he couldn't think straight. The fever might have to go undampened for a while longer, but he could do something to quench the fire temporarily.

Reaching over, he clamped his fingers over Maxie's wrist in an unbreakable grip and refused to release her when she tried to pull away.

"Mother would like to see Maxie, Bram," he spoke in a level tone. "If you'd like to get home, I can bring her along later."

Bram and Cassy exchanged a look, and in answer to the desire in Bram's eyes, it was Cassy who replied.

Clearing her throat, she said as casually as she could manage, "As a matter of fact, Jussie, Bram and I have something to discuss. We'll wait out here for Maxie, all right?"

"Fine," Justin said, looking into Maxie's eyes in a way that dared her to say what she was thinking, while he tightened his hold on her and opened his door. Pulling her with him, he literally hauled her out of the car.

"Thanks for the dinner, Bram," he said before shutting the car door. "I enjoyed it."

"You're welcome, Jussie," Bram replied, his expression troubled. While Maxie hadn't said anything, he'd sensed her reluctance. But an instant after Justin and Maxie walked away, Cassy claimed all of his attention.

"I haven't had a chance to tell you how beautiful you look tonight," he said to her. He stroked her shoulder with tactile enjoyment, while his eyes admired the sophisticated blue silk dress she wore, as well as the svelte figure inside it.

Cassandra was pleased by his compliment. She had spent a long time dressing especially for him that evening. She was also affected by the warm touch of his hand on her shoulder. It amazed her how strongly she reacted to such small gestures when Bram was the one who made them.

"Thank you," she replied in a soft voice, her smile unconsciously inviting. "And you look wonderful in a suit, Bram," she added with warm teasing. "Somehow I suspected you would."

Bram's hand moved to her neck. He wanted to pull her up along the length of his body, but the console between their seats was in the way, frustrating him. In order to distract himself from the desire, he mentioned Justin and Maxie.

"Did you get the same impression I did tonight?" he asked, nodding his head toward the house. "That there's something personal going on between Justin and Maxie?"

"Yes," Cassandra replied, not altogether pleased at the change in subject. "It's hard to believe, but the awareness seems to be there between them."

Bram frowned. "God, I hope not!" he said forcefully, startling Cassandra.

"Why?" she asked, and at his expression, she grimaced slightly. "I mean aside from the fact that they're mortal enemies in a business sense. Otherwise, they make a nice couple. There's something ... electric between them, don't you think?"

Bram felt impatient with her. "I don't want my sister hurt by a man like Jussie," he declared, and there was a definite tinge of contempt in his voice when he said Jussie's name.

Cassandra stiffened a little. While it was true that she disagreed strongly with Justin about a lot of things, he was her brother, and her family loyalty and pride were stung by Bram's attitude.

"Bram, be careful," she said in a low voice of warning.

He looked at her, puzzled by her tone. "What do you mean?"

She stared at him, her expression withdrawn. "Justin's my brother, Bram," she pointed out quietly, "and I love him just as you love Maxie. And while I may not agree with him about a lot of things, I don't like to hear him spoken of with contempt."

Bram took her point, but he felt frustrated. Cassandra had been very adamant that she wasn't like her father or her brother. Yet here she was, defending Jussie. It strengthened his inner conviction that no matter how much Cassandra protested her difference from them, blood was thicker than water. He sat back, taking his hand from her shoulder, his expression distant.

"There you go again," Cassandra said in a tight voice. And when Bram merely looked at her, she gave a little sound of frustration. "My God, Bram! What are we doing sitting here together? We always seem to end up arguing about the same thing. Can't you accept that while I disagree with Justin about how to run the company, and I never agreed with him or my father about class distinctions, they are members of my family, and I love them despite our differences?"

Intellectually, Bram understood. Emotionally, he was trapped in the past. "Since you admit that Justin does have definite ideas about class distinctions, can't you see how he might hurt Maxie?" he demanded. "You consider her a friend. If Justin weren't your brother, would you encourage her to get involved with him, knowing how he feels about our family?"

"If Maxie cares for Justin," Cassandra said stiffly, "I don't imagine it would do me or anyone else any good to warn her about him. I have plenty of reasons to think it isn't a good idea to get involved with you, but I can't seem to help myself. The moment I see you or you touch me, it's as if I don't have a scrap of common sense."

She stopped speaking abruptly, reacting both to her own anger and her embarrassment at having confessed her feelings so blatantly, and to the stillness that came over Bram as a result of her words. She assumed he would take them negatively, rather than focusing on her last statement. She was taken by surprise when, acting out of frustration, she started to open her car door and Bram reached across to wrap his fingers around her upper arm, preventing her from getting out.

She looked at him warily, not knowing what to expect.

"I seem always to be apologizing to you," he said half angrily. But then his expression softened and he pulled her closer. Cassandra didn't resist, but she stiffened her body against the desire to yield completely to him.

Bram looked into Cassandra's eyes, disliking the wariness he saw there, just as he disliked the stiffness he felt in her body.

"Cassandra...Cassy..." He shook his head, his voice soft. "I've never been like this about a woman before."

"Like what?" Cassandra couldn't resist asking, and there was the slightest relaxation of tension in her muscles that Bram felt.

Bram smiled in a self-mocking way as he prepared to confess his feelings as blatantly as Cassandra had. "Consumed with the need to be with her—you," he corrected himself, speaking in a voice as soft and sensual as dark velvet. "Delighted with the way you look, your smile, your warmth, your intelligence. Did you know that when I kiss you, I feel it down to my toes? I think I may be becoming obsessed with you. I keep wondering if this is how it feels to be in love. I've never been in love before, so I'm not sure."

Cassandra had softened with every word of Bram's confession. "I haven't, either," she said, "and I've been wondering the same thing."

But when Bram smiled and leaned closer to kiss her, Cassandra placed a light, restraining hand against his chest.

"But you left out something," she added, her gaze troubled. When Bram frowned slightly, she explained. "You left out the fact that you don't trust me...and how can you love someone you don't trust, Bram?"

Her quiet question pierced his heart, and Bram stayed silent for a moment, studying her lovely face, which now expressed such vulnerability.

"Are you going to remain victimized by the past all your life, Bram?" Cassandra asked so softly, that Bram could barely hear her.

He understood what she was saying, however. He understood and became determined, somehow, to stop tainting what they'd found together with his preoccupation over who she was. "I hope not," he said with quiet sincerity. "God, I hope not, Cassy!"

Abruptly, he pulled her closer and found her mouth, kissing her with a hunger that was heightened by his underlying feeling that they might have too little time together, too little time to overcome the obstacles in the path of a full-blown relationship between them.

Cassandra kissed him back, unable to do anything else. It was exactly as she'd explained to Bram earlier. Whenever he touched her, her common sense dissolved, and she was ruled by emotion and desire for him.

"Damn this car!" Bram muttered against her cheek, half ruefully, half angrily, a moment later. He wanted to feel all of Cassandra against him, the way he had the first time he'd kissed her and the way he had that afternoon. "Come on!" he said with soft impatience. "Let's go for a walk."

But of course, they didn't walk far. Only to the shadows of the nearest tree, where Bram pulled Cassandra against him and wrapped her in an embrace that left her longing to be even closer to him, and kissed her with a fervor that left her breathless and aching for all of his love, as he was aching for hers.

MAXIE HAD PULLED AWAY from Justin's grip without loosening it as he hauled her to the door of the house, opened it and thrust her inside. When the door had closed behind him, Maxie pivoted and gave him a look that would have withered a lesser man.

"Let go of me," she said in a violent hiss so that his mother, if she was within listening range, wouldn't hear her.

"Not yet," Justin said softly, pulling her into his arms.

"Jussie, your mother—" Maxie protested, but Justin cut her words off with his mouth.

The kiss was hungry on Justin's part, but Maxie was too angry at him, and too worried that his mother might discover them, to participate the way Justin wanted her to.

At last, he raised his head to find Maxie glaring into his eyes.

"Maxie, Mother's gone to bed," he whispered urgently. "She always retires early, so she won't be walking in on us. Kiss me back."

Seizing her mouth again, he was able to elicit a more rewarding response this time, but he could feel Maxie's reluctance to give one at all, and he finally stopped kissing her and rested his forehead against hers for a moment while he held her close and thought out what he was going to do. When he had, he lifted his head and looked into her eyes, his own containing a mixture of desire, perplexity and resentment.

"All right, Maxie," he said in a grating, exasperated tone. "Maybe you'll believe how serious I am when I tell you I'll hire that incompetent pipsqueak Manion back. I'll have to grit my teeth every time I go out to the shop and wade through the piles of sawdust he creates, and he'll cost the company more than he's ever going to be worth, but as a gesture of reconciliation, I'll force myself to accept it. Does that satisfy you?"

Stunned by a capitulation from Justin she had never dreamed of obtaining, Maxie stared at him in amazement. She was both touched and exasperated.

"Justin, you can't throw bribes at me like that, instead of exercising simple justice because it's the right thing to do," she snapped.

Justin raised his eyes to the ceiling as though praying for help. When he looked back at her, his blue eyes glinted with anger.

"What's just about paying a man to cost you money?" he demanded in a barely contained whisper. "If you had a practice and hired a law clerk or a secretary or even another attorney who couldn't do the job, would you keep the person on, when you could hire someone a lot better?"

Maxie hesitated. Her prejudice against Justin's methods was so ingrained, and her habit of arguing with him so firmly entrenched, it was hard to grant him a point.

"Is he really incompetent?" she asked, her voice quieter now.

Justin sighed. "Maxie, does it make any sense to you that I would fire someone who was *good* at his job?" he asked wearily.

"It would if he did other things you didn't like," Maxie persisted.

Justin shook his head. "This kid is too dumb to do anything I don't like, other than screw up the simple job of planing a damned board."

Maxie hesitated, then had an idea. "Could you try him at something else?" she suggested.

"I wouldn't let him near an expensive piece of wood with anything more damaging than a piece of cloth," Justin grated.

Maxie's face fell, then brightened. "How about a broom?" she asked, her mouth quirking into a smile. "Could he do much damage sweeping up other people's sawdust?"

Justin thought about it, then shook his head. "He might be able to handle that, if nothing else, Maxie, but it would mean putting old Bill Sampson out of a job, and he's got a few years yet until retirement. You can't ask me to fire Bill, can you?"

Maxie shook her head, her expression disappointed.

"Maxie," Justin said more gently as he took her face into his hands, "we may have our differences, but if you'll put your prejudices aside for a moment and check your facts, you'll learn that while my people have some gripes about pay and benefits, there's not one of them who believes I don't respect competency. I've never fired a man who didn't deserve it, and as much as it may hurt you to accept it, some people deserve to be fired. It may be because they're simply trying to do something they have no talent for, in which case getting fired may be a blessing in disguise if it forces them to look for something they may be good at. But even if there's nothing they're good at, it isn't reasonable to expect me to pay them without getting anything in return. Well, is it?" he demanded an answer from her when she was silent.

Maxie still hesitated, thinking about the example he'd given her about law clerks or other employees she might someday have.

"I suppose not," she finally admitted in a low voice, and when she felt Justin's body relax with relief at having won at least one concession from her, she looked up at him with a firm gaze. "But your people have a right to complain about their pay and benefits, Justin. You aren't fair with them and never have been." She held up a hand to stop him from saying anything when he opened his mouth to reply. "I'll back off about Manion," she conceded. "But I'll never back off on the other things I'm fighting for, Justin. Never."

For a long moment they looked at each other, and then Justin slowly nodded. "All right," he agreed. "I can accept that." And then it was his turn to stop her from speaking. "I won't accept a union," he said firmly, "but I'll listen to your ideas." He hesitated, then shrugged. "And Cassy's," he added grudgingly, "and see if we can't come up with something short of that."

Maxie couldn't believe her ears. She had no intention, of course, of ceasing to fight for a union, but until this moment she had believed Justin would never concede anything unless forced to it by the strongest measures, and then he would kick and scream rather than accept defeat with good grace. She thought about the reasons for his about-face, and there was only one conclusion to come to.

"You're doing this for me?" she asked hesitantly.

Justin gave her a grim smile. "What difference does it make?" he asked. "If I am, would that make the offer unacceptable?"

"I'd rather you did it because you believe sincerely that it's the right thing to do," Maxie said soberly. "Otherwise, you may someday change your mind, especially—"

She stopped and looked away; Justin frowned at her until he figured out what was on her mind. "Otherwise," he said with soft dryness, "after I've made love to you and gotten it out of my system, I'll revert back to the old rotten Justin?"

"Something like that," Maxie whispered.

Angered by her opinion of him, though it was nothing new, Justin stubbornly decided he wouldn't give her the reassurance she obviously wanted.

"Take what you can get, Maxie," he advised her. "If you're so dedicated to getting the workers what you think they need, take it any way you can get it. If it makes you feel any better, I doubt I could get away with taking anything from the employees, once they've gotten used to better times. That would be playing right into your hands. A union would surely be voted in in that case."

Maxie looked up at him, her expression sad. "You got away with it once," she reminded him.

Justin froze for a moment before his anger, fueled by guilt perhaps, roared into life full force and he stepped back and threw the door open.

"Go home, Maxie!" he grated. "If you prefer our old method of dealing with each other, you've got it. Anything to please a *lady*."

Stiffening, Maxie gave him a frozen look; then without a word, she swept by him and left the house, flinching involuntarily as the door slammed behind her. She wasn't sure who had been the bigger fool this night, she or Justin, and at the moment, she didn't care.

Bram had heard the door of the house slam, and as Maxie stumbled toward the car, he released Cassy and hurriedly came to meet her. Cassy followed close behind him.

"What is it, honey?" he asked Maxie as he met her by the car and held her. At seeing the glint of tears in her eyes, he rasped in a dangerous tone, "Did he hurt you?"

The grimness in Bram's voice woke Maxie to the need for discretion.

"Justin Stewart?" She tilted her chin proudly and replied in a scathing tone of dismissal. "He couldn't hurt me if he used every penny in his bloated bank account and every muscle in his overgrown body. No, he didn't hurt me, Bram," she said fiercely as she pulled out of his grip, passed a wide-eyed Cassy and patted her arm, then slid into the front seat of the Jaguar.

But as she sat stiffly, staring straight ahead through the windshield while she blinked back her tears and waited for Bram and Cassy to say good-night, a devastating thought pierced her heart like a lance.

But he did hurt me, she acknowledged as she turned her face to look at the blank door separating her from the man who was coming to mean altogether too much to her, a man who had reversed some of his lifelong principles for her sake, only to have her throw his offer back in his face. *And I hurt him,* she acknowledged, stricken by the realization that hurting Justin, far from being satisfying, left her sharing his hurt in a way only loved ones did.

"Oh, my God," she whispered, stunned by the revelation. "What a fool I've been. What a total, inexcusable fool."

Chapter Ten

"Well, Maxie, I confess, I'm not sure how to advise you."

It was long past midnight and Maxie, at Bram's urging had told him everything that had been happening between herself and Justin.

As they sat at the kitchen table drinking coffee, Bram studied Maxie's pale, tired face and saw that his words had disappointed her.

"If Jussie were any other man," Bram said with slow thoughtfulness, "I'd probably tell you to give him the benefit of the doubt, take what he's offered—which you have to admit is a big concession for him—and continue to work on his softer side in the hope that he'll someday act from his own principles rather than yours. And maybe that's what you should do." He shrugged tiredly and leaned back in his chair.

"But you're having trouble getting past the fact that this is Justin Stewart we're talking about," Maxie said, "whom we've been accustomed to view in a certain way all of our lives, instead of a stranger whose history we don't know so well."

Bram smiled slightly and nodded. "I guess you're right," he said. "And I'm not really happy to admit that, since I resent the idea of anyone judging me on my past instead of taking into account what I've done with my life since I left here. Yet, here I am judging Justin by *his* past.''

Maxie looked at Bram curiously. "Why should you mind having anyone judge you by your past?" she asked with genuine puzzlement. "You were always an achiever, and that hasn't changed." As Bram looked at her in surprise because she had just given him an entirely new perspective on his secret resentment, Maxie added, "But until a short few hours ago, Jussie's behavior didn't justify our perceiving him any differently than we did in the past. It would take a little time to believe in the sincerity of his change, even if he hadn't done an about-face and gone back to his original position only minutes after making his offer.''

But Maxie felt a little guilty about voicing that last statement. She knew why Justin had changed his mind so quickly, and that it was mostly her fault that he had.

"Why not sleep on it," Bram suggested. It was late and he was tired, as was Maxie, but he really needed some time to think about the insight Maxie had given him on one of his own problems.

"All right," Maxie agreed with a sigh, pushing back her chair to get up. "Not that we'll get much sleep," she added with a rueful smile as she carried their coffee cups to the sink. "Dad will insist we go to church in the morning, you know.''

Bram felt startled. In his youth he had attended church regularly. Actually, he'd had no choice in the matter, since his parents had insisted on it. But since he'd been away from home, especially during the years when he'd worked so hard to get his business going, he'd gotten out of the habit.

He shrugged as he got to his feet as well and followed Maxie upstairs. After all, he was getting impatient to start a family of his own, and when he did, it would be his turn to see that his children had a spiritual, as well as a secular, education.

As he lay in bed in his attic room later that night, Bram sought to clarify and build on the thought that had occurred to him when Maxie had said, in effect, that he hadn't changed all that much since he'd grown up in Barton's Corner. If he hadn't, was it logical to assume that the people in the town had recognized his worth even back then? Certainly, those old men he'd talked to on Friday had given the impression they had.

Bram then thought about the fact that Justin, Sr., had offered to send him to college in return for a promise to come back and work for him. The man hadn't been known for his generosity, and as far as Bram knew, Justin, Sr., had never made that offer to anyone else before or after Bram's time.

And Mary Louise Stewart had remembered him immediately, especially the fact that he'd beaten her son out for things Justin, Jr., had badly wanted. But she hadn't seemed to resent him for that, and moreover, she treated him with a respect and warmth Bram didn't think she was faking.

And Cassy…Bram immediately felt a surge of desire just thinking about her. Cassandra freely admitted that she'd had a schoolgirl crush on him years earlier, and it had been she who had sought him out before he even knew who she was on his first day back in town. But was that attraction absolutely free of reservations about his background?

Bram frowned, aware that his logic was now becoming clouded by his emotions. Logic told him that he was misjudging Cassandra by attributing any prejudice about his past to her. Logic told him his own hang-up was the problem. But logic couldn't entirely free him from a lifetime of resentment that the Stewarts, with their money, power and position, had behaved toward him and his family as though they were inferior because they had none of those things.

The Stewarts. Bram thought about how he unconsciously lumped them all together as one entity, as though they all thought alike. And again, logic told him how unreasonable a view that was to take. Cassandra's fondness for Maxie in the face of her father's disapproval—and to be fair, Mary Louise's kind attitude now—demonstrated their difference. So why didn't he rely on his mind for direction instead of illogical emotion?

Tired, Bram shook his head, frustrated for the moment, wondering if he would ever get to a point where he could overcome the prejudice that resided in him as strongly as the prejudice he attributed to the Stewarts. He fell asleep with his frustration riding him, and woke to it the next morning.

FOR A SMALL TOWN, Barton's Corner had a plethora of churches encompassing a variety of denominations. The largest was the plainly fashioned, yellow brick First Southern Baptist Church, but it was largest only in membership. The one that the Stewarts attended, the Presbyterian church, with its red-brick exterior, sweeping marble steps and old-fashioned but elegant architecture was blessed with a smaller, wealthier membership. But it was the small, gray-brick Methodist church on the corner of a pleasant, tree-shaded residential street that ministered to the Palmer family that Sunday morning, as it had ministered to Palmers for over half a century.

As Maxie, Bram and Harry Palmer sat in the small, plainly furnished edifice listening to a sermon on tolerance and forgiveness, as well as the folly of trying to pluck specks from the eyes of others while harboring logs in one's own eyes, Maxie's mood deteriorated. It seemed the message was directed straight at her, and its aim was deadly accurate. She left church that morning laden heavily with the knowledge that, for the second time in three days, an apology to a Stewart seemed warranted.

Bram, too, listened thoughtfully to the message and wondered if he was guilty of the sort of self-righteousness the pastor was detailing. Certainly, common sense told him he was the one making problems between Cassy and himself, rather than the other way around.

On the other side of town, the Stewart family—Justin, in particular—was listening to a sermon delivered by its new pastor, a man possessed of a fiery dedication to social justice. The young cleric was an effective speaker, and if Justin thought his pastor seemed to glance in his direction more than in anyone else's, he was quite correct. The type of man to learn everything there was to know about any place he served, Reverend Miller hadn't taken long to find out the nature of the conflict between the citizens of Barton's Corner and the owner of the town's main source of employment, and to determine in his own mind where the fault lay.

Cassy glanced at Justin from time to time, trying to fathom whether the sermon was having any effect on her stubborn brother. But his face was fixed in a remote expression that made her wonder if he was even listening. If he wasn't, she considered it a real pity. Pastor Miller had been most effective when discussing the sacred trust placed in the hands of those whom God had blessed most bountifully to treat those depending upon them with fairness and justice.

When they filed out of the church at the end of the service, Cassy felt distinctly nervous about what Justin might say to their good reverend, who was standing at the door to greet his parishioners and shake their hands.

"Ah, Mr. Stewart." Reverend Miller's merry blue eyes positively beamed at Justin when it came his turn. "I'm delighted to meet you. Your lovely mother is one of our deaconesses, of course, and was partly responsible for my appointment here, so I've met her. But it's nice to meet the rest of the family."

Justin eyed the young man wryly as he took his hand and received a firm handshake. It was impossible to dislike someone so openly full of goodwill who also had the gift of appearing to be fully human, but Justin couldn't resist making a comment on a sermon he felt had been directed at him, and which, despite his reluctance to receive its message, had affected him more than he cared to acknowledge for the moment.

"I could have guessed you knew my mother," he said dryly. "In fact, I was wondering if she wrote your sermon for today."

"Justin!" Mary Louise, her tone filled with remonstrance, poked a finger in her son's back with a good deal of force. She would have preferred to deliver a stronger blow, but they were, after all, in church.

Reverend Miller, however, never faltered. In fact, if anything, the merry intelligent look in his eyes strengthened. "No, I write my own sermons," he replied, chuckling, "and whatever blame or credit they collect is mine."

Cassy hurriedly stepped forward before Justin could say anything else and held out her hand. "I'm Cassandra Stewart, Reverend," she said with every bit of charm she could muster, "and I enjoyed your sermon very much."

The minister looked into Cassandra's lovely eyes, his own displaying warmth and approval. "I know who you are, Miss Stewart," he said with quiet respect, giving Cassandra the impression that he knew a great deal more besides. "Though I know you grew up here, you're newly back, aren't you?" When Cassandra nodded, the minister smiled. "Permit me to say I think Barton's Corner has recaptured a distinct asset with your return."

Cassy studied the man's face for a long moment, certain, especially in view of his sermon, that he was quite well versed in the politics of her hometown. She wasn't the least surprised that her mother had voted for his appointment here. "Thank you," she said with a quiet respect that matched his.

Others were waiting behind them, and the Stewart family continued on their way outside to walk to Mary Louise's Lincoln Continental for the drive home.

In the privacy of the car, when Mary Louise started to chide Justin for his remark to their pastor, he raised a hand from the steering wheel to stop her. "I'm sorry, Mother," he said, his voice preoccupied yet firm. "I'll behave myself next Sunday."

Mary Louise subsided then, though she still gave her son a look of disapproval from time to time, and Justin and Cassandra remained silent for the rest of the drive home.

Justin remained silent through the noon meal, which Mary Louise had started before leaving for church, while Cassandra and her mother chatted. From time to time Cassandra glanced at Justin, noting his preoccupation and wondered what was on his mind. Probably the fight with Maxie the night before, she decided, frustrated over Justin's stubborn pride. If he was as enamored with Maxie as Cassandra suspected he was, it would be just like him to cheat himself of the pleasure of pursuing the attraction because of Maxie's background and her current legal efforts.

If he behaves like a fool, he doesn't deserve her, anyway, she thought, her irritation with her brother spoiling her pleasure in her mother's excellent meal.

Cassandra was caught by surprise, when after clearing the table, Justin requested her presence for a private chat. "What about?" she asked blankly.

Justin tightened his jaw with annoyance. "I just want to talk to you," he said, sounding irritable. "Let's go for a walk around the estate."

Cassandra shrugged and nodded, wondering what was on his mind. "All right," she agreed. "Let me get a jacket."

A few minutes later, as they strolled the perimeters of the land they would one day own jointly, Cassandra waited with well-concealed impatience for Justin to begin.

Finally, keeping his eyes straight ahead of him, in a quiet, reflective voice, Justin said, "Tell me what sort of changes you have in mind for the mill."

Stunned by the question, and the manner in which her brother had asked it, Cassandra didn't answer for a moment. And then, after gathering her wits about her, she decided there was no point in being anything but perfectly frank with him.

"I have a very simple business philosophy, Jussie," she began quietly. "When I was young, I began to disagree with some of the ideas you and Daddy held because they seemed not only unfair, but inaccurate."

"In what way?" Justin asked, still with a quiet lack of animosity that Cassandra hoped would last. But in view of what she was about to say, she doubted it would, and she wasn't sure she would blame Justin if his temper did erupt.

"First," she said levelly, trying to choose a tactful way to put things, "Bram Palmer demonstrated that he wasn't inferior to you in sports or intelligence."

She felt a certain tension rising in her brother, but when he didn't comment upon her observation, she went on. "Then, when I got to be friends with Maxie, I realized the only real difference between us was the fact that my family had money and position, while hers didn't." She felt Justin's tension abating and was more certain than ever that his feelings for Maxie were strong. "But it wasn't until I got older and studied history that I combined my instincts with hard knowledge."

"Explain," Justin said quietly, his attitude amazing Cassandra and giving her the impetus to continue this discussion in a more relaxed way.

"Justin, you have to admit that people with power over others—people in our family's position if you want an example—very often abuse their power, which history shows is a mistake, since abuses almost inevitably provoke rebellion in those who are oppressed."

Justin raised an eyebrow at her, and Cassandra shrugged, realizing he thought she was putting things a little strongly if she was talking about his, and his father's, management of their company.

"Wouldn't you call the grumbling that's going on at the mill, and the very real possibility that Maxie may be able to establish a union among the workers, a rebellion of sorts?" she asked, to make her point. When Justin frowned, she added, "It's all relative, Jussie. I'm not saying our abuses rank up there with the czar of Russia's, or that our employees are about to take up arms against us, though workers have gone that far at times."

Justin gave her a sardonic look, and Cassandra smiled wryly back at him and went on with her discussion of her ideas.

"But I don't subscribe to the idea that people who have no power, upon suddenly obtaining it, are automatically going to behave with virtuous wisdom, either," she continued. "I believe power can corrupt almost anybody."

"Well, that's encouraging," Justin drawled, pausing to check a sagging log in the rail fence that surrounded their property, then walking on.

Sobering now, Cassandra added, "It's sad that when the unions did eventually become established as a result of a very real need for the workers' protection, some of them were eventually headed by people who were as exploitive as some of the owners had been and might still be if some kind of check wasn't placed on them. There's just no guarantee that justice and wisdom necessarily follow the establishment of a union."

Cassandra paused in her walking to look into Justin's eyes, and he paused with her. She was encouraged when she saw that he apparently was listening with respect to what she was saying. At least, he wasn't arguing.

"So I'm against a union at the mill, Justin," she said with quiet self-confidence, "because, even though it may sound arrogant to some, I think this town's welfare would be better served by enlightened management, instead."

Justin looked at her thoughtfully. "I don't have to ask whether you think my management has been 'enlightened,'" he suggested dryly.

Cassandra looked away for a moment, then back at her brother, her expression serious. "Let's just say I can see where improvements are needed," she said quietly. "I think the unrest among our employees has some justification."

"Be specific," Justin responded in a rather clipped tone, but without reacting in the unreasonable manner Cassandra had feared he would adopt. Encouraged, she began to ask questions and make suggestions.

For the next hour, as they slowly walked the grounds of their home, talking about existing personnel policies at the mill, profit-and-loss statistics and any plans Justin had for expanding their market, the discussion had an unsettling but positive effect on both of them. Though there had always been love between them, it had always been the unthinking, familial sort. Neither could remember ever discussing anything together in an adult fashion, with the emphasis on facts and alternative methods, and with respect for the opinion of the other, even when disagreement existed, rather than a hostile exchange of mutual challenge.

Just before they reached the house again, Justin wound up the discussion in a way that left Cassandra feeling optimistic.

"I'll think over what you've said, Cassy," he said levelly. "God knows, we're not likely to expand our market as long as our labor force has its mind on things other than making furniture, and if we don't grow, we'll stagnate."

He took a deep breath before he was able to expose himself in a way that was almost completely new to him—only with Maxie had he showed the sort of vulnerability he showed now to his sister.

"I could use your help, Cassy," he said in a low, deep voice. "I feel that I'm alone, being battered from every side. Even Mom—" He stopped, sighed, then went on. "It hasn't been easy lately, Cassy. In the early years, especially when Dad was alive and on my side, I could handle just about anything. But in the past few years it's gotten harder and harder to shoulder all the responsibility, with nothing to ease the burden and no one even to talk to about my problems. I've been lonely."

Cassandra immediately felt sorry for him. "That's why I'm here, Jussie," she said, unconsciously slipping her hand under his arm in response to the new warmth she felt toward him. "To help. You think about what I've said, and I'll think about what you've said. I'll be coming to work at the mill tomorrow, and once I've checked the books and gotten familiar with the whole operation, we can talk again."

"I won't get in your way," he said, and then with a teasing look at her, he added, "That is, if you'll refrain from treating me like a loathsome monster without a brain in my head or a finer instinct in my heart."

Cassandra felt slightly guilty. "Have I been that bad?" she asked, her expression rueful.

"Sometimes." Justin nodded gravely, and then he laughed and pulled her to him for a hug before they headed back toward the house.

Cassandra wanted to get her mother alone and tell her about the talk she'd had with Justin, but when they came into the den, Mary Louise had guests. Maxie and Bram Palmer were there.

Bram stood up when Justin and Cassandra came into the room, and his special smile for her drove all else from Cassandra's mind.

"Bram," she said with spontaneous excitement, wedging another chink in the armor of suspicion he wore under his skin because she was a Stewart.

Justin was taken aback at seeing Maxie voluntarily seated in his home, when she'd been so adamant about not wanting to visit there. And as unusual as it was for him to be uncertain about anything, on remembering the fight they'd had, he wasn't sure whether he was glad or sorry that she'd come.

"Sit down, children," Mary Louise said pleasantly. "I've made some coffee."

Cassandra gave Bram an especially warm smile and moved to sit down beside him on the sofa. Leaning close, she whispered, "I'm so glad you came." She received a look of such open warmth from him that her heartbeat escalated.

For a while the five of them sipped coffee and spoke of mundane matters of no particular significance to any of them. And then Maxie got up and came to stand in front of Justin, who eyed the troubled expression on her beautiful face with conflicting emotions. He wanted both to comfort and shake her.

"May I talk to you alone, Justin?" she asked quietly, uncomfortably aware that not only had she had to smother her pride to come here in the first place, but that there were witnesses to her potential humiliation if Justin chose to be nasty. For a very long moment, she thought Justin was going to bear out her worst fears. Her relief was intense when he finally stood up beside her.

''We'll go for a drive,'' he said, his face and voice unrevealing. Turning to his mother, who was eyeing him curiously, he added, ''Excuse us, will you, Mom? I don't imagine we'll be gone long.''

Maxie felt a dart of irritation at Justin's last sentence, but she kept her feelings out of her expression.

''Thank you for the coffee, Mrs. Stewart,'' she said with quiet dignity. ''It was nice to see you again,'' she added, meaning it.

Mary Louise stood up. ''It was very nice to see you again, Maxine,'' she said warmly, and there was a perceptive expression in her eyes that convinced Maxie that the older woman was aware how much it had cost her to come to the Stewart house. ''You must come back soon,'' Mary Louise added firmly, and Maxie's beleaguered heart was eased by Mary Louise's invitation. Suddenly, after years of festering, the hurt she had sustained at seventeen began to heal, and as she left with Justin, she felt much better than she had upon arrival.

When Justin and Maxie had left, Mary Louise returned her attention to Cassandra and Bram, and seeing that they were eager to be alone, she cleared her throat. When Cassandra looked up, startled by her mother's action, she flushed slightly at the look of satisfied smugness in Mary Louise's eyes.

''I have a meeting at the church to attend,'' Mary Louise said, failing to mention that she hadn't, until this moment, intended to attend the meeting, since it had nothing to do with any of the various committees on which she served. However, as a deaconess, she would be welcome, anyway.

''Oh,'' Cassandra said, relieved that she and Bram would be left alone to talk. ''All right, Mother. Do you want me to start dinner for you?''

''That would be nice,'' Mary Louise said pleasantly as she started for the door. ''Why don't you plan to cook for five.

You'll stay, won't you, Bram?'' she inquired with sweet persuasiveness. ''And I'd like Maxie to eat with us as well. As a matter of fact,'' she added with a sudden smile, ''let's have Harry over, too. I haven't had a chance to talk to him in a long while.''

Before Bram had a chance to agree or disagree, Mary Louise was gone, and he turned to look at Cassandra with surprise in his eyes.

Cassandra sighed and shook her head. ''It surprises you that my mother invited your family to dinner,'' she guessed.

Bram felt uncomfortable at her perception, but he would have felt more uncomfortable lying to her.

''Yes,'' he admitted, ''but not as much as it once would have.''

''Well, that's something,'' Cassandra said dryly.

Bram shrugged, then abruptly added, ''Cassy, I'm trying. I know with my mind that you and your mother aren't snobs. But the past still has a hold on me I'm trying to break. And I'm fairly certain,'' he added, his tone as dry as hers had been, ''that Jussie lives in the past as well, though I think even he may be easing up a little.''

Cassandra nodded. ''I know he is,'' she responded and told Bram about the conversation she'd just had with her brother. ''Maybe it's Maxie's influence,'' she concluded with a happy smile. ''I hope so. I still think they make a striking couple.''

Bram had to laugh. And when Cassandra asked what amused him, he said, ''I just realized how Jussie must feel about your going out with me. I have my brotherly doubts about a relationship between him and Maxie as well.''

Cassandra said nothing for a moment, merely looked into Bram's eyes searchingly. When he raised his brows at her, silently asking what was on her mind, she sighed.

''It's just that I'm so confused,'' she said quietly.

"About what?" Bram pulled Cassandra into the curve of his arm, unconsciously feeling protective toward her.

"About us," she admitted. "I don't know what we're doing."

Bram frowned, and Cassandra reached up to smooth the wrinkles out of his forehead. "I'm trying hard not to fall in love with you, Bram," she said softly.

Bram immediately tensed. "Why?" he asked, his voice slightly harsh.

For once, Cassandra elected to ignore the real meaning behind his question. "You keep saying you can't stay away from me," she almost whispered. "And I feel the same about you. It keeps amazing me that we've come to feel so strongly about each other in such a short time."

Bram relaxed slightly and took her hand in his own. "It doesn't amaze me," he answered, a growing huskiness in his voice. "I don't see how any man could resist you."

Cassandra smiled, her eyes on him returning the compliment. Then, her smile faded. "But you're going away soon," she started to say.

"There are precedents for long-distance relationships," Bram quickly interjected, focusing on her mouth.

Cassandra nodded. "But would that be wise, in view of the fact that the more we're together, the more we might want to be together? Our lives are going to be lived in separate places. Plus," she added sadly, "I'm not sure you're ever going to trust that I respect and admire you and have no reservations about you or your family." She paused, her helpless frustration in her eyes. "So where does that leave us, Bram?" she asked, desperately hoping she wasn't already in love with Bram, since there might not be a solution to their dilemma.

Bram looked into her eyes, knowing quite suddenly that he was already in too deep to end their relationship for spurious reasons. "There are ways to work things out," he said, believing it for the first time. He leaned back and pulled Cassandra into his arms, suddenly needing to touch her, knowing that when they touched, their problems invariably faded away.

"They may not be perfect," he said a little shakily as he began to brush his mouth against her cheek. "But then, right at this moment, I wouldn't consider anything less than a desert island, where I could have you completely to myself for the rest of our lives, as perfect."

Cassandra sucked in her breath, as much from the implications in Bram's words as the impact of his mouth against her skin. "But," she started to say, and Bram's mouth closed over hers, cutting off whatever objection she'd been about to make. By the time he drew back slightly, she had no breath to say anything.

The expression in her eyes shook Bram, and he found himself saying, "We can do anything we set our minds to, Cassy. Don't give up on us yet." Before she could reply, he took her mouth in a kiss that made her believe exactly what he'd said.

"Cassandra," he whispered raggedly a moment later, moving his lips to the tender lobe of her ear.

"What?" She more breathed the word than said it.

"I want to make love to you, desperately..."

She met his gaze, searching for something to help her make her decision. She was as certain as she'd ever been of anything in her life that if Bram Palmer made love to her, she would never be free of him. And while she was already aware that it might be too late to keep herself from falling in love with him, would he ever come to love her unreservedly, without the past coming between them?

What she saw in Bram's eyes undermined her desire to behave sensibly. She thought she might drown in the passion she saw there. His raw need sparked an answer inside her, dulling her mind and arousing her own passion to an unbearable pitch.

"You want me, Cassy. I can see it in your eyes." The husky rasp of arousal in his voice, and the warmth of his hand against her skin under her sweater further undermined Cassandra's common sense.

Her attention became focused on the present and on the pleasure Bram offered, rather than the future and its possible problems. Indeed, she blessed the years of lonely dedication to her career she'd endured that had left her open to the joy Bram was offering, with its promise to make the end of her self-denial all the sweeter.

"Yes," she whispered, closing her eyes and allowing her body to melt against his. "Yes, Bram. I want you."

Bram kissed her closed lids, her cheek and her slightly parted, softly tender lips. And then he stood and pulled her up into his arms, stroking her passion into a conflagration with his kisses and his gentle but forceful wandering hands and the pressure of his aroused body against hers.

In response to his whispered question, she led him to her bedroom, hardly aware of the journey. When the door had closed behind them, Bram again pulled her into his arms, backing her slowly toward the bed where she had spent the nights of her childhood, and where Cassandra somehow knew she would now learn from Bram, in a way she'd never experienced before, the real joys of being a woman.

With gentle hands, he quickly undressed her, his eyes darkening with the desire he felt as he looked at the exquisite lines of her body and felt the soft velvet of her skin.

"You're so beautiful," he murmured as he tenderly lifted her onto the bed. He kept his eyes on her as he quickly shrugged out of his own clothes, then joined her, exulting in the unhindered delight of lying next to her, skin to skin. "And you feel as good as you look," he whispered, before taking her mouth in a kiss that was invasive, possessive and demanding, seductively calling forth a flood of passion from Cassandra.

"Bram..." She said his name on an inhalation of breath as he released her mouth and trailed kisses down her throat, over her shoulders, to the lovely promise of her breasts.

Cassandra's breathing turned ragged as Bram caressed the swelling curvatures of her aching breasts with his fingers, then took the tips into his mouth alternately, to lave them with his tongue. She pressed her nails into his muscular shoulders as waves of heat washed through her, and she arched with delight when at last, he moved above her and made a place for himself between her thighs.

The pressure of his large body on hers made her feel protected and enhanced her abandonment to her senses.

"It's been a long time for me, my love," Bram whispered a ragged warning as she writhed beneath him, searching for the hard, throbbing warmth that would bring her completion. "Don't tempt me so."

"Oh, but I want to tempt you," Cassandra replied. "I want to tempt you beyond thought, beyond anything you've ever felt."

"Cassy, you already have." Bram's declaration ended in their joining, as he proved unable to resist the needs she'd aroused in him. And for a long moment after plunging into her, he remained still, savoring the moist warmth of her body's welcome, the yielding sweetness of her softness beneath him, before he began the slowly escalating rhythm that would bring them the release they sought.

To his delight, Cassandra's eruption into ecstasy came first, freeing him to sink totally into his own senses and seek his own. And the enveloping warmth of her arms around him, as well as the continuing acceptance she gave him with her body, aided the escalation of his pleasure, until he was shuddering in the grip of a joyous explosion that was all the more powerful for its delay.

Later, as they lay wrapped in each other's arms, jointly experiencing the contentment of their mutual satisfaction, Cassandra accepted that she had answered the question of whether it was already too late to stop herself from falling in love with Bram. But she regretfully decided it would be best not to voice her love until Bram had resolved his own questions.

And Bram, as he lay in the delicate confines of Cassandra's bed, in the middle of the Stewart household, with the privileged daughter of the Stewarts' in his arms, felt a wondering sense of disbelief that such a thing could have happened. How could he be here, welcome in this bed, when once he wouldn't have been welcome anyplace on the property?

But as Cassandra stirred in his arms, murmured his name and lifted her mouth to his for a kiss that he knew would spark a renewal of the lovemaking he had enjoyed to the depths of his soul, he forgot her surname. As her body melted against his, he murmured words of desire to a woman he determinedly thought of only as Cassandra, a woman who had dissolved his loneliness, and substituted in its place a feeling of contented belonging and unimaginable excitement. Soon there was no room for thinking at all, only for feeling, the glorious feeling of being joined with someone who was as absolutely focused on him as he was on her.

Chapter Eleven

"What did you want to talk about?"

They were parked in Justin's favorite thinking spot overlooking the river, and he was acutely aware that this was the first time he'd ever brought anyone else to this place. He'd done it automatically, which he was also aware said a lot about how far he'd progressed along the road to viewing Maxie as intimately entrenched in his life.

Maxie sat with her arm on the window ledge of the pickup, her chin cupped in her hand. She didn't want to look at Justin while she humbled herself, but some deeply ingrained sense of justice, no matter how unwelcome at the moment, made her turn her head to him and drop her hand.

"I wanted to apologize to you, Justin," she said quietly and saw him stiffen in surprise before he turned to stare hard at her.

"I behaved badly last night," she admitted. "Later, I realized what a big step it was for you to make the concessions you did, and how wrong I was to expect you to go as far as I wanted, and for the reasons I'd prefer."

Justin frowned. While he was warmed that Maxie had apologized, the words of her apology were still, somehow, a subtle condemnation of him.

He said nothing, thinking over his position. It grated on him that while he was more and more coming to grant Maxie respect for her views, even if he didn't agree with all of them, she seemed unprepared to grant him any respect for his. Indeed, it wasn't just that she disagreed with him. She apparently condemned him on a personal level for his views.

"Justin," Maxie whispered, and when he gave her his attention, he began to realize that her conflicting desires were causing her pain. He noticed the dark circles under her eyes and the troubled look deep within the green depths that so fascinated him, and his anger softened.

"What?" he asked, his voice growing gentle as he searched her face and turned his body toward her.

"I wish you'd accept my apology. I can't help our differences—the way I think, the way you think—but I'm trying to be more understanding."

Maxie paused, her eyes on him, her senses reacting to the pull of Justin's sexuality. She longed to have him hold her and kiss her and tell her in that husky rasp that stirred her so, how much he wanted her.

Aided by the look in her eyes as much as by the plea in her voice, Justin felt a familiar ache begin inside him. But in addition to desire, he was aware of wanting to comfort Maxie. He wanted to tell her about his talk with Cassy that afternoon and thereby ease her worries. But he wanted just as strongly to have her accept him, respect him, as the man he was without having continually to humble himself before her and become someone different before she could accept him.

"I accept your apology," he said, and unconsciously he spoke in the voice that seemed to take hold of him only when he was speaking to Maxie Palmer, "and I guess I owe you one, too."

Maxie was gratified, as well as surprised. "For what?" she asked softly.

Justin had his arm over the steering wheel, and now he raised a hand to rake it through his thick hair.

"Something about you provokes a devil in me, Maxie," he admitted with harsh reluctance. "I feel as though I'm always on trial with you, and that the sentence is always going to be negative. So I go out of my way to give you what you seem to expect from me. Last night, for example, when you brought up the time I was responsible for cutting your father's pay—I know now how much that hurt you and your family and I'm sorry for it. But the way you reminded me of it set my temper off instead of making me want to apologize, the way I should have."

Maxie stared at Justin, absorbing his words, testing the conclusions they elicited. Yes, she decided, finding the thought sobering, she could see how a man as proud as Justin would find it hard to be condemned at every turn by anyone, especially a woman he desired, and how he would react by exaggerating the very qualities she found lacking. And she had certainly never tried to approach him in a manner fashioned to elicit his goodwill. She had attacked him at their first meeting, never letting up, and thereby probably hindered her own cause by strengthening his defenses.

"I'm afraid you're right," she admitted in a tone of surprised regret.

Justin looked at her sharply, afraid to trust.

"Justin, I'm sorry," she said with an honest dignity that weakened Justin's distrust. "I let the past dictate the present," Maxie went on. "I've hated you since I was seventeen, and I let that hate obscure my judgment. Had you been anyone else, I don't think I would have approached you in the way I did. Common sense would have told me it would hinder my goal, rather than aid it. But I haven't been able to use common sense where you're concerned in all these years."

She looked into his eyes, hesitating a moment before making a further confession, one that would leave her much too vulnerable but that seemed necessary to make.

"And since yesterday afternoon, my common sense has taken another turn for the worse," she admitted softly. "I should never have let myself feel anything for you on a personal level, neither hate nor love. And yet I did. I do. Wise or unwise, I can't seem to help myself."

That was the confession that unlocked Justin's pride and made him act spontaneously, without thought of consequences. He reached for her, and had she come less willingly, he would still have pulled her into his arms and lowered his head to drink hungrily of her mouth.

But Maxie didn't come to him unwillingly. She came with glorious relief, thoughtlessly happy to be in his arms again and oblivious of all the reasons why she shouldn't be there.

Just as had happened the afternoon before, she met his kisses with a fierceness that matched his. She clung to his body as meltingly, as desperately, as Justin held hers. She reacted to the touch of his hands with ecstatic eagerness.

And just when she would have done anything he demanded of her, he thrust her slightly away from him and with his face flushed with desire, his eyes a seductive force that held Maxie a willing captive, he forced her to think about what she was doing.

"You want me to make love to you, don't you, Maxie? Here and now?"

Maxie hesitated, resentful for the moment that Justin was forcing her to make a conscious decision, rather than sweeping her mindlessly off her feet.

"And if I do?" Justin persisted. "Can you live with giving yourself to a man you don't respect or trust?"

Shocked by Justin's bluntness, Maxie drew back, her expression uncertain.

Justin tightened his jaw, determined now that if he couldn't have the rest of what he wanted from Maxie, he would forgo what he could have. For the first time in his life, he understood the real purpose of sex, instead of viewing it as an animal hunger to be eased unemotionally.

"Justin?" Maxie said his name softly, afraid to believe what she thought she saw in his face . . . afraid to hope there was that much substance to his feelings for her.

"Make a decision on the way things are now, right now. On the man I am right now," Justin urged her, plunging Maxie into uncertainty again.

But as she stared into the fierce clarity of his eyes, Maxie finally understood Justin Stewart for the first time in her life. He might be proud, but the pride wasn't all shallow. There was enough dignity in it for him not to want her body without her respect and her heart. And any man who wanted a woman as much as she was positive Justin wanted her, yet would sacrifice his desire for principle, was worthy of her respect, she concluded.

"I won't feel ashamed of giving myself to a man like you, Justin," she finally said, her voice firm, her eyes steady. "Is that what you needed to hear?"

Slowly Justin relaxed, studying Maxie's face to verify the truth he heard in her voice.

"That's what I needed to hear," he agreed quietly, with relief.

They stared at each other for a long moment, and when Justin made no move to pull her back into his arms, Maxie's eyes lit with soft humor, and she went to him of her own volition, realizing why he was waiting.

Cupping his face with her hands, she bent to his mouth and caressed it with her own, taking infinite care to convince him of her inner certainty. Between kisses, as Justin at last began to respond, she bared her heart to him.

"I love you, Justin," she murmured, her eyes on his, open and trusting. "I'm not afraid of loving you any longer."

And as Justin's arms came around her, she felt the tremble in their strong haven, verifying the emotion she saw in his eyes.

"I won't stop fighting you," she whispered, her smile taking the sting out of the words, "but I won't be fighting out of anger anymore...and it will be for *you*, as much as for myself or anyone else."

Justin gently tucked her head into the curve of his neck, and when Maxie relaxed against him, snuggling into his embrace with the confidence of belonging there, he stroked the red hair he had once viewed with contempt and made a confession of his own.

"You won't have to fight so hard anymore, Maxie," he said in a voice roughened by emotion. "Neither will Cassy. As hard as it may be for either of you to believe it, I'm beginning to see what you've been trying to tell me for so long."

Maxie opened her eyes, which she had closed in contentment, a slight tension in her body alerting Justin to her thoughts.

He smiled and tightened his hold on her. "No." He shook his head slightly. "I don't mean I'll give in to a union."

Now Maxie stiffened before she relaxed again upon remembering how much progress had been made, and that if Justin had changed his mind once, he might change it again.

His smile broadened as Justin again divined her thoughts. "But," he added, with a lack of emphasis that delayed Maxie's understanding of his next words, "I doubt if one will be needed when I have to answer to Cassy every day in the office, and to you every night in my bed at home."

Patiently Justin waited for his proposal to penetrate Maxie's prejudiced mind. He knew it had when she jerked upright in his arms and stared at him with shocked disbelief.

Feeling completely relaxed and more at peace than he had in years, Justin leaned back against the window and watched Maxie's face with an indulgent, loving expression on his own while she struggled for words.

"Justin, you can't mean what I think you do," she finally said, shaking her head while she watched him closely.

"Can't I?" He shrugged, his blue eyes twinkling. "I've wanted a wife for a long time. I haven't had anybody to talk to, you see. At least no one I knew would understand me and love me, no matter what."

"Well..." Maxie stumbled, still unable to believe he was serious. "I love you, of course, and I'm trying to understand you, but Justin, you must know that I won't always agree with you."

Justin adopted a mock-woeful expression. "Ah, well," he gave out on a long-suffering sigh, "I guess I can't have everything, can I?"

Maxie continued to stare at him, shaking her head with bewilderment. Then, as something that worried her came to mind, her expression grew grave.

"And what if you have a passel of redheaded children?" she asked soberly. "How will that make you feel?"

Justin pretended to give her concern due consideration and reached up to rub a strand of Maxie's silken red hair between his thumb and finger, his eyes thoughtful.

"I suppose," he said, giving a mournful shake of his head, "that I'll have to get used to it. Maybe it won't be so bad if our son turns out to be as smart and play football as well as Bram, and if our daughter turns out to be as stubbornly principled as her mother."

Uncertain, Maxie eyed Justin cautiously, and when she saw his beautiful mouth twitching with suppressed humor, she slapped his hand away from her hair with subdued force and glared at him.

"And what if your children's mother won't be content to stay at home and be a housewife?" she demanded. "What if she wants a job as Barton Furniture's employee representative?"

Justin raised his eyebrows, pursed his mouth and finally shrugged. "I might consider it if she would agree to be Barton Furniture's general counsel as well," he said with lazy unconcern.

At his unexpected response, Maxie felt overwhelmed. She found it almost impossible to believe that the Justin Stewart she thought she had known as thoroughly as anyone ever could know him had changed so quickly and thoroughly into an entirely different sort of man than he had been all his life.

Justin viewed Maxie's confusion with a certain amount of sympathy. "Hard to believe, isn't it?" he said in a consoling voice.

"You can say that again," she avowed emphatically.

Justin shrugged and smiled. "Maybe I'm just being my old shrewd, crafty self," he proposed in a teasing way, "undermining my enemy by marrying her. After all, a wife can't testify against her husband, can she?"

"This wife can," Maxie said with firm conviction, eyeing Justin with anxious alarm. "Justin, you mustn't think I'll change too much, just because I love you…might marry you," she added with slow wonder at the very idea of taking such a drastic, unexpected step.

Justin suddenly grinned. "And you mustn't think I've undergone a complete change of character," he said lightly. "I'm willing to admit I've been wrong about some things, true. But I'm still a businessman, with one eye on profits and the other on expenses. You'll still have battles to fight where I'm concerned."

His grin suddenly disappeared, and pulling Maxie up against his body, he studied her lovely face with a mixture of pleasure and warning.

"Just don't ever carry one of our fights into the bedroom, Maxie," he said with soft firmness. "I can take anything from you but that. When I make love to you, I want your full and unequivocal participation."

Maxie's expression softened and she slid her arms around his neck, leaning into his body with uninhibited pleasure at the contact.

"If we do get married, Justin," she said softly, "that's one thing you won't have to worry about. If I could want you so desperately when we were at each other's throats all these months, I don't think I'll have any problem wanting you without reservation, once we close the bedroom door behind us, especially now that I know how much I love you."

"But you still have doubts about marrying me?" Justin asked, his disappointment in his tone.

Maxie smiled into his eyes and touched his mouth with gentle fingers. "Maybe if you tell me you love me," she said very softly, "my doubts will disappear."

Justin showed his surprise, as well as a certain amount of discomfort. "The words don't come easily to me," he admitted, "but I thought you'd understand when I asked you to marry me."

Maxie shook her head and waited, gazing at him with patient love.

Justin sighed, then his smile broke out like sunlight, making Maxie catch her breath. "Maxine Palmer," he said with gentle formality.

"Yes?" she answered, her voice trembling slightly.

"I don't know how it ever could have happened. You must have snuck up on my blind side." Justin paused, amused as Maxie's expression turned irritable. "But I seem to have fallen in love with you,'' he finally said the words she'd been waiting to hear, and as she smiled, he shook his head in wonder. ''And that's the last thing I thought I'd be saying to you when you showed up wanting to talk to me this afternoon.''

Maxie's smile grew amused. ''And are you glad I did?'' she teased.

''I'm not sure yet,'' Justin said with mock perplexity. ''I think I'm as surprised as you are.''

Maxie's laughter gurgled from her throat, and as she tipped her head back, Justin bent to taste the hollow poised so temptingly before him.

Maxie's laughter died abruptly and when Justin raised his head, she met his mouth with a kiss that thrust both of them into a state of instant desire and that shortly had them both shaken by the intensity of their feelings.

''We can wait until after the wedding if you like,'' Justin whispered reluctantly, thinking his willingness to be patient might convince Maxie more than anything else of how serious he was about her.

''Only if the wedding is very, very soon,'' Maxie whispered back, her voice trembling with emotion and desire.

''Is next Saturday soon enough?'' Justin smiled, suddenly anxious to be traditional, in tribute to the woman of his choice. He was also aware that he wanted to bind her to him quickly enough to prevent any second thoughts she might have. Once they were married, he was positive both of them would work hard to solve the inevitable problems they would have.

''Saturday would do nicely,'' Maxie agreed, reluctantly pulling away from Justin's embrace. ''But where will we live?''

Justin shrugged, his gaze tender. ''Would it be too much to ask of you to share my home?'' he asked sensitive to any reluctance she might feel to do that.

Maxie gazed at Justin, her heart in her eyes. "Your father wouldn't approve," she tentatively reminded him.

"I'm not concerned with Dad's approval anymore," Justin said quietly. "If you wouldn't feel comfortable, I'll build us a new house."

Maxie only needed the offer, not necessarily the follow-through. "Let's see how it works out," she suggested. "Your mother's feelings have to be considered."

Justin smiled and shook his head. "Mom would be delighted," he assured her. "And if you won't mind living with her, nothing would please her more than to take care of us while we devote ourselves to the family business."

Maxie felt a little trill of superstitious fear trace her back at the thought of being part of the "family business"—a business she was accustomed to viewing with hostile combativeness.

"This is going to take a lot of adjustment, Justin," she said with honest bluntness.

Justin laughed and hugged her close and protectively. "Isn't it, though," he agreed with more anticipation than dismay. "But we can handle it, can't we?"

"Oh, Justin, I hope so," Maxie whispered, tightening her arms around him and closing her eyes. "It will break my heart if we can't."

THAT NIGHT at the family dinner party Mary Louise had instigated, to the amazement of all, and to the consternation of Harry and Bram, Justin Stewart announced that he had asked Maxine Palmer to marry him and she had agreed.

But Justin won Maxie's respect completely when, after making the announcement and waiting for the shock to wear off slightly, he turned to her father and said with utter sincerity, "I'll take good care of her, Harry. She means as much to me now as she does to you. Trust me, and try not to worry that she's making a mistake. I assure you, she isn't, and neither am I.''

As Justin's kiss sealed the engagement, Maxie's eyes filled with tears, and she wasn't the least surprised that Harry's, Mary Louise's and Cassy's, did as well. Only Bram gazed steadily across the table at her, asking with silent concern if she really knew what she was doing.

Maxie nodded at him, trying to ease his worry, then sat back in her chair with her hand in Justin's, reflecting that life was certainly full of surprises. As a young girl, and later as a young woman, she had speculated many times about what sort of man she would someday marry, where she would live and how many children she would have. And she had never once suspected that her name would someday be changed to Stewart, that she would someday live in the home that had once been forbidden to her, and that her children would be fathered by a man who had once considered her beneath his notice.

O Lord, she breathed a silent plea as she exchanged a look with Cassy, her friend, whose good wishes she didn't doubt in the slightest, *please let it all work out for the best. Help Justin stay as he is this night and never regret he chose a Palmer for a wife, and help me always to feel as certain as I do now that he's worth the risk I'm taking.*

Regaining the contentment that had deserted her for a moment, Maxie gazed at her father and knew from the bewildered, almost betrayed look on the aged face she loved so much that she would have to do some tall talking to convince Harry she was doing the right thing. And as her gaze moved to Bram, she realized there was another member of her family she would have to convince as well.

But it was Justin's face that made her certain she was right to take her risks and live with her choices. Now that their love was in the open and acknowledged, she couldn't imagine how she had fooled herself for so long that it didn't exist at all.

Later that evening, before Maxie went home with her father and brother and had to face the questions and doubts she knew they would have, she was grateful that Cassy drew her down the hall to her bedroom, thinking her friend was going to give her the encouragement she needed.

But when they were seated together on Cassandra's very feminine white organza bedspread, Maxie mistook the meaning of the expression on Cassy's face, which was actually caused by the fact that Cassandra felt a bit awkward sitting with Maxie on the bed where she'd made love with Bram earlier.

"Oh, Cassy, not you, too?" Maxie sighed. "I thought you'd be happy for Justin and me."

Startled by Maxie's incorrect conclusion, Cassandra blinked, then started smiling. "I am, you dope!" she exclaimed. "I was thinking about something else entirely."

Cassandra was grateful when Maxie didn't ask what she'd been thinking about and, instead, said, "Well, I really couldn't blame anybody for wondering how a marriage between me and Justin is going to work out. It *is* going to be tricky."

"How so?" Cassandra grinned, knowing very well the problems Maxie and Justin would have to face, but feeling optimistic that they would work things out.

Maxie grimaced. "First, I'm going to have to convince the people I've been trying to influence to form a union, including my dad, that I haven't sold out to the Stewarts," she said dryly. "And then I'm going to have to walk a tightrope to make sure a conflict of interest doesn't develop that compromises my principles."

Maxie paused, and seeing that Cassandra's grin was broader, she said a little irritably, "What's so funny?"

"I was just thinking that if anybody can walk that tight-rope, you can." Cassandra laughed. "And you'll have some help, Maxie," she added, leaning forward to hug Maxie with affection. "I'm on your side."

Maxie smiled her gratitude, but when they straightened from their hug, her smile disappeared as a thought occurred to her. "But what about you and Bram?" she asked curiously. "Obviously, you plan to stay here, but I could have sworn you two were getting seriously involved with each other."

Cassandra shrugged, looking away from Maxie's discerning eyes. "He says we'll work things out somehow," she said lightly, though she wasn't at all sure they would, and the possibility that they wouldn't, now that she was head over heels in love with Bram, was heartbreaking.

Maxie relaxed. "Well, if Bram says you can work things out, you will," she said confidently. "Bram can do anything he sets his mind to, and so can you."

Cassandra appreciated Maxie's confident optimism, and her smile was warm as she looked at Bram when she and Maxie rejoined the others.

A few moments later Harry, still with a bewildered look on his face, stood with Mary Louise, whose expression conveyed nothing other than supreme satisfaction, and watched Bram and Cassy, and Maxie and Justin, pair off for good-night hugs and kisses.

"Don't worry about a thing, Harry," Mary Louise whispered to him upon noticing his bewilderment. "We're fortunate in our children, and I have faith that everything is going to work out beautifully for them. Just you wait and see. You and I are going to be the proudest grandparents in Barton's Corner before too much longer."

On being reminded of the prospect of grandchildren to come, Harry's mood lightened. "Never thought I'd have a grandchild by the name of Stewart," he remarked bluntly.

Mary Louise's mouth twitched with laughter. "Think of them as Bartons if it makes you feel better," she suggested. "You didn't have anything against my father, did you?"

"A finer man never lived," Harry asserted with a firm nod of his head, and his mood lightened further.

Later, at home, as Harry, Maxie and Bram sat at their kitchen table, Maxie tried to make her family feel better about her engagement to Justin.

"I don't expect everything to go smoothly," she admitted, "but I want you to know that I love Justin, and I believe he loves me, and somehow, we'll make things work out."

Her gaze softened as she looked at Harry and saw that though his doubts were easing, he was still somewhat worried.

"I know it's hard for you to believe, Daddy," she said quietly, "but Justin's changing. He may never accept the union we've been working for but if I didn't think that he will make some much-needed changes at the mill, I don't believe I could marry him. I'm not going to give up my principles, Daddy, even for the man I love."

"I know you won't, honey," Harry assured her. "I'm just hoping Jussie's worthy of your trust, because I don't like divorce. I don't believe in it. And if he doesn't change, that's what it might come to."

To Maxie's surprise, Bram spoke up, focusing on the positive. "I saw the way Jussie looked at Maxie, Dad," he said, "and I believe he loves her and wants to please her. Besides," he added with a thoughtful look in his eyes, "Cassandra will be helping her to implement those changes Jussie seems to be willing to accept now."

Harry nodded and patted Maxie's hand before he got to his feet. "Well, children," he said, "I hope you're right, and I'll be prayin' extra hard for God's blessings on this marriage." Then he looked at Bram with a proud smile. "And for the other one that looks like it's on the way as well."

Maxie noted that a troubled light appeared in Bram's eyes at their father's words, but as Harry started toward the door, he said, "It's time for this old man to be in bed. I have to go to work in the mornin', and I don't do my best unless I'm good and rested."

"Good-night, Daddy," Maxie said, her attention diverted from Bram for the moment. "And, Daddy..." she added. When he stopped walking and turned to look at her inquiringly, she said with tears in her eyes, "Thank you for being my father."

Harry smiled. "I reckon I got better kids than I deserved," he replied. "But your mama didn't. No, sir, your mama deserved the best, and that's exactly what she got."

With a nod, he turned away and left the room, and Maxie, wiping tears from her eyes, returned her attention to Bram.

"Now what about you, Bram Palmer?" she asked with mock sternness. And when he looked at her with surprise, she said, "What are you going to do about Cassy? How are you two going to get together if you return to California and she stays here?"

Bram shrugged, an unconcerned smile on his lips. Though he wasn't at all sure he was telling the truth, he said, "We'll make things work out, Maxie, I've worked hard all my life to get somewhere, only to find out now that I have, that it doesn't mean all that much unless you have the right person by your side to share things."

"And you're positive Cassy's the right person?" Maxie asked.

To Bram's surprise, Maxie's question focused things for him. "I'm positive," he said slowly, meaning it, and much disturbed because he did.

"Then good luck, big brother." Maxie grinned at him. "Personally, I think you have excellent taste in women."

Bram smiled, reluctant to spoil Maxie's happiness by voicing any of the doubts that still rode him. It didn't help that the doubts had nothing to do with loving Cassandra, or even with her loving him. They had to do with whether or not their love could surmount present problems which had their basis in the past.

Chapter Twelve

The next morning, as Bram greeted Jodie and prepared to supervise the rehabilitation of his father's house, Justin Stewart, president of Barton Furniture, sat behind his desk and faced two lovely women whose beauty in no way concealed their mutual determination.

Justin just had time to silently thank the fates that his father hadn't lived to see this day, before the concentrated, pleasantly worded, but in no way waffling, attack on him began.

"I've gotten together a few proposals concerning employee benefits I consider absolutely essential to put into effect as soon as possible," Maxie began, placing a sheaf of papers in the center of Justin's desk.

"A *few* proposals," Justin said, with a careful lack of facial expression as he eyed the thickness of Maxie's offering.

Cassandra quickly spoke up, to head off any objections Justin might be about to voice. "I read them this morning, and they seem very fair to me. There's nothing there I wouldn't have suggested myself, given time."

Justin raised eyes absolutely blank of expression to acknowledge his sister's interjection.

"Of course," Maxie said with dignified formality, "we understand that you'll need time to read them over before we have an in-depth discussion concerning them, and at that time, if you have valid objections to any of them, Cassy and I will do our best to—'' Maxie faltered, not wanting to give Justin the impression that he was going to be allowed to get away with any unsubstantive objections ''—to negotiate.'' Maxie had at last found the right word and directed a beaming smile in Justin's direction.

Cassandra spoke up quickly again. ''That's right. Meanwhile, while you study Maxie's proposals, I'll study the books, to make sure the costs of the proposals are in line with what the company can stand.''

Cassandra directed a warning look at Maxie, wishing she had had more time to discuss things with her ally before having this meeting, but Maxie had been intent upon pressing her advantage as quickly as possible.

Maxie subsided, reflecting that Cassy had a point. She didn't want to put the company out of business, after all, and she was willing to adjust her demands to what the traffic would bear, so long as she became convinced that all that could be done would be, and quickly.

''Very well,'' Justin said at last, keeping his tone neutral, though he was amused by Cassandra's tactic as well as by Maxie's precipitate testing of him. He recognized, however, that both of them had reason to mistrust his promises, and while he had no intention of giving the appearance of caving in to them right now, he knew he was going to give them what they wanted, eventually.

''I'll look these over as soon as possible,'' he said, carefully moving Maxie's proposals to the right side of his desk.

His amusement increased when he saw Maxie and Cassandra exchange a look of puzzled concern that he hadn't spoken angrily to either of them, nor had he jumped to attention with quite the alacrity they might have been hoping for.

"But meanwhile," he continued, leaning back in his chair, still speaking with neutral authority, "I'd like to discuss something that needs more immediate attention than this," and he gestured at Maxie's papers with a graceful movement of his hand.

Now his amusement was hard to conceal as both Cassandra and Maxie frowned simultaneously.

"As you both know," he said with mock formality, "I'm getting married next Saturday."

Startled, Maxie gazed at him, torn between smiling happily at the reminder that Saturday was her wedding day as well, and grimacing her exasperation at the way Justin had voiced his reminder.

"And I intend to take at least a two-week honeymoon," Justin went on, now gazing at the ceiling in a thoughtful manner, as though he were discussing weighty business matters rather than the most important event in his life.

Cassandra leaned back in her chair, concealing a smile as she recognized the game Justin was playing. She could tell that Maxie hadn't caught on yet, because her friend was alternately smiling and frowning as though she wasn't certain which was the appropriate reaction.

"There's a lot to do in the next week." Justin spoke firmly now as he sat forward and placed his hands squarely on his desk. "You, Cassy," he nodded at his sister, "must get familiar enough with the business in that short time that you can take over for me while I'm gone."

Cassandra nodded gravely, her lips twitching in her efforts to keep from grinning widely. "And I must also find time to help Maxie shop for her wedding dress and a maid-of-honor dress for myself," she said, exactly matching Justin's weighty tone.

"Naturally," Justin said in a formal manner before turning his attention to Maxie. "And you, Miss Palmer," he said gravely, "if I'm not mistaken, are going to have a very busy week ahead of you, indeed."

Maxie heaved a breath of disgust. "If I decide to go through with this wedding," she said ominously. "I'm not certain I want to marry a man who can't separate the boardroom from the bedroom."

"You can't possibly be referring to me," Justin responded with a chiding note in his voice. His eyes as he spoke, however, raked Maxie with a blatantly unmistakable sexual look that took her breath away. "I have no difficulty whatsoever in making such a distinction."

My mistake. You certainly don't, Maxie responded silently.

"Now, as I was saying," Justin resumed in his formal tone, "*all* of us have a very busy week ahead of us, and I suggest we get started. Do you agree?" He politely addressed the question to both women.

"Oh, indubitably." Cassandra nodded, barely able to control her laughter.

"Good," Justin said with a distant smile as he got to his feet. "Then I suggest you, Miss Palmer, run along to Personnel and sign all the various forms required of a new employee, before departing this place entirely to start getting our wedding together, while you, Miss Stewart, accompany me on a tour of the mill."

Cassandra, sensing that Maxie needed a moment alone with Justin—whether to brain him or kiss him, she wasn't sure—stood up as well.

"Do you mind if I visit the washroom first?" she inquired of Justin in a pleasant voice and with a pleasant smile.

"Take your time." Justin nodded, leaning back on his heels and thrusting his hands into the pockets of his beautifully tailored gray trousers, the picture of an insufferably priggish businessman.

Cassandra made a hasty exit from the office, but not quickly enough to miss the expression of murderous anticipation in Maxie's flashing green eyes.

No sooner had the door closed behind Cassandra, than Maxie got to her feet and marched around Justin's desk to glare up at him.

"You think you're funny, don't you?" she demanded with her hands on her hips.

Justin smiled slyly as he looked her up and down. "I was just trying to maintain a little propriety in the office," he said, adopting a tone of wounded innocence, which warred with the expression in his eyes.

"Propriety?" Maxie burst out indignantly, reaching up to tug at the perfect knot of Justin's tie. "I'll show you propriety."

"Now, now," Justin sputtered through the laughter he couldn't hold back any longer as he tried to fight Maxie off. "I believe there's a rule against sexual harassment in the work place, though I never expected to be a victim of it myself!"

"There are a lot of things you're going to have to get used to now," Maxie responded grimly, and then gasped as Justin pried her fingers loose from his tie and quickly drew her hands around his neck, before dropping his own to her waist and pulling her abruptly against his body.

"If you mean I'm going to have to get used to being raped in my own office, I can't tell you how much I'm looking forward to the experience," he said fervently, and with a sparkle of laughter in his eyes, he bent his head and kissed Maxie so thoroughly, she was left without a whisper of breath to voice any further objections.

"Now," Justin said with satisfaction when he had silenced Maxie, "how do you feel about an Alaskan cruise for our honeymoon? I've always wanted to get up there for a visit, but I've always been much too busy to make the trip before. Of course, now that my sister has joined me in the business, I should be able to get away a lot more often than I have in—"

"Justin, it'll be cold in Alaska this time of year," Maxie interrupted with a weak protest, her voice muffled by his chest.

Justin's smile was pure bliss, tinged with just a hint of sly satisfaction. "I'm counting on it," he said fervently, and when Maxie tipped her head up to gaze at him with resigned humor, he bent to kiss her much more tenderly this time and finished by rubbing her nose with his.

A few minutes later, when Maxie came out of Justin's office with a dazed look of happiness in her eyes, Cassandra met her with a grin.

"Have you forgiven him?" she asked teasingly.

"Forgiven him?" Maxie gave Cassy a mischievous smile. "Oh, I wouldn't say that. I'll wait and see how he reacts to my proposals before I decide on forgiveness or revenge."

Cassandra laughed. "Judging from the look on your face when you came out of there just now, I don't think Justin is going to have to worry about facing your revenge."

"Probably not." Maxie sighed, then joined in Cassy's laughter before heading for the personnel office as Justin had suggested.

BRAM WAS PLEASANTLY TIRED that evening when he came to pick Cassandra up for a drive, but on seeing her face, he realized she was more than he.

"Hard day?" he asked solicitously, once they were in the car.

Cassandra nodded, wishing they were in a car without a center console so that she could snuggle up to Bram and further enjoy this chance to rest.

"Jussie's keeping me hard at it so I can fill in for him while he's on his honeymoon," she said. "It's tiring, but I'm enjoying it. There's something different about working at a place you partly own. It's somehow more satisfying than working for someone else.''

Bram nodded as he started the car and turned it to head down the driveway, but there was a look in his eyes that made Cassandra wonder what he was thinking. She decided not to wonder and asked him outright.

Bram hesitated, then shrugged. ''I agree with you,'' he said quietly.

''But?'' Cassandra prodded him.

''Let's wait and talk about it when we get where we're going,'' Bram suggested, feeling at a disadvantage when he had to drive.

''And where is that?'' Cassandra asked.

Bram smiled ruefully. ''There isn't much privacy around here, is there?'' he stated the obvious. ''How about Lover's Lane?'' he suggested with a grin.

Cassandra laughed. ''Don't you think it might be a little crowded there?'' she teased.

Bram shook his head. ''Not on a school night . . . at least I hope not.''

He was relieved that his hope was confirmed as he pulled the car into a parking spot on a bluff overlooking the scattered lights of Barton's Corner. They were the only ones at the popular courting spot for the town's teenagers.

''This brings back memories.'' Bram smiled as he turned off the engine and looked over at Cassandra, thinking she looked lovely in her loosely woven white sweater and navy-blue slacks.

''I don't think I want to hear about them,'' she retorted, feeling slightly jealous of the times Bram must have been here before, even if those times were long in the past, especially since she didn't have the same sort of memories to think about. She had never dated anyone in Barton's Corner seriously enough to come here.

Bram looked at her thoughtfully, divining that she had never been to Lover's Lane before and the probable reason why.

"Jealous?" he asked softly, in order to keep from inquiring if his deductions were correct.

Cassandra looked squarely at him then, and nodded. "Very," she said equally as softly, then unknowingly confirmed Bram's guess. "But I'm glad that my first time here is with you."

Bram nodded. "I am, too," he said, meaning it. "But I'm a little curious about why you've never been here before."

He was immediately ashamed of asking the question and wondered irritably why he persisted in trying to find things to separate the two of them, rather than looking for ways to bring them closer together.

Cassandra unconsciously did what he should have done himself. "None of the boys I went to Barton's Corner High with could compare with you, Bram," she said with perfect sincerity. "I didn't realize at the time why I wasn't like the other girls, falling madly in love with one boy or another. But when I got to college and met young men who were comparable to the standard you'd set, I behaved as my high school girlfriends had earlier."

Now, it was Bram's turn to experience jealousy. "You fell madly in love with one young man after another?" he inquired dryly, wishing with a fervency that took him by surprise that their ages had allowed them to attend school together. But he realized he wouldn't have been ready for a serious relationship then, and Cassandra might not have, either.

She confirmed this with a light laugh. "I wouldn't say I fell in love with anyone," she responded. "I fell into infatuation sometimes, but I intended to come home and work at the mill, so I never let any relationship become too serious." She sobered then and added, "Until you."

Her confession provoked an almost overwhelming desire in Bram to take her into his arms, but he wanted to feel all of her against him, and the car's design wouldn't permit that.

"Let's get out for a while," he suggested in a husky voice that brought a shiver of pleasure to Cassandra's spine.

He met her on her side of the car and immediately took her into his arms and bent to her mouth, pressing her against the car in order to brace her to withstand the need that rode him.

"Damn this town," he breathed raggedly a few moments later as his hands roamed Cassandra's body inside her sweater. "If we were teenagers, I'd make love to you in the back seat of the car, but we're not, and there's no place else decent enough to take you around here, even if I cared to make us the subject of gossip by tomorrow morning."

"I know," Cassandra whispered, kissing the underside of his jaw and unbuttoning his shirt so she could slip her hands inside it and touch him intimately. "It's frustrating. I want you, Bram."

"And I want you," he grated just before seizing her mouth for another kiss.

Within a very few moments, Bram pushed himself away from Cassandra, using all of his willpower, and took a few steps toward the edge of the bluff, leaving her to sag against the car while she tried to regain her equilibrium.

Bram suddenly pivoted and returned to face her. "This is a hellish situation," he said in a frustrated voice. "And it's going to be a lot worse when I return to California. Cassy, come with me, please."

Cassandra raised her head, torn by the need she heard in Bram's voice and by her own needs, which were still raging through her. But she had unfinished business in Barton's Corner, and she couldn't turn her back on it, no matter how much in love with Bram she was.

"Bram, I can't," she said, her tone pleading with him to understand. "Not yet, anyway. But I can visit you," she added upon seeing the disappointment in Bram's expression. "And you can visit me."

"Great." He shrugged, turning away from her, his stance revealing to Cassandra his continued frustration and a burgeoning anger.

"What else can we do?" she asked helplessly. "I have commitments to meet, the same as you do, Bram. And anyway..." She started to add that it would be the height of foolishness for her to leave everything and follow him to California, when he'd never even said he loved her and she wasn't sure he would ever get over his resentment of her family.

"Anyway, what?" Bram turned, his expression hard.

Quietly, Cassandra told him what she'd been thinking, and then it was Bram's turn to be silent for a few minutes. And the longer the silence lasted, the more Cassandra despaired that they were headed for the same sort of happiness Justin and Maxie had found.

Finally, Bram stepped closer, and cupping her head in his hands, forced her to look up at him.

"I do love you, Cassy," he said with such quiet sincerity that Cassandra's heart leaped within her breast, "and as far as my resentment toward your family...well, I've come a long way. But perhaps you're right that we should be certain before we make a firm commitment to each other."

Cassandra searched his face, frustrated because the lack of light concealed too much of his expression from her.

"So I suppose we're going to have to settle for those visits you suggested," he said with soft reluctance in his voice, "until you've done what you have to here, and I'm certain I've conquered my resentment of who you are."

"And then?" Cassandra asked, uncertain how she felt about Bram's implied expectation that she would give up her career in the family business for him.

"Then, if you feel you still have to work at the mill here, we'll have to work out how to conduct a long-distance marriage," Bram answered softly, filling Cassandra's heart with love for him as well as relief that he wasn't going to insist she make all the sacrifices for their love.

"Oh, Bram," she whispered, wrapping her arms around his neck and leaning into his body. "I do love you so much."

"And I love you," Bram whispered back and kissed her with gentle thoroughness, to seal their mutual confession.

Later, on the drive home, however, Cassandra's worries returned. "It would be awfully hard to raise children if we do marry and have to live apart," she pointed out.

"Not as hard as it would be if those children had any mother besides you," Bram retorted humorously.

Cassandra misunderstood him. "You think I'll be a good mother?" she asked, pleased by the compliment.

"I imagine you will be," Bram drawled, "but I meant I can't imagine having children with any woman other than you."

Cassandra inhaled sharply, even more pleased by this compliment than she had been by what she'd thought he'd meant at first. Heedless of the console between them, she launched herself across it to throw her arms around Bram's neck and kiss his cheek.

"Hey!" He laughed, dividing his attention between his driving and Cassandra's interference with it. "Wait until I stop the car to give me these little signs that you aren't entirely indifferent to me, all right?"

"Yes, darling," Cassandra said with feigned meekness as she settled back in her seat, though her heart was bursting with an optimistic expectation that everything was going to work out all right between the two of them. She wondered if Bram knew how much he had revealed about his inner state of mind with his confession that he couldn't imagine any other woman bearing his children, then decided it didn't matter. *She* knew.

At the Stewart house, Bram again took her to the shelter of the nearby trees to kiss her good-night. He wanted more than the sort of chaste kiss they would be able to exchange in the car to last him until he could be with her again. "Good night, love," he whispered against her lips as he held her lightly, but not lightly enough that she couldn't feel the heat of his desire against her, which precipitated a renewed outburst of her own.

"Cassy," he protested without much conviction as she pressed herself against him. "Honey, I'm a man, not a boy, and I can't take much more of this before I do something foolish."

"And I'm a woman, not a girl," Cassandra whispered, though she allowed him to push her away and hold her upright. "Maybe it wouldn't be so bad if we did something foolish."

"I'm perfectly aware that you're a woman," Bram murmured, drinking her in with his eyes. "But I think you'd change your mind about being foolish in the morning. I know I would."

Cassandra glanced regretfully at the lighted window nearest to them, which told her either her mother or Justin or both were still up.

"I suppose you're right," she said with a sigh, "but I don't intend to let you go back to California without making love to me again."

Bram grinned. "Don't worry about it," he said huskily. "I'll work something out."

Cassandra smiled back and, reaching up on tiptoe, planted a chaste kiss on his cheek. "Call me tomorrow?" she suggested lovingly.

"Without fail," Bram responded. He watched as Cassandra walked up the stairs and opened the door of the house, then lifted a hand in farewell. She stepped inside to turn and watch as Bram walked to his car.

"I love you, Bram Palmer," she whispered as he drove away. "I love you past understanding."

And in her bed that night, she hugged the pillow where Bram had laid his head the day before, using it as an unsatisfactory substitute for the warm living body that had claimed her own forever.

Chapter Thirteen

One of the guests at Maxie and Justin's wedding reception, a young man who had been much taken with Maxie and had consequently volunteered a lot of his free time to help her with her union activities, forgot to check to see who was near him as he voiced a cynical remark to a friend. "Well, I guess if old Jussie couldn't stop Maxie any other way, he decided he'd marry her to get her off his back."

Bram had no compunction about interjecting a sharp reply to a remark that had aroused his temper to a formidable level. "Would you care to say that to either of them face-to-face?" he said in a dangerous tone that made the young man jerk around to look at him. Bram gave the fellow a smile that was anything but friendly when he saw he didn't have the courage of his convictions. "No, I didn't think so," Bram drawled and walked away to find Cassandra, intending to stay by her side and prevent her from hearing anything such as he had overheard.

Cassandra, however, was in her bedroom helping Maxie finish dressing in the suit she would wear to go off on her honeymoon. The reception was being held at the Stewart estate because the Palmer house was in a shambles as a result of Jodie's remodeling.

When the two of them, after exchanging a hug of delight that they were now related, left the bedroom, there was the bedlam of the happy couple's leavetaking to get through, and finally, bombarded by rice and laughing with joy, Maxie and Justin drove away, heading for Springfield on the first lap of their journey to Alaska. They would spend their wedding night in Seattle.

Hours later, when everyone had at last gone home, and Harry and Mary Louise, both exhausted, had gone off to bed, Bram and Cassandra finally had the den to themselves.

"It was kind of your mother to invite us to stay here until Dad's house is habitable again," Bram said, smiling as Cassandra came to sit by him on the sofa. He thought she looked as beautiful as a vision in her pale blue, elegantly styled maid-of-honor dress.

"Why not?" Cassandra smiled tiredly as she snuggled under Bram's comforting arm. "You're family now."

Bram's smile grew rueful. "That sure takes some getting used to," he said, shaking his head. "I would never in a million years have believed I would someday be related to the Stewart family."

"It's not so bad, is it?" Cassandra asked softly, gazing up at Bram's decidedly handsome profile.

He looked down at her, his smile fading to a look of desire as he studied Cassandra's lovely, and at the moment, vulnerable, expression. "No," he said, his voice softly husky, "it's not bad at all. In fact, I'm beginning to think it's inevitable that I'll soon be even more closely related to one particular Stewart."

Cassandra gave him a slow smile of encouragement and was rewarded by a kiss that infused her with the warm languidness of desire. When she stood up and tugged at his hand, Bram looked inquiringly in the direction of her mother's bedroom and the guest room Harry was sleeping in.

"I don't care, Bram," Cassandra said with quiet firmness. "We've been too busy all week to be together in the way we both want. I don't intend to go to bed without you again tonight."

Though Bram would have preferred to make love to Cassandra without the distraction of knowing his father and her mother were under the same roof, he was desperately hungry for her and doubted he could sleep in the same house with her without making love to her, anyway. Besides, he knew something she didn't that influenced him to stand up quickly and accompany her to her room. And before long, as Cassandra came to him with a passion that made his blood surge in his veins, he couldn't care about anything except pleasing her the way she was pleasing him.

Later, as they lay together in contented exhaustion, Bram had to tell her his bad news. "I got a call from my partner this morning," he said quietly, and when Cassandra looked at him in alarm, he shrugged and held her closer. "He needs me back there next week to help put together a program for a potential new client—a big one."

Cassandra's expression showed her disappointment, and Bram ran his thumb over her downturned lips. "You knew I would have to return to California eventually," he whispered, kissing her forehead.

She nodded, but her expression didn't clear. "I just haven't had time to think about it this week and get ready for it," she admitted. Indeed, she hadn't had time to think about anything much during the past week, other than learning the ropes at the furniture mill and helping everyone get ready for the wedding. "I'll miss you, Bram," she said with a catch in her voice.

"No more than I'll miss you," he responded. "But we'll visit each other on weekends."

"I can't come until Justin gets back," Cassandra said regretfully. "I know just enough about the operations at the mill to realize that I'm going to have to work eighteen hours a day there, including weekends, for the next two weeks, or everything will fall apart.''

Bram grimaced, but he wasn't surprised. ''That's about what I figured,'' he said. ''And from what my partner told me, I'm going to be in the same situation for a while.''

They looked at each other, and seeing the look of woeful disappointment in each other's eyes, they suddenly smiled simultaneously.

''Are you thinking what I'm thinking?'' Bram teased, moving his hand in a seductive sliding motion over her hip.

Cassandra nodded her head. ''Let's make the best of what time we have,'' she whispered, and raised her head to meet his kiss with an eagerness that warmed Bram's heart as well as his body.

IN A SOFTLY LIT, luxurious hotel room in Seattle, Washington, Justin Stewart, clad only in black silk pajama bottoms, was sitting on the side of the bed pouring two glasses of champagne when Maxie came out of the adjoining bathroom. Justin looked up and caught his breath at the sight of his new wife. Swathed in a pale green nightgown and a peignoir that matched her eyes, making them sparkle with more of a challenge than Justin had any intention of resisting, she made his blood race in his veins.

''Beautiful,'' he said with soft, but emphatic, approval.

Maxie's smiling eyes bathed Justin's body with an approval that matched his. ''Exactly what I was thinking,'' she reciprocated.

Justin's chuckle was satisfied as he stood up and met Maxie halfway across the room, extending one of the glasses of champagne to her. ''Shall we drink to our mutual good fortune?'' he teased in a low voice, his eyes embracing Maxie before his arms could.

"Absolutely." Maxie nodded, and twined her arm through Justin's to draw him back toward the bed as they each sipped their champagne.

When they were seated side by side, they solemnly drained their glasses before setting them down on the bedside table.

"I'm glad we waited," Maxie said with a half-shy smile.

"Are you?" Justin said tenderly as he reached a finger to push back a strand of silken red hair from Maxie's cheek and tuck it behind her delicate ear. "Then if you are, I am. But it wasn't easy. In fact, if last week hadn't been so busy, I don't think I could have."

"Me, neither," Maxie agreed, and suddenly smiled a pixie smile that charmed Justin totally.

"You made a beautiful bride," he whispered as he leaned forward and kissed the corner of Maxie's mouth.

"And you made a handsome groom," Maxie said dreamily. But then, on remembering something, her smile faded slightly.

Justin drew back and searched her face, and though Maxie tried to hide her feelings, he knew something was bothering her.

"Come on," he said with soft insistence. "Something's wrong. Tell me what it is."

"It's just that I could tell some of the guests at the wedding—people who work for you—" Maxie reluctantly started.

"Us," Justin reminded her quickly, his eyes teasing her.

Maxie looked surprised for an instant, then shrugged. "I guess that's right," she said wonderingly, and it was clear to Justin that she really hadn't taken in what marriage to him meant until this moment. "Well, anyway," she went on, "I could tell they thought I'd betrayed them, and it made me feel..." She hesitated, searching for the right word, and Justin supplied it, his tone dry.

"Like a Benedict Arnold?"

Maxie winced and frowned, wishing she hadn't thought of any of this. She didn't want her wedding night spoiled.

"Well, maybe this will ease your mind," Justin drawled, and getting up, he walked over to his suitcase, opened it and withdrew some papers. Returning to Maxie, he laid them in her lap, then sat down beside her, watching her face closely as she picked up the papers and looked at them.

Maxie couldn't believe her eyes when, as she slowly turned over page after page, she saw that each one of the proposals concerning changes in personnel policies at Barton Furniture had been marked Approved and initialled J.S. Only the last page had been changed; where Maxie had suggested setting up a permanent committee, chaired by Justin and containing employee representatives, to air complaints or hear suggestions. Justin had scratched out his own name and put in Cassandra's.

Mutely, she looked at her husband, and Justin shrugged. "I figured the employees already have too much resentment against me, or fear of my reactions, to let that committee work the way it should if I chaired it," he explained casually. "They'll be more honest with Cassy."

Still, Maxie said nothing, merely stared at him, and after waiting for a moment and still being unable to guess her reaction, Justin said softly, "That's your wedding present, honey. I couldn't think of anything else you'd rather have."

Now there were tears in Maxie's eyes, and Justin frowned before taking the papers from her and setting them aside. Then he gently gathered Maxie into his arms and lowered her onto her back on the bed.

"Did I make a mistake?" he asked, a line of worry appearing on his forehead. "If I did, it's too late to change it. I told Cassy to issue a letter to the employees while we're away, informing them of these changes."

Maxie shook her head, and now the tears in her eyes spilled over onto her cheeks, and Justin became really alarmed. "Honey, if you're upset because I did this for you, rather than because I wanted to do it myself, I'm sorry, but I still have a few of my old spots left. I'm not going to start off our marriage by lying to you. I *did* do it for you, and to a certain extent, for Cassy and Mom. And I'm really hoping for everyone's sake that it works out the way you hope it will." He paused, then grinned. "But I have to admit also that it didn't hurt as much as I expected it to. I only contemplated suicide once or twice when I was marking Approved on all those pages."

At that, Maxie started laughing through her tears, and she reached up to circle Justin's neck with her arms and pull him down so that she could cover his face with kisses.

"Hey." He sputtered with mock disgust. "You're getting me all wet, and I've already had my shower!"

Still laughing, Maxie pushed Justin over onto his back and gave him such a long and thorough kiss that it ended with both of them more ready for loving than talking.

"You can't fool me," Maxie whispered between fervent kisses. "You're not as much of a filthy capitalist pig as you pretend to be."

"Who's spreading that rotten rumor around about me?" Justin growled softly, resuming his position of dominance by rolling Maxie under him.

"I got it from the best of sources," Maxie said with loving smugness. "Your wife told me."

"Wives should be seen," Justin said sternly, leering at Maxie as he began to remove her peignoir, "and not heard."

Maxie pouted as she helped Justin take off her nightgown. "Not even a little groan of ecstasy or two?" she complained, then grew quiet when she realized Justin hadn't heard her. He was staring at her body with awed disbelief, his eyes rapidly darkening with desire as he raised a hand to trace it reverently over her ivory breasts.

"I think," he started to say, then had to clear the husky rasp from his voice. "I think," he continued as he moved his hand down to Maxie's flat stomach, then lowered it to brush his fingers with delicate lightness over the triangle between her long legs, "that a few groans of ecstasy would definitely be in order. But I have the feeling I'm the one who's going to be doing them."

Maxie's slow smile was lovingly complacent as she lightly ran her fingers over the back of Justin's neck when he bent to kiss her breasts, then the smile was gone and she arched and gasped when his tongue slowly traced one of her nipples.

Justin's smile was satisfied as he tilted his head to look up at her face and saw the glaze of passion in her eyes.

"Gasps, though," he said in a low, sensual voice, "gasps of pleasure are a wife's prerogative."

"Oh, Justin." Maxie sighed with trembling impatience. "No commentary is needed. Just get to the part where I'm too breathless to make any sounds at all."

And with a soft, pleased chuckle, Justin did his wife's bidding, to her complete, inarticulate satisfaction. His low-voiced praise was the only sound that pierced the silence of the softly lit room where he made his wife his own, and she, in her turn, wound the bindings of love around his heart so tightly, he knew he would never be able to loosen them.

Much, much later, as they were drifting off to sleep together for the first of many times during their married life, Maxie sleepily wrapped her arms around Justin's waist and whispered a good-night that pleased him enormously.

"Thank you for my wedding present, Justin," she mumbled. "You were right. You couldn't have given me anything that would please me more."

And Justin, smiling contentedly, drifted off to sleep, thinking there was a lot to be said for giving, even when it hurt. The reward—at least the sort of multi-dimensional reward Maxie was giving him—was worth the effort he was having to make to change his spots into a pattern more to her liking.

THREE MONTHS LATER, Cassandra Stewart sat at her desk in an office adjacent to Justin's long after he and Maxie had gone home for the day, her normal even-tempered mood frayed considerably. Gazing abstractedly out one of the wide windows, she thought about how much had been accomplished in such a short time.

After receiving the concessions Justin had granted them, the mill's employees had shown their appreciation by instigating a rise in quality production that was beginning to stretch Cassandra's marketing talents in order to sell what they produced. She had been kept busy working with Barton Furniture's designers to choose new styles of furniture to introduce into their inventory, and was now implementing new advertising campaigns and hiring and training additional salespeople to call on potential clients. She should have been on top of the world.

But Cassandra hadn't seen Bram in two weeks, and she knew that was the source of her present discontent.

Nothing means very much without him, she thought disconsolately, unwilling to face just yet where her thinking was taking her, but an idea was nibbling at the edges of her mind.

Everyone—her family as well as Harry Palmer, because he knew that Bram's frequent visits home now were partly due to his desire to see her—was delighted that Cassandra lived in Barton's Corner. But Cassandra wasn't delighted anymore. She had already accomplished most of what she'd set out to do. Justin's management practices weren't a source of worry now. And while there were still marketing opportunities to be exploited, she knew any competent marketing person could take her place. Furthermore, every time she visited Bram, she became more aware of certain limitations connected with living in a small town. But mostly, she was frustrated at having to conduct her relationship with Bram long-distance—she missed him terribly when they were apart. And though it made her feel guilty to admit it, she was downright jealous of Maxie's pregnancy.

Cassandra grimaced as she finally faced her problems squarely. She wanted to leave Barton's Corner and join Bram in California. And what was stopping her? Nothing more than the fact that on returning to Barton's Corner, she had made up her mind so firmly that she had come home forever, and she was so reluctant to disappoint her loved ones that she had had difficulty recognizing what she really wanted. She had known for some time what Bram wanted, however, though he hadn't pressured her about it. But she would have had to be blind not to see how much he wanted her to come to California permanently.

"Why, you idiot!" she laughed at herself as she realized her decision was already made. "What are you waiting for?"

Typically, Cassandra acted without delay. She was home within twenty minutes and had gathered the family for a conference.

"Justin," she addressed her brother first, wondering whether he was going to protest her decision, "I want you to know how much I appreciate having worked with you. At first, I thought we would be at each other's throats eventually, but you have my complete respect now, as well as my resignation, effective immediately."

Cassandra stopped, waiting for an explosive reaction from her family that never came. Somewhat bewildered, she glanced from Justin, whose grin was widely complacent, to her mother, who merely sat smiling and nodding in a satisfied way, to Maxie, whose eyes twinkled back at her affectionately.

"Well," Cassandra said, "isn't anyone surprised?"

Three heads moved in a negative reaction, and Cassandra placed her hands on her hips and glared at her family.

"All right," she demanded, "why not?"

"It's been obvious for a month." Justin shrugged.

"You belong with Bram," Mary Louise said simply.

"You frown every time I say something about my pregnancy," Maxie teased. "You think I don't know a jealous woman when I see one?"

Cassandra opened her mouth to protest, then closed it again and smiled, instead, as she realized she was looking for problems where there were none.

"Well, then," she said happily, "I guess no one will mind if I leave for California in the morning."

"Whoa!" Justin held up a hand and shook his head. "You're going to find me someone to take your place first. *Then* you can go to California."

Cassandra's smile slipped and she started to protest, but on seeing that her family was as united about when she would leave as they had been about their conclusion that she was ready to go, she sighed and shrugged.

"Okay," she gave in. "But this is going to be the fastest recruiting job you've ever seen." And without waiting to discuss the matter, she hurried to the study that had once been her father's, then had been shared between father and son, and was now shared by Justin, Maxie and Cassandra.

Before bedtime that night, she had put together an ad for a marketing executive that would be run in newspapers and trade magazines, and she had made a good start on a manual outlining the special nuances of marketing furniture that she had discovered.

It took a month before Cassandra found a young man anxious to leave the hassles of big-city life and raise the family he and his wife had just started in a small town—a month of agonizing sacrifice, as it was impossible for her to visit Bram while she was interviewing, and he was in the middle of a big job that prevented him from coming home.

Cassandra eagerly presented her candidate to Justin, and upon receiving her brother's approval of her choice, she set about training the new young man; when she was satisfied that she had helped him all she could, she made plane reservations for California, only to have to cancel them when Bram called her, informing her rather grimly that he would be in Barton's Corner that evening.

"But, Bram—" She started to tell him that she had been about to come to him, but he cut her off abruptly, sounding to Cassandra's astonished ears both angry and determined about something.

"No buts, Cassandra," he stated. "I'll be there on the six o'clock plane. I've had all of this I'm going to take!"

He slammed the phone down before Cassandra could ask him what he was talking about, and when she tried to call him back, there was no answer.

Biting her lip, Cassandra stood by the phone until Maxie walked by, glanced at her and stopped.

"What's the matter?" she asked in a puzzled tone. "Is there a problem with your reservations to California?"

"No, no problem there," Cassandra said slowly as she began to get an inkling of what was on Bram's mind. "But I won't be going just yet."

"Why not?" Maxie inquired, amazed. She knew how anxious Cassy had been to join Bram.

"Because your brother is coming here," Cassandra said absently, then looked at Maxie, a frown between her eyes. "Maxie do you know if Bram likes surprises?"

Maxie grimaced and shook her head. "No, he doesn't," she declared with no uncertainty in her tone. "Once, my parents held a surprise birthday party for him, and he showed up looking as if he'd been dragged through the mud—which he had, actually. He'd been practicing football after a rain. And ever since then, he's hated surprises with a passion.'' She looked at Cassandra's suddenly pale face and asked with dawning comprehension, ''Why? What have you done?''

''Oh, nothing much,'' Cassandra said weakly. ''I just neglected to mention to him that I'd made a decision to join him in California permanently. I thought it would be a nice surprise when I just showed up out there...''

Her voice trailed as she and Maxie exchanged a look of dawning dread.

''He sounded angry when he called to tell me he was coming,'' Cassandra informed Maxie with a resigned sigh.

''Uh-huh.'' Maxie nodded, then shrugged her shoulders in a fatalistic manner. ''Well, I wouldn't worry too much. After you tell him your news, he should get over being mad at you fairly quickly, but you sure picked the wrong man to try to surprise, especially about something like this.''

''That's what I was afraid of.'' Cassandra sighed again. And without another word, she headed for her bedroom to ready herself for Bram's arrival that evening.

Chapter Fourteen

As Cassandra watched Bram coming toward her from the plane, she was both relieved to note that his expression wasn't hostile and ecstatic at seeing him again. It had been far too long since they'd been together.

"Bram!" she exclaimed as she walked into his arms and held him tightly. "Oh, it's so good to see you!"

Bram looked a little puzzled as she loosened her hold on him enough to kiss him, but Cassandra was too full of her own joy to notice, and by the time the kiss was over, it was evident that the only thing on his mind was his need for her.

"Let's go," he said urgently, turning her toward the exit of the terminal.

"Don't you have any luggage?" Cassandra asked, delighted by his eagerness to be alone with her.

Bram shook his head and held out his hand. "Just this," he said, indicating a small carry-on bag he held, and then he rushed her outside to her car. Without asking, he ushered her to the passenger side and held out his hand for her keys. Cassandra gave them to him, thinking smugly that he was probably afraid she would drive too slowly for him, and he didn't want to wait to make love to her. But then she wondered where he planned to make love to her this time. It seemed too long a wait to drive from Springfield to Barton's Corner, where they might have to wait for everyone at home to go to bed, the way they usually had to when he visited.

When he was behind the wheel, she leaned over and touched his arm. "Bram, kiss me again before we go," she murmured. "It's a long way to Barton's Corner—unless you planned to take a room here in Springfield for a couple of hours?"

Bram looked at her, and this time she did notice that he seemed puzzled about something. But before she could say anything, he spoke.

"No, I don't plan to get a room here." And he leaned over and kissed her with a fervency that pushed everything else out of her mind. When he straightened and started the car, his expression strained, Cassandra contented herself for a while with studying his beloved face as he headed for the road to Barton's Corner.

"Bram," she said when they were on the highway, "aren't you tired of what we have to go through to be alone together when you come home?"

Bram flashed her a glance that now showed the hostility she had expected to see when he came off the plane, and Cassandra drew back, startled to see it.

"I certainly am," he said grimly, "and as I said on the phone, I've had all of this I'm going to take!" As Cassandra started to say something, he cut her off. "But I don't want to talk about it right now, Cassandra. I'm tired and I want to concentrate on my driving. We'll talk when we get where we're going. You can believe that!"

Hurt and made angry by his attitude, at first, Cassandra snapped, "Maybe we'll talk, and maybe we won't!" But instead of answering, Bram merely flashed her another one of those glances that froze her inside, and Cassandra turned away from him to gaze out the window, biting her lip to keep from crying.

As the silence went on, her anger faded, to be replaced by fear. Had Bram changed his mind about loving her? After all the plans she'd made and after finding a replacement for herself at the mill, was it all for nothing? Why had she settled on that dumb idea to surprise him? she wondered anxiously. If she'd told him what she was doing, might he have told her not to act so drastically, because his feelings for her were waning?

She stole a glance at Bram's rigid profile and felt her stomach turn over. No, she thought, desperately holding on to her composure. Of course Bram still loved her. He had to!

By the time they reached Barton's Corner, Cassandra's head and body ached from tension. And when, instead of turning toward her home, Bram headed for Main Street, she thought she would scream.

"Where are you going?" she asked stiffly.

"Wait and see," he responded in a tight voice that effectively cut off any further questions from Cassandra.

She was thoroughly at sea by the time Bram had made two circuits of Main Street and waved at the few people in sight to attract their attention. Had he lost his mind? she wondered uneasily. Was he working too hard and experiencing some sort of breakdown?

When he pulled up at the only motel Barton's Corner boasted, which was perfectly respectable, but which was owned by a couple who were never reticent about gossiping, she was positive he had gone completely around the bend.

"Bram, what are you doing?" she demanded when, without a word, he got out of the car. He didn't answer and came around to her side. Belatedly, Cassandra started to lock the door, but she was a second too slow and Bram pulled it open.

"Come on," he said in a calm voice, as though what he was doing was perfectly natural. "We're staying here tonight."

Cassandra stared up at him in shock, and was about to tell him in no uncertain terms that while he might be crazy, she wasn't, when at last she began to get a glimmer of understanding about what he was doing.

"Why?" she asked, trying to sound as calm as he had.

"I'll tell you when we get inside," he hedged, and Cassandra's glimmer of understanding began to edge toward certainty.

She sat perfectly still, debating with herself about how much her reputation in Barton's Corner mattered to her, which didn't take long. Then, with a stunning smile, she swung her legs around and climbed out of the car, shutting the door behind her with a flourish.

"Lead on, darling," she said lightly, and slid her hand under his arm to tug him with her as she started walking toward the office. She ignored the look of shock that was now on *his* face.

"Cassandra, wait a minute." He resisted her tugs and swung her around to face him.

"But why, dearest?" she asked innocently. "I'm as eager to be with you as you apparently are to be with me."

A look of shame crossed Bram's face, and he couldn't meet her eyes for a second, while Cassandra tried hard to keep from laughing.

"Honey, don't you realize what I was doing?" he said in a low, miserable voice. And when she raised her brows inquiringly, he said, in a tone of confession, "I thought, when you didn't come to me this past month, that you had changed your mind about us, that you'd decided I wasn't—" He stopped, but Cassandra was well aware of what he'd been thinking, and she was both angered and dismayed by what her attempt to surprise him had caused.

"Anyway," Bram went on, "I was angry. I wasn't really going to get a room here, though," he added soberly. "I wouldn't do that to you. I was merely... Oh, hell, I don't know exactly what I was trying to do!" he said in a voice filled with hurt and frustration. "Scare you, I guess, or something. Whatever it was, it was a stupid idea, and I'd never have done it if I didn't love you so much that I'm going out of my mind!"

Cassandra looked at him, her heart filled with love for him, yet despairing that he was ever going to get over believing she thought he wasn't good enough for her, unless...

"It doesn't seem like such a stupid idea to me," she said quietly.

Bram frowned, and it was clear he didn't take her meaning. "What are you talk—"

"I think we should go ahead," she said very calmly. "It might cause a little bit of a stir at first, but when we're married, the talk will die down."

"Cassandra, what..." Bram started to say, and then his eyes widened. "When we're what?" he asked in a very quiet voice.

"When we're married," Cassandra replied almost in a conversational tone. "I've already turned in my resignation at the mill and found someone to replace me, and I was planning to bring all my things to California with me this time, but then you said you were coming here instead, and since I know that the family will want to be at the wedding, this really works out better, don't you think? I'm sure Reverend Miller can work us in sometime tomorrow, and I rather like the idea of an impromptu wedding. It will save a lot of time and trouble."

She almost burst out laughing when she saw the conflicting expressions flickering across Bram's handsome face. She correctly deduced that he was torn between shaking her to pieces and kissing her senseless.

"I'd rather you kissed me, Bram," she said, flashing him a sweet smile. "I'm sure I'd enjoy that more than a shaking."

"Cassandra," Bram said in a low, threatening voice, "did I ever tell you that I don't like surprises—especially ones that put me through hell, when I'm sure your intention was to take me to heaven?"

"No, darling," Cassandra responded gravely. "You never told me that. But I know it now, and I assure you, I'll never surprise you again."

"Good!" Bram exploded. Then, looking around him to see if anyone had witnessed his momentary lack of control, and seeing no one, he stepped closer to her and put his arms around her. "Then let me give you that kiss you want," he said, his voice still slightly rough. "I need it as much as you do so I can start enjoying what you just told me."

Cassandra placed her fingers over his lips, stoically ignoring the danger signals that erupted again in Bram's eyes.

"But you haven't accepted my proposal yet," she said softly. "A woman likes to know a man's intentions before she spends a night in a motel with him."

Bram grated his teeth and closed his eyes while he gathered his sadly torn patience about him. Then, his eyes flashed open and he said, very slowly and very distinctly, "Yes, I would be pleased to marry you, Miss Stewart, and no, I have no intention of spending the night with you in this motel. I never did. Now kiss me."

Cassandra kissed him with laughter bubbling inside her the whole time. She managed, however, to devote enough attention to the kiss so that she could feel the tension beginning to drain from Bram's body by the time it was over. But she wasn't done with him yet, not by a long shot.

''Lovely,'' she murmured when Bram at last raised his head and looked into her eyes with nothing but love in his. ''Now take me to bed, Bram Palmer, before *I* lose *my* temper.''

''Where?'' Bram asked immediately, thinking she might have discovered some place they'd heretofore overlooked in this benighted town where they could be alone together.

''Right here,'' Cassandra answered, gesturing at the motel with a graceful motion of her hand.

Shocked, Bram drew back. ''Cassandra, you can't be serious!'' he protested. ''Why, the Masons would tell it all over town before—''

Cassandra was nodding her head, and there was a fierce light of determination in her eyes that made Bram pause. ''You *want* the town to know?'' he asked incredulously.

''I don't care what this town knows or doesn't know,'' she responded in a flat voice filled with conviction. ''But I care what you know, Bram Palmer,'' she added more spiritedly, ''and if the only way I can convince you that I'm not ashamed of the least little thing about you is to provide Barton's Corner with some juicy gossip, then let's get on with it.''

When Bram just stared at her for a moment, then started smiling and shaking his head, Cassandra erupted as vehemently as he had a few moments earlier.

''Take me in there right now, Bram, and I don't ever again want to hear you even hint that I have a snobbish bone in my body.''

''Shh.'' Grinning broadly, Bram pulled her into his arms. ''Don't worry sweetheart. You've convinced me. Now, I'm the snob. I don't want anyone making any scandalous remarks about my future bride.''

Cassandra struggled for a moment, then gave up and relaxed against him, joining him in the laughter shaking his body. When they drew back simultaneously and exchanged

a long look of loving humor, Cassandra was about to tell
him again that she loved him when she sensed someone behind them. Turning in his arms as Bram lifted his head, since
he had caught a hint of movement out of the corner of his
eye, they both froze when they saw Mr. Mason, the owner
of the motel, standing a short distance away looking at them
with an amazed expression on his face.

"You folks don't want a room, do you?" he asked,
sounding as though he was prepared to believe that they
might, since in his profession he'd seen a lot of things
stranger than a Palmer and a Stewart appearing at his door
wanting to rent a room for the night.

Cassandra recklessly tossed caution to the wind. "I do,"
she said sweetly, glancing at Bram with a mischievous sparkle in her eyes.

"She's joking, Mr. Mason," Bram quickly spoke up,
giving Cassandra an annoyed look. And then he smiled, and
said in a more natural voice, "We're getting married tomorrow, though, so we may be back then."

Mr. Mason visibly relaxed. He even heaved a sigh of relief. "That's nice to hear, folks," he said, nodding his head.
"I get too many couples that haven't been before a preacher
comin' in here, and I have to turn 'em away. Me and Ma
don't hold with that sort of thing, you know."

"I know," Bram said, his smile broadening as Cassandra gave him a startled look, which quickly turned to one of
indignation. "Talk gets around."

"Well good night, then," Mr. Mason said, raising his
hand in a wave, "and congratulations on your wedding."
Then he chuckled. "The way you Palmers and Stewarts are
getting together, it wouldn't surprise me to hear that Mary
Louise and Harry are next in line."

As Bram and Cassandra exchanged a look of surprise,
Mr. Mason shuffled to the door of the motel office and disappeared inside.

"They wouldn't...would they?" Cassandra asked in a wondering tone.

"Of course not." Bram laughed, relaxing again. "They're friends, but I don't think either one of them ever plans to marry again."

Cassandra breathed a sigh of relief. "Well, that's good." She nodded her head. "That would be carrying family togetherness just a little too far, especially for a conservative little town like Barton's Corner."

She knew she had managed to allay Bram's suspicions about her real feelings toward him and his family when he didn't react to her remark with anything other than a hearty laugh while he escorted her back to the car.

When they were inside it, Cassandra automatically turned to him for a kiss, which Bram happily provided, but when it was over, her expression was rueful.

"What is it now?" Bram inquired, his smile and tone indulgent.

"I was just wondering where we *can* go to make love," she answered mournfully. "I don't think Mom and Justin and Maxie will be in bed yet."

Bram looked thoughtful for a moment, then raised an eyebrow at her.

"If we were seventeen, we'd go to Lover's Lane," he said casually.

Cassandra blinked at him. "But we're not, and it's cold, and we agreed before that it wasn't appro—" She broke off to stare at him, her eyes slowly widening with delight. "But on the other hand," she said, lowering her voice to a tone of loving anticipation, "I couldn't have turned you down if you'd asked me when I was seventeen, and I can't deny you anything now, especially when by this time tomorrow, you'll be my husband."

Bram raised a hand to stroke his fingers lightly over her cheek. "And while it might be an inappropriate place to take a lover," he said softly, "it seems just right for an engaged couple. It will be good practice for us. I've heard variety adds spice to a marriage."

Cassandra chuckled and clasped Bram's wandering fingers in her hand, pressing his palm tightly against her cheek. "If that's so," she teased him softly, "then California will be the perfect place for us. There should be a lot of opportunity for variety there—hot tubs and beaches and—"

"Us," Bram interjected, leaning to close his mouth gently over Cassandra's. When he drew back slightly, her eyes contained that dazed expression he loved. "Cassandra, I love you," he murmured. "Thanks for making the sacrifice of coming to live with me."

"Sacrifice?" Cassandra whispered the word, her eyes teasing him lovingly. "Now I know you've lost your mind, Bram Palmer. I'm not making any sacrifice. Surely you have a position for a good marketing executive in that company you worked so hard to establish?"

Bram raised his eyebrows in surprise, then relaxed into a chuckle. "And what, may I ask, are your qualifications for marketing computer software, Miss Stewart?" he teased back, beginning to enjoy the idea of working with her, having her close to him during the days as well as the nights.

"A good marketing mind can sell any product," Cassandra responded gravely. "Just look at how you sold me on the idea that you were going to ruin my reputation in Barton's Corner, when you knew all along the Masons wouldn't rent us a room." She frowned then and straightened slightly. "And by the way," she added, "how did you really know the Masons wouldn't—"

"Cassandra," Bram interrupted her with an impatient sigh.

"What?" she answered, a hint of sulkiness in her voice.

"Don't you think we've had enough problems between us for a while?"

Cassandra thought that over and finally began to smile. "Yes, I do," she said with honest simplicity. "But I'm likely to change my mind if you don't start this car and head for Lover's Lane right this minute."

"Anything you say, darling," Bram answered with a slow smile of anticipation, and reached to turn on the key.

A short while later, Bram stopped the car a little short of Lover's Lane, while the two of them eyed the crowded bluff with gloomy resignation.

"I forgot it was Friday night," Bram confessed.

"So did I," Cassandra said with a sigh.

"It's a good thing we're getting married tomorrow," Bram ventured, releasing a frustrated breath as he turned the car around and headed for the Stewart house.

"But Mother will have a fit about our giving her so little notice," Cassandra predicted.

"We'll win her over," Bram assured her, reaching to pat her hand.

"And she'll likely drive herself crazy making plans," Cassandra finished dispensing her bad news in an apologetic tone.

Bram stayed silent for the rest of the drive, and it was only when he zoomed by the Stewart driveway, instead of turning in, that Cassandra stirred and looked at him inquiringly.

"I just remembered Butler's Meadow," Bram said with satisfaction, "or rather the deserted road beside it. We wouldn't want to keep your mother up all night, would we, Cassandra?"

"No, darling," Cassandra agreed, settling back in her seat with a contented smile on her face. "We certainly wouldn't want to do that."

Epilogue

Justin and his brother-in-law, Bram, stood at the windows of Justin's study looking out at Maxie Stewart and Cassy Palmer, who were having a wonderful time splashing with Justin's redheaded two-year-old daughter, Bram's one-year-old blond son and several children of the employees who worked at the ever-expanding Barton Furniture mill.

"It's nice to have you all home for a visit again," Justin said with satisfaction. "That boy of yours is a corker, and I think little Mary is as much in love with him as Maxie and I are."

Bram smiled with pleasure at the remark, then spoke musingly. "I've been trying to decide whom he most resembles. He's not like your darling Mary, who's the spitting image of Maxie. He doesn't take after either Cassy or me particularly, and I can't quite—"

Bram stopped speaking abruptly, and slowly turned to gaze at a picture of Justin Stewart, Sr., he'd noticed from time to time hanging on the wall behind the desk that used to be the senior Stewart's. "Oh, my God," he muttered as he turned back to Justin, who was eyeing him sympathetically. "You knew," Bram said in an accusing tone.

Justin shrugged. "We all did," he said simply, "but no one had the guts to tell you."

"Even Cassy?" Bram asked, frowning as he thought about her keeping anything from him.

"She was afraid it might make you dislike the boy," Justin said, feeling relieved when Bram's expression showed how shocked he was by the idea of anything making him dislike his little boy. "I'm glad she was wrong," he added quietly. "And if I were you, I'd tell her she was."

"I intend to," Bram said forcefully. A second later he was looking at the picture again, wondering, in spite of himself, how Justin, Sr., would have felt about his grandson. Would he have disliked the boy simply because he was the son of a Palmer?

"Why worry about it?" Justin asked, guessing what was on Bram's mind. "But in my opinion, he would have loved little Harry just like the rest of us. How could he have helped it, especially when the boy is the spitting image of him?"

Bram laughed in response to Justin's sly grin. "I guess you're right Jussie," he said as he returned his attention to his family out by the pool. "How could anyone help loving a boy like that?"

And as he gazed tenderly at his small son, he finally put away the last of his resentment against any of the Stewarts. After all, as he had realized more than once, whatever else you could say about them, you couldn't fault their taste. His lovely wife had chosen him above all others to father the son whose sweet face was a reminder of a man who had been as handsome a specimen of masculinity as Bram had ever seen.

"Let's join them," Justin suggested, turning to go to his room to put on a swimsuit. "Come on, Bram. The summer's almost over here. Just because you've got sunshine all year round in California doesn't mean you can't enjoy ours, too."

Smiling with contentment, Bram didn't follow Justin at once. Instead, he stood thinking that it would always feel like summer to him here, where he'd started with love from one family and come back to find the rest of the love he needed to start another one, the joy of his life forever.

Readers rave about Harlequin American Romance!

"...the best series of modern romances
I have read...great, exciting, stupendous,
wonderful."
— S.E.,* Coweta, Oklahoma

"...they are absolutely fantastic...going to be
a smash hit and hard to keep on the
bookshelves."
— P.D., Easton, Pennsylvania

"The American line is great. I've enjoyed
every one I've read so far."
— W.M.K., Lansing, Illinois

"...the best stories I have read in a long
time."
— R.H., Northport, New York

*Names available on request.

Harlequin American Romance

COMING NEXT MONTH

#185 STORMWALKER by Dallas Schulze

Sara Grant chose the wrong time to lie when she insisted that she knew all about horses and hiking. She badgered Cody Wolf into taking her on his search for the downed Cessna in the Rocky Mountains and Sara's missing nephew. Unfortunately she then had to prove she could be just as tough as her surefooted, half-Indian companion.

#186 BODY AND SOUL by Anne McAllister

Her mother had always said that disasters come in threes, and now Susan Rivers could attest to it. First her teenaged brother was thrust upon her for the summer. Then, she was evicted. And when Susan finally found another apartment in southern California, the unspeakable happened: Miles Cavanaugh moved in next door.

#187 ROUGE'S BARGAIN by Cathy Gillen Thacker

Only a scoundrel like Ben McCauley would have promised Lindsey Halloran three weeks of work on the idyllic island of Maui and then asked her to play a starring role in a high-stakes vendetta against a business rival. Pretending to go along with Ben's elaborate scheme, she plotted to beat the master at his own game. But what she didn't plan on was Ben's irresistible manly charm.

#188 A MATTER OF TIME by Noreen Brownlie

Jennifer Bradford thought that stress was an acceptable hazard of her job as a magazine editor in Los Angeles—that is until Dr. Julian Caldicott diagnosed her severe "type A" behavior. Although she resisted the efforts of the enticing doctor to defuse her, what should have been a simple procedure turned into a battle of wits and wills . . . and much more.

ATTRACTIVE, SPACE SAVING BOOK RACK

Display your most prized novels on this handsome and sturdy book rack. The hand-rubbed walnut finish will blend into your library decor with quiet elegance, providing a practical organizer for your favorite hard-or soft-covered books.

Only $9.95

Approximately 16" x 8" when assembled

Assembles in seconds!

To order, rush your name, address and zip code, along with a check or money order for $10.70 ($9.95 plus 75¢ postage and handling) (New York residents add appropriate sales tax), payable to *Harlequin Reader Service* to:

In the U.S.

Harlequin Reader Service
Book Rack Offer
901 Fuhrmann Blvd.
P.O. Box 1325
Buffalo, NY 14269-1325

Offer not available in Canada.

BKR-1